OF VALOR AND VAMPIRES
THE GODDESS'S DAUGHTER
BOOK III

WARD PARKER

Mad Mangrove Media

ISBN: 978-1-957158-24-2

Cover by TrifBookDesign

CONTENTS

CHAPTER 1

SOPHIE

The meeting of the Executive Council got off on the wrong foot—or arm, I should say—after Timothy wrenched off his left limb and threw it at me. There was no harm involved, because I easily dodged the flying appendage and Timothy would regenerate a new one in a week's time. He was a zombie, after all. A spiteful one with no impulse control, as was the case with most of the members of the guild he led: the Union of Undead Flesh Eaters.

The meeting already augured a poor outcome for my hopes of reuniting the guilds in the face of our common enemies.

The meeting also came to a disturbing end. But first things first.

"You have a conflict of interest," Timothy said to me, his words slurred and garbled like you'd expect when coming from a decaying mouth. "You're nominating Diego because you have the hots for him."

Jeez Louise! Was my crush so obvious that even a zombie

could recognize it? My face grew hot. I tried to shut down my empathy as it became flooded with the prurient feelings of the others in the room.

I couldn't help but notice Diego's emotions, though. He was angry—more so at me than at Timothy.

"I have no desire to lead the Executive Council," Diego said in a flat voice. "I have just begun my role as Duke of the Clan of the Eternal Night. I cannot take on the additional responsibilities."

"Then I nominate Dr. Noordlun," I said. He was the head of the Memory Guild, to which Mom belonged, and was a brilliant scholar at the college. Maybe not the most charismatic of men, but we wouldn't have to worry about him going rogue like Baldric did.

Speaking of Baldric, he sat in the corner of the room, glowering at anyone who looked his way. He was the same brilliant, deceitful, and treacherous faerie he'd always been, but now he had an impairment: a magical implant in his brain.

He had attempted to insert a complex, powerful spell into my head to control me, but thanks to my empath powers and a lot of luck, I'd tricked him into putting the spell into his own brain. Now I had a means to control *him*. It was how I'd convinced him to resign as the president of the Executive Committee.

He would have betrayed the supernaturals of San Marcos in his quest for power. Instead, he was sitting in the corner of a cheap motel conference room watching us awkwardly attempt to replace him.

"What gives you the right to take part in this, anyway?" Timothy asked me while he retrieved the arm he had flung. The motel would charge us a hefty cleaning fee if he left the arm on the floor, and I suspected he wanted to throw it at me again.

"Orlena appointed me her proxy while she recovers in the hospital," I replied, giving a hateful look to Baldric, who had given her a cerebral hemorrhage during his attempt to take her life.

"I think you should take over from her as the Arch Mage of the Magic Guild," Bob said to me with a fatherly look of pride. He had held that position until he'd been turned into a vampire. Now that he wasn't a leader, he still attended council meetings but couldn't vote.

"My magic isn't powerful enough yet," I said with exaggerated humility. "Right?"

"I think it is," Bob said. "You've been tutored by the best." He was referring to himself.

"Does anyone else have a nomination?" asked Sybil, Queen of the Elven League.

Gaarg raised his hand. The troll who led the Troll, Ogre, and Gnome Alliance said, "I nominate Rufus."

"Thank you, but I'll pass," the shifter, in his burly, bearded human form, replied. His hair was jet black, though when he shifted to a wolf, his fur was white. "My pack and I are eager to fight, but not to lead."

"Then we shall vote," Sybil said. "All in favor of Dr. Noordlun as the council president, say 'aye.'"

"Wait!" Baldric interjected. "I nominate Sophie."

A few people laughed.

"The president must be the leader of a guild," Sybil said. "Everyone knows that."

"By proxy, she is," Baldric said with a cunning smile. "And she's been involved in fighting the Unseelie Court more than any of us."

I had an uneasy feeling, wondering why Baldric was doing

this. He'd walled off his emotions from me, so I couldn't sense what he was up to. I just knew it wasn't benevolent.

Everyone in the room stared at Baldric and me in confusion. Except for Diego. He had a sly, ironic look because he was the only one who knew about the spell lodged in Baldric's brain that I could control, even though it was Baldric's spell. Diego must have suspected me of making Baldric nominate me.

I caught his eye and shook my head no. "I'm flattered by your faith in me, but I respectfully decline."

"Once again, then," Sybil said. "All for Dr. Noordlun?"

"Aye," said nearly everyone in unison.

"That's a nay for me," Baldric muttered.

"Let the record state that Dr. Sven Noordlun is the new president of the Executive Council of the Supernatural Guilds of San Marcos, Florida."

The kindly white-haired professor smiled and nodded at everyone as we applauded lightly.

I glanced at Diego. He returned my gaze with a cynical smile. Did he really think I forced Baldric to nominate me? He knew me better than that. Diego was giving off such a strange vibe tonight, it made me uneasy. Maybe it was the stress of being the new leader of his guild.

Baldric slipped into an empty chair beside Dr. Noordlun. "Professor, may I schedule a brief meeting with you this week?"

"The history department is having conferences this week," Dr. Noordlun replied. "Perhaps next week?"

Baldric frowned, then transformed it into a bright, fake smile. "That would be fine. I'll have my assistant call yours."

What is Baldric doing? I wondered. For this faerie, a day without scheming was like a day without breathing.

The door opened, and a stranger entered the room. That's what you get when you hold your meetings in a hotel conference room. I guess we should have posted a guard, but it goes to show how casually the guilds have done business. Until now, when our existence was in jeopardy.

The stranger was a tall, handsome man with short brown hair and a scar above his forehead at the hairline. He emanated the magic of a different species having shifted into human form. He wasn't a faerie, though. What species he was, I had no idea.

"Sorry to barge in," he said in a mild Southern accent. "I'm here on guild-related business."

"How did you know we were meeting here?" Rufus asked warily. "The directory in the lobby says we're the Rotarians."

"I have my connections," the man answered. "I represent a supernatural community that fled the earth centuries ago. You see, most can't shift to human form like I and my bloodline can."

"What kind of supernatural people are you?" Rufus demanded.

"Dragons."

All the side conversations in the room shut off, leaving only silence.

"My name is Ronnie, by the way. I am the leader of my people."

The guild leaders and the rest of us in the room introduced ourselves.

"*Ronnie?*" Rufus asked with derision. "That's not the kind of name I'd expect of a dragon."

"Watch your manners, Rufus," Dr. Noordlun said.

"There's a story behind my name," Ronnie explained. "My mother spent a great deal of time in Florida. She was a big fan of a Florida man named Ronnie Van Zant."

"Of the audaciously awesome band Lynyrd Skynyrd!" Bob said.

"Exactly."

"Do you live in the In Between now?" I asked. "I saw dragons there recently."

"Yes. I recognize you. A witch. I was one of the dragons you saw. We migrate between the In Between and earth, visiting places we won't be seen by humans, such as the Everglades, the Brazilian rainforest, and parts of Africa and Asia."

"Even in those remote places, there's a chance you can be seen, right?"

The man smiled at me. I only just now noticed his eyes had vertical pupils. "We have ways of camouflaging ourselves."

"Well, welcome, Ronnie," said Dr. Noordlun. "How can we help you?"

"We've sensed the increased strife and danger on this planet, particularly here in Florida. Humans and Fae almost made dragons extinct over the centuries, and now they're trying to do the same to all supernaturals. I want my people to join with you, for all our sakes."

"That's exactly what I've been trying to get the Executive Council to understand," I said. Everyone ignored me.

"Do you wish to establish a guild of dragons?" Dr. Noordlun asked.

Ronnie laughed. "If that's what it takes to fight alongside you against our common enemies."

"We need fighters more than we need dues-paying guild members," Diego said. Everyone stared at him with rapt attention. "How do we get in touch with you?"

"Through her." Ronnie pointed at me. "I sense in her the power of telepathy, which my people use regularly." He turned to the door. "Thank you for hearing me."

After Ronnie left, Dr. Noordlun adjourned the meeting. Seconds later, a loud gasp came from the back of the room. It was from Evelyn, Priestess of the Psychic Guild. Now that I had bloomed as an empath I had the right to join her guild, but I admit I was intimidated by the ancient crone who was famous for her clairvoyant powers.

"I sense a great disturbance in the psychic energy field," she said in a loud but quavering voice. "A traumatic conflict is ensuing nearby."

"In San Marcos?" Diego asked.

"No," she replied. "But somewhere close."

"What kind of disturbance? An attack against supernaturals?"

"Yes. And against humans."

"By vigilantes?" I asked. "The governor's militia? The Fae of the Unseelie Court?"

Evelyn looked at me like I was stupid. "All of the above."

"You can't tell us where this is happening?"

"Only that it is in a town near San Marcos."

I frantically scrolled through my phone, looking for news alerts. I found no reports of anything amiss. Others pulled out their own phones, texted, and made calls, presumably to people they knew in nearby towns.

I had a better resource: a friend of the family, Detective Michael Samson of the San Marcos Police Department. I called him but went straight to voicemail.

Anxiety grew in the conference room. Supernaturals are naturally a very paranoid bunch, and as an empath, I was highly susceptible to their fears. It was driving me crazy.

I called the main number at the police department.

"May I speak with Detective Samson, please?"

The receptionist paused. I picked up the worry in her voice. "He's not on duty today. Would you like to leave a message?"

Although Mom and I were known as Samson's friends, our brand, you could say, was damaged thanks to the hysteria about supernaturals brought about by the Great Unmasking. Now that witches, monsters, and others had been proved to exist, our family-run inn had been shut down by the state because of supernatural activity.

I decided to lie.

"This is his daughter, Ann." I used the actual name of his daughter, who was around my age.

"You haven't spoken with him?" the receptionist asked with alarm.

"No. Why?"

A long pause. "Let me transfer you to the Chief of Detectives."

I worried that Samson's boss would know Ann too well for me to bluff my way through a conversation. I was correct.

"Who is this?" he demanded after I asked him about Samson. "You don't sound like Ann."

I hastily disconnected.

The impression I got was that something had happened to Samson and that it wasn't an accident that occurred in the line of duty. My understanding was that Samson had kept the fact he was a werewolf secret from everyone on the police force. So, if his secret had been revealed, his coworkers probably wouldn't handle it well.

I scoured my memory for what I knew about Samson's personal life. I didn't have a way of getting in touch with his daughter, but I did remember that he lived in Altman, a small town on Lake Altman in a rural area not far from San Marcos.

"Does anyone know someone who lives in Altman?" I asked the council members who hadn't left the room.

"My sister-in-law lives there," said Rufus.

"Do you mind calling her and asking if anything weird is going on in town?"

His brow furrowed. "Why Altman?"

"Detective Samson lives there, and he seems to be unreachable," I replied. "It's just a hunch. A real long shot."

Rufus made a call on his cell phone, speaking at a low volume. He walked away from the group to a far corner of the room, then returned.

"She says the militia has been there, driving through the neighborhoods in pickup trucks."

My heart sank. Had Samson been taken by the militia, like so many other supernaturals had been?

I voiced my concern.

"My sister-in-law didn't say anything about arrests," Rufus said, "but they very well could have taken him. I don't see how they would know he's a shifter, though. He was very careful about keeping that secret."

"All it takes is neighbors seeing a wolf run around at night," interjected Gaarg. "Being that there are no wolves in Florida."

"Our usual response to nosy neighbors is that they saw a large coyote," Rufus said.

That didn't make me feel any better. I felt I should let Mom know about Samson's possible disappearance.

"Oh, no," Mom said over the phone. "I hope you're just being paranoid."

"I've got a bad feeling," I replied.

"I'll go check on him. I'm just outside of Altman."

"What are you talking about?"

"I'm trying to drum up business for the inn. Since we're marketing ourselves solely to supernaturals now, we can't advertise in the usual places. I'm driving around, leaving flyers in stores and restaurants in places where I know a lot of supernaturals live. You know, in case they want a weekend getaway in San Marcos at an inn just for them. Or if they're refugees because of oppression."

"*Flyers?*" I was incredulous.

"With coupons. Stay for three nights and the fourth night is free. The wording is very discreet, so only supernaturals will know they're the target audience."

"Mom, don't go into Altman. I just told you the militia was there."

"I'll stay clear of any guys in uniforms with guns."

"Evelyn of the Psychic Guild said she senses additional activity that concerned her. It could be Fae from the Unseelie Court."

"After we kicked their butt recently?"

"We defeated a small detachment of soldiers. The Queene has a huge army. Please stay away from the area."

"Sophie, you're the one who called and got me all alarmed about Michael."

"I didn't mean to alarm you, only to inform you."

"Michael is a dear friend. I can't turn around when I'm this close to his home without checking on him."

"Mom, please don't. Evelyn senses that some bad stuff is going to happen there."

"I'll reach his house in ten, fifteen minutes. I'll call you then to let you know I'm fine." She ended the call.

I didn't need a drop of psychic blood to know that Mom was making a huge mistake. Her stubbornness had helped her make it through life, but today it could do the opposite.

Should I drive to Altman in case Mom got into trouble? I wasn't sure if two people knowingly stumbling into danger was such a good idea.

However, after I left the meeting room, twenty minutes went

by without a call from Mom. Then thirty minutes. I called her and she didn't reply.

Finally, minutes later, as I was wrestling with deciding if I should go after her, I got my answer.

Sophie, I'm in trouble, she said, her voice pouring telepathically into my head. "*Altman is under attack.*"

CHAPTER 2

DARLA

Altman was dead. I hoped that was only in the metaphorical sense. It was just after 9:00 p.m., and the city looked abandoned. Restaurants and gas stations that should have been open at this hour were dark, and it was only the streetlights that assured me the city hadn't lost power.

Sophie was right that I was taking a risk coming here after the militia had been spotted. But I was panicking about Samson, and I had planned to stop here anyway on my amateurish promotional tour.

The town, with a main street leading straight to the shore of massive Lake Altman, had a historical inn that had recently gone out of business. I had hoped to poach the inn's type of clientele with my coupon flyers taped to the door. There was also a funky gift shop and bookstore where I would have placed a big stack of them, but the store was closed and dark.

My day had been spent going from town to town. Most were based on agricultural economies, and their retail establishments wouldn't be receptive to my flyers. But now and then, the historical towns along the lakes and the river that connected them were tourist-friendly. There, I would find the occasional psychic shop or New Age store.

Even in the middle of the day, these places had been closed. I feared the militia had scared the owners away, or worse, had arrested them.

It was an odd feeling: on the surface, everything in these towns appeared normal, but there was a sense of menace. It was as if they had been occupied by a foreign invader who instilled an atmosphere of fear. I saw nothing specific, but the mood hung over the towns nevertheless.

In Altman, I got my proof of what was going on. Mine was the only car sitting at a red light at an empty intersection when a cacophony of horn-honking approached from behind me. Flashing hazard lights filled my mirrors as an armada of pickup trucks roared past me through the red light. The six trucks were stuffed with uniformed armed men in the cabs and open truck beds. It was like something you'd see on the news from war-torn regions of the Middle East or Africa.

My hands on the steering wheel trembled. The ominous vibe I had been feeling was real. I had hoped the militia had been decimated in the recent battle with shifters after the militia burned the church they believed held vampires. But there appeared to be plenty more of the extremists.

Michael Samson's home was just outside of town. It was a small ranch of sorts, with a house, a barn, and several acres of fields and woods. The barn used to house a couple of horses, but they had been sold after Samson's daughter moved away and got married.

No lights were on in the house. I rolled toward it along the dirt driveway, dreading what I might find.

Samson's SUV was parked in front of the house. As I neared

it, I saw the vehicle had been destroyed. It was riddled with bullet holes; the windows were shattered, and the tires were flat.

His house had also been peppered with bullets. The front door hung open on one hinge, and broken glass covered the front porch. The shards of glass in the windows looked like jagged fangs.

My gut was solid ice as I got out of my car and crept onto the porch.

"Michael?" I called with a quavering voice.

The only response was a buzzing of cicadas from the nearby trees.

Please, may he be alive, I prayed.

My feet crunching on broken glass, I walked into the house. Whatever had happened to Samson, he had put up a fight. The interior looked as bad as the exterior, with spilled shell casings and the signs of a battle everywhere. Too bad home insurance didn't cover acts of war.

I explored the entire house, calling out his name, although I knew by now that he wasn't there—at least not alive.

Thankfully, I didn't find a body. There was plenty of spilled blood, but I hoped it had come from the bad guys.

A spare bedroom appeared to be the site of Samson's last stand. Samson's hunting rifle and his police sidearm were lying on the floor atop shell casings and, strikingly, a clump of hair lay beside them. Most people would think it came from a dog, but I knew it was a wolf's fur.

Samson had shifted to wolf when he knew the militia was winning the battle.

Again, I prayed he was okay. Something—maybe the psychic senses in me—told me he was alive. Now all I had to do was find him. *Good luck.*

After I retraced my path down his driveway, I came upon a

small pickup truck sitting beside the rural highway at the entrance to a driveway near Samson's. I almost panicked at first, thinking it was a militia vehicle. But the man leaning against the hood of the vintage truck was unarmed and dressed in civilian clothes.

I rolled down my window. "Do you know what happened here?" I asked him.

"The militia took Mr. Samson," he drawled. "But not without a fight. Woke everyone up within miles of here."

"It happened tonight?"

He nodded. "A couple of hours ago. I saw your headlights turn into his driveway and came out to see who you were."

"I'm a friend, checking on him. Do you know if he's alive?"

"I think so. I was watching with a night-vision scope and saw a man wearing a hood, tied up with ropes, in the bed of one of the trucks. I believe it was Mr. Samson."

I felt the tiniest bit of relief. "Where would they take him?"

"I heard they were holding folks in a strawberry-packing warehouse not far from here. Don't know if they're still there. Heard it's just a temporary stockade."

"Why would they take Michael?" I asked, playing dumb, curious if Samson's neighbor knew he was a shifter.

He squinted, trying to figure out my angle. "I guess Michael was an undesirable in these times of ours."

"What do you mean?"

He laughed nervously. "He's different from most folks. Some people don't like the ones who are different. Those different ones ended up in the warehouse. Feels like the town is half empty now."

"Look, I know Michael's secret. His other identity. The militia is taking people like him all over Florida."

The man smiled and nodded. "I got nothing against werewolves. Never believed they existed until I found out Michael was one. He never bothered my livestock, and if it weren't for some howling at the moon and a few glimpses of a wolf in the fields, I wouldn't have figured it out. Michael's a good man, a good neighbor. What he does in his private life is none of my business. Same goes for the other folks who got rounded up. They say witches and bloodsuckers are among them. I didn't know they lived here, but I don't have a problem with it."

"I wish everyone had an open mind like you," I said. "Where can I find the strawberry warehouse?"

"Oh, you shouldn't go there. Too dangerous."

"I have to. Michael is a good friend."

He studied me, then spoke. "Take this road back to town, then go south a few miles on County Road 80."

"Thank you," I said, putting the car into gear.

"Be careful."

I waved goodbye and pulled onto the road.

County Road 80 was a narrow, unlit strip of asphalt that ran straight through strawberry and vegetable farms. I traveled on it for more than three miles without seeing any structures before I came upon the single-story windowless building.

Something *Growers* was all I could read of the fading sign as my headlights passed over it. I pulled into a sandy parking lot, which was perhaps a risky move, but there were no other vehicles in sight. The county road was silent except for the intermittent hiss of an occasional vehicle passing.

I got out of my car and approached the building. It had only two narrow windows that were dark and several garage-style doors that were closed. The building was clearly no longer used by its owners, and I had doubts the militia was still using it.

Between the two windows was a normal front door. It was locked, of course. Being the human vessel of an ancient goddess had its perks, but the ability to pick locks was not one of them.

My psychometry, however, might prove useful in finding out if supernaturals were kept there.

The locked door handle was loaded with psychic energy. The problem with doorknobs, latches, and the like was they received a lot of handling, but it was usually very brief. And people usually weren't thinking about much when they handled them.

I decided to search for memories anyway. First, I put myself into a semi-trance state and opened my psychic senses. The most important part was blocking out my thoughts of the here and now so I could read the thoughts of others from the past.

Hovering my hand close to the metal handle, I sensed a lot of recent activity after years of disuse. The thoughts I picked up weren't the banal, empty meanderings of the office workers and fruit packers who had worked inside. What I felt were urgent, excited thoughts of men involved in evil acts.

Militiamen, in other words.

I sensed a vivid, very recent memory and put my hand directly on the handle. The last man to touch this had been locking up early this morning before dawn. He was in a—

—*hurry, because we've got more supernaturals to catch. The vampires inside will be fine for a few days. Damn rusty lock! Got it*—

—That's all there was of the man's thoughts. I removed my hand from the handle.

So, there were vampires inside. But presumably no shifters. And the militiaman had locked up hours before Samson was caught.

Where were Samson and the other shifters, plus the witches the neighbor claimed had been captured?

I put my hand near the handle again, searching for any other relevant recent memories. There were many jumbled fragments from various men—a word or two each about supernaturals or orders from superiors. But wait, here was something—thoughts about being—

—*ordered to transfer the prisoners from this packing house and empty the town of supernaturals before the*—

—That was all there was. Before the *what?*

I searched in vain for more memories that might answer my question but found nothing.

The rumbling of a large engine disturbed my thoughts and grew louder. The silhouette of a large pickup truck approached along the county road. When I saw the fluttering American flag behind the cab, I knew it was time to get out of there.

I ran to my car and jumped in, pulling out of the dirt parking lot just as the pickup truck pulled in. In addition to the flag, a half dozen militiamen crowded the bed.

They all stared at me with great interest. The same interest a lion has when staring at a gazelle.

I was just a middle-aged innkeeper who had done nothing to the packing house. But when I glanced in my rearview mirror, the truck was right behind me. I guessed they figured I'd seen something incriminating. But I'd seen or heard nothing. All I'd done was read the memories of someone who had thought about the vampires held captive in the building.

It didn't matter. These guys must have assumed the worst and were now coming to get me.

The grill of the giant truck hit my car's trunk. Not hard enough to make me crash, but enough to make me consider surrendering.

Nope. Not going to happen. I slammed my foot on the accelerator.

For nothing. My poor car was at its top speed. In fact, it was shaking and rattling so much I thought it would disassemble at any moment.

The truck rammed into me again. My car fishtailed, the tires screeching on the asphalt. I swung the wheel back and forth, trying to regain control, but the next thing I knew my tires were on the dirt shoulder, sending up a cloud of dust.

And then I was in a ditch, the car jolting to a stop in the shallow water and mud. The airbag didn't deploy, so I just sat there, hyperventilating, listening to the ticking coming from the engine after it died.

Voices came from above the ditch. My car was lying at a slight angle, the right side lower where water seeped beneath the door. I craned my neck and saw militiamen looking down at me, bathed in the truck's headlights.

"Do you reckon she's a supernatural?" one asked.

"Could be a witch. It'll be easier just to shoot her now, so we don't got to deal with her. We should've left town by now."

What an ignominious way to die, I thought. *Shot in a ditch.*

I texted Sophie that I was in trouble, and the strangest thing happened. The men began coughing and doubling over, holding their stomachs. Then, one by one, they dropped to the ground.

Before I could rejoice at my good fortune and escape from the car, a wave of weakness and nausea swept over me amid a spasm of coughing. I recognized the symptoms. They portended far worse than the militiamen.

CHAPTER 3

SOPHIE

I performed my locator spell using strands of Mom's hair from her hairbrush. Kneeling inside a magic circle in my room, surrounded by discarded clothing and my usual clutter, I was depressed and angry. Cervantes, my black cat and witch's familiar, looked on, sending me good vibes. But they didn't improve my mood.

Mom wasn't yet sixty, but she required more and more care, as if she were elderly and suffering from dementia. Her catatonic episodes when astral traveling to visit the Goddess or the Elves were bad enough, right? But now I had to deal with her wantonly going into Altman when she knew the militia was there.

And don't forget about when she was abducted by the Fae of the Unseelie Court. I had to recruit a small army of gnomes to rescue her. Though in all honesty that hadn't been Mom's fault, I wanted to blame her anyway. Why did she get sucked into sticky supernatural trouble so often?

When my locator spell activated, I received a vision of Mom.

She was unconscious in her car beside a remote country road outside of Altman. She was alive, but I sensed illness in her. This wasn't one of her catatonic moments; there was something wrong.

The car was in a ditch, so the rare passing car might not see it until the sun rose. However, a pickup truck on the shoulder nearby might attract attention, especially since unconscious militiamen lay scattered on the ground around it.

During my vision, no cars came by, though.

After I broke the spell, I considered calling an ambulance for Mom, but I knew in my gut that she didn't have a conventional illness. She had been overcome by magic, which would explain the incapacitated militiamen.

Did you find her? Cervantes asked me telepathically in his Spanish accent.

"Yes," I said aloud. I explained her predicament.

My heart skipped a beat when I realized they must have been felled by Fae magic—the spell laced with phytolucine, a substance created by trees to defend themselves. The Fae harvested it from tree roots and incorporated it into their spell, hoping to wipe out humans. I had been exposed to traces of it when we destroyed an underground Fae laboratory, but it hadn't affected me or the other supernaturals in our party.

It had affected only Mom, because although she was a psychic—and a victim of the state's anti-supernatural persecution like all paranormals and supernaturals—she wasn't a true supernatural creature like a vampire, or a witch with magic genes like me.

Would the spell kill Mom? We had always assumed killing humans was the purpose of the spell, but maybe it only knocked them out temporarily. I changed my mind and called 911, just in case.

"My mother suffered a medical emergency, and her car went off the road near Altman," I told the operator.

"I'm switching you to the local dispatcher there," she told me.

There was a *click*, then the line rang and rang, with no one picking up.

Of course. The local 911 operator had probably been overcome by the spell. I had to get to Altman immediately. My only comfort was the fact that the vision from my spell had told me that Mom was alive.

I flew downstairs to get Cory, but it would be nice to have additional help when going into a danger zone. I called Diego.

The vampire actually answered my call for once.

"Altman? We're on our way there now," he said. "I received a report that the town's vampires had been rounded up and are being held captive in a packing house on County Road 80 outside of town."

"Wow. That's near where Mom is." I gave him more details of what my vision had told me about her.

"We have to hurry. It sounds like the Faerie Queene's army is going to attack the town."

The truth dawned on me. "That's why the militia was rounding up all the supernaturals. The Fae must know their spell only works on humans, so they're having the militia clear out the supernaturals to leave the town undefended."

"Sounds rather lazy of the Fae to rely on the militia and the spell to do their conquering for them," Diego said.

"Lazy and smart. Let's try to meet up in Altman after our rescue missions, in case the Fae are there."

IT WAS ABOUT A THIRTY-MINUTE DRIVE TO ALTMAN, AND ONCE we were on County Road 80, Cory and I kept our eyes peeled searching for Mom's car. The Fae magic was in the air, but it wasn't as strong here as it was in the center of town. Fortunately, Cory and I were unaffected.

We passed an old warehouse. Diego's car was parked beside it, along with two passenger vans. Hopefully he could defeat whatever method was used to lock the vampires inside the building. A locked door wouldn't be strong enough to keep vampires confined.

It wasn't hard to find Mom's car. The truck I had seen in my vision was still parked beside the road, lights on and engine running. Cory jumped as soon as his SUV had come to a complete stop, sliding down the embankment into the ditch where Mom's car sat in shallow water, the driver's side higher because of the slope.

I quickly touched the necks of the eight militiamen to check their pulses. All were alive, but deeply unconscious.

Mom's window had been left open, and Cory reached inside to check on her.

"She's alive and breathing normally with a good heartbeat," he said. "Thank God."

I glanced at the unconscious militiamen. "It looks like the Fae magic doesn't kill normal humans like we'd feared. I guess it just knocks them out of commission while the Fae invade us."

"Still, I wish we had a spell to counteract it." Cory stroked Mom's face.

"That's next on my horribly long to-do list," I replied. "Let me help you pull her out of the car."

The driver's side of the car was too close to the slope of the ditch to get her door open, but the two of us pulled her through the open window. At times like this, her petite size was a blessing. We carried her up the slope and placed her carefully in the backseat of the SUV.

"I don't see any signs of injury from the car crash," I said. "With luck, she'll be freed of the spell when we get her away from this area. If she doesn't snap out of it, we'll take her to the ER near home."

Cory stared at the prone militiamen. "Do you think we should take their weapons in case they wake up and come after us?"

"Yeah. The guns might come in handy if things get worse. Let's make sure we get all their ammo, too."

We loaded up the cargo area like a pair of gunrunners and returned the way we had come. When we reached the abandoned building, Diego's car and the vans were still there. The vans were empty. Apparently Diego hadn't freed the prisoners yet.

We pulled into the parking lot. "Stay with Mom. Let me see if Diego needs some magical help."

The building was completely dark inside. Diego and the vampires would have no trouble seeing, but I was just a living human, my magical abilities notwithstanding. Speaking of which, I was about to use the flashlight on my smartphone, but I thought, *what would a witch do instead?*

With a quick spell, I produced a glowing orb that floated in front of me a few feet above the floor. This would be a more impressive entrance in Diego's eyes.

I moved through the open space past dust-covered wooden crates, boxes of plastic containers, a conveyor belt, and several sorting stations. No vampires in sight. At the end of the space was a door leading to an office area. Diego, Helga, and Eduardo stared at me as I entered a room emptied of furniture. They had obviously already known of my arrival, thanks to their superior hearing.

"They're locked in the bathroom and we can't get them out," Diego said. "It's some kind of magic spell."

Which was unfortunate, because I really needed to use the bathroom.

I studied the bathroom door, which wasn't sealed with silver or adorned with religious iconography—the few traditional ways to lock up vampires. Instead, it radiated magic.

Fae magic.

As far as I knew, the militia didn't work directly with the Unseelie Court and their sorcerers. The only faeries the militia would interact with were the indigenous ones who pretended to be human, such as Governor Witlessin.

And Baldric, who was a sorcerer. The mind control spell he had accidentally cast on himself wasn't stopping his slimy, backstabbing behaviors. In fact, as I studied the spell, I recognized its unique handiwork as his.

"I think Baldric did this," I said. "How could he use magic in front of the militia without them realizing he was a supernatural and turning on him?"

Eduardo shrugged. "Humans have an infinite capacity for hypocrisy and the ability to blind themselves from realizing it."

"I'll try to deconstruct this spell and break it," I said, adding that the Fae had used a phytolucine-laced spell to disable the humans in the area, including Mom. "We must escape before the Fae attack."

"Oh, it's much too late to escape," Diego said. "The roads were sealed off shortly after we arrived. We will need to fight our way out of here before the full army arrives."

"Okay, then. I'll get to work. No pressure at all."

I stared at the brown door with the man and woman symbols

on it illuminated by my floating orb, the three vampires watching me. When I went into a trance, the structure of the Fae spell came into my perception.

Lines of energy, like strings of yarn, were woven together into a fabric that covered the door, as well as the walls on either side, to prevent even the strongest vampire from bursting through. The Fae spell structure was more intricate and ornate than the simple, sturdy spells I created. The woven pattern seemed rather old-fashioned, but inarguably beautiful.

If you had seen one, you would think, *just cut the strands, Sophie, and it will unravel.*

Nope, it was not that simple. I needed precisely the right magic to cut the strands, and it was crucial to anticipate and contain the reaction of all that magical energy collapsing on itself. In the past, I'd caused fires and minor explosions when I didn't defuse a spell properly. Once, I triggered a mini thunderstorm that rained bleach and turned my hair white. Kind of embarrassing.

After studying the spell structure, I cast an energy-severing spell that would cut the support strands across the entire length of the magic barrier at exactly the same time. This would make the energy collapse upon itself across the maximum area, reducing the impact in any one place and dissipating the energy evenly.

As soon as I did so, a clicking sound entered my head. It was then that I realized Baldric—or whomever the Fae sorcerer was—had set a trap for a human witch, wizard, or mage attempting to break the spell.

Perhaps, even, the trap had been devised specifically for me.

As the energy from the sorcerer's barrier spell collapsed, it didn't land upon itself in a heap. No, it gushed outward across the floor, away from the wall, and toward me.

It hit me like a tsunami, knocking the wind out of me and temporarily blinding me. It covered me like a wet blanket, heavy and hot. I struggled to open my eyelids, as if they had been glued shut.

When my eyesight finally returned, the bathroom door opened and at least ten vampires poured out of the tiny room. They were men and women of different races and various ages, hurrying past me like I was a statue standing in their way.

In fact, I quickly realized that was indeed what I was: a statue. I was paralyzed, standing there frozen with my palms pointed toward the door and walls where the Fae spell had been. I couldn't move my head, but my eyeballs could rotate, and the view of my arms and hands revealed nothing unusual.

Except that they were unmoving.

"Sophie, is something wrong?" Diego asked.

My mouth had been left slightly open from when I uttered my spell incantations. My lips couldn't move, but my tongue could.

"I am rozen," was all I could manage to say.

"What happened?"

"Aggic." In case you couldn't translate, that was meant to be "magic."

"Well, you certainly have bad timing. The Fae army just began invading."

CHAPTER 4

SOPHIE

"Inhading?" I mumbled through my frozen lips.

"Yes," Diego replied. "Although not with tanks and troop transports. With delivery vans."

The vampire picked me up like a mannequin and moved me to one of the small windows so I could see.

It was true: headlights pierced the night from a long line of trucks and vans rolling along the road toward Altman. The moonlight illuminated the familiar logos we saw every day, everywhere, in cities, suburbs, and rural areas. The Fae must have stolen the trucks or placed counterfeit logos on their own.

Any humans who had been awake to see the convoy would have had no idea it carried invading soldiers.

If I had any doubt the trucks belonged to the Fae, it disappeared when a UPP van pulled into the parking lot of the packing plant beside our SUV. Cory must have been walking around and attracted their attention as a seemingly normal human who hadn't been enchanted by their spell.

The driver wasn't wearing a brown UPP uniform; he was all

in black and carried a handgun. The back door of the van slid open and a half-dozen similarly clad men and women exited, half of whom were carrying long guns.

How did I know they were faeries? Because I'm highly sensitive to supernatural creatures and sensed what they were, even from inside the building. I also felt the magic they emanated from being in human form.

When the gnomes and I had fought the Fae before, they had been in their natural, diminutive forms—possibly because they were fighting other supernatural creatures. On this mission, the Fae had adopted the forms of the humans they were conquering.

"Cory. Arla," I mumbled.

"Don't worry," Diego said. "I'll protect Cory and Darla."

An explosion of light came from our SUV, blinding me. The faeries flew backwards, away from the car, landing in the dirt. A fusillade of fireballs shot from the vehicle's windows, obliterating the creatures.

"Looks like Cory is doing just fine at protecting your mother," Diego quipped.

However, the drivers of the next vehicles to pass the packing plant saw what had happened, and they all began pulling over. The one that stopped closest to us erupted in a magic-induced inferno.

The vehicles further down the line kept their distance. Bursts of light and the popping of gunfire filled the night.

"Now he needs help," Diego said. He turned to the vampires who had gathered behind him—Helga, Eduardo, and the ten they had freed. "Brethren, let's kill some faeries."

Suddenly, I sensed they weren't inside the building anymore. I couldn't turn my head to follow them, but in an instant I had a view of vampires leaping into trucks and vans, followed by mangled Fae bodies flying out.

After four trucks had their passengers slaughtered, no more of them stopped. The rest of the convoy sped up, passing the packing plant, wisely avoiding the vampires.

Diego and two others stepped in front of the last vehicle. I thought they would be run over but the van slammed into them and stopped, as if it had hit iron pilings. The vampires entered the cab, and I'll spare you the details.

The gunfire had ceased, and the roar of the last truck of the convoy faded into the distance. The van Cory had incinerated continued to burn outside the window, casting the wreckage of the battlefield in a demonic light.

Cory stepped out of the SUV, no worse for wear. He followed Diego into the building.

"I ha ohay?" I mumbled.

Cory stopped beside me. "What?"

"She's paralyzed by the spell the Fae used to seal the vampires in here," Diego explained. "It's sealing her into immobility."

"How is she going to break the spell?"

"I don't know. I don't believe she knows either. As a witch yourself, *you* must figure it out."

"I need to break the spell on Darla too," Cory said, full of despair.

"Sophie is supposedly quite good at telepathy now. She can help you with her magical knowledge."

It frustrated me to be talked about like I was a potted plant, almost as much as it infuriated me to be a potted plant. Diego was right, though: I was a more accomplished witch than Cory. He'd always been a reluctant one and hadn't constantly improved himself like I had.

As the threat from the Fae increased, Cory had stepped up.

His fireballs were almost as powerful as the lightning I shot from my sword. When I wasn't frozen, that is. Cory also had the ability to draw energy from underground ley lines, which was very valuable indeed. With the two of us working together, we had a chance of defeating the spells that incapacitated Mom and me.

"I can't figure out how to break spells if we're under attack by the Fae," Cory said. "We need to get out of Altman."

"Of course," Diego replied. "No one is safe here, and we must return to San Marcos before dawn. Follow our vehicles. We will take an indirect route home that avoids Altman."

Since Mom's sleeping body was flexible, Cory moved her from the backseat to the passenger seat of the SUV. He stowed me horizontally where Mom had been, which was rather awkward because my hands were still extended like they'd been when I was frozen.

Lying on my back, I could see little of what was outside of the car. The last view I had as Cory pushed me through the door was the vampires piling into the passenger vans, which followed Diego in his Aston Martin heading away from town, in the direction from which the Fae convoy had come.

We drove for a while along the curving roads. It felt like forever, but we had probably gone only a short distance. All I wanted was to break the spells on Mom and me before crawling into my bed at the inn. I knew it wouldn't be that easy, though. Nothing in my life was.

"How's it going back there?" Cory asked.

"Oh-ay," I mumbled. Speaking was simply not going to work. I tried to send a message to Cory with telepathy.

Are we still following the vampires?

"Yes," he replied aloud. He didn't realize he only needed to think, and I would understand. "They're driving awfully fast, though. Nowadays, you don't want to get a speeding ticket if you're a vampire."

Only if we've traveled past the reach of the Fae's spell. Otherwise, law enforcement will be incapacitated.

"True."

Mom groaned from the front seat.

"I think she's coming out of it!" Cory said excitedly. "We must be far enough away from Altman and the spell. We're in the middle of nowhere."

Mom began snoring loudly. The spell left a bit of a hangover effect.

"Oh no!" Cory said. "The vampire vans are stopping. Maybe the sheriff pulled them over."

It might be the Fae, I conveyed to him. *Can you turn around?*

Gunfire came from ahead of us.

"I think it's the militia," he said in a low voice.

Turn around! Let's get out of here!

"No. They'll see us. I've shut down the headlights and pulled off the road behind some bushes. I just saw a militiaman flung into the air. Looks like the vampires are kicking their butts."

Better hope so.

"The vampire vans are moving ahead now. I'm going to follow them."

Are you sure it's safe?

"It looks like it. We need to stay close to the vampires for protection, so I don't want to lose them."

Call or text Diego to be sure.

Cory tapped out a text. He waited a moment and grunted with frustration. Believe me, I knew that feeling when trying to reach Diego. He tapped his phone some more and put it to his ear. I heard the unanswered ringing and the line going to voicemail.

"No response," Cory said. "I'm getting back on the road. Like I said, I don't want them to leave us behind."

I tried to reach out telepathically to Diego. I'd never had luck with that before. His emotions were readable when I was near him, but reading his thoughts and sending him mine hadn't worked yet. The same was true tonight.

The car moved across bumpy grass and climbed back onto the asphalt road. Cory turned on the headlights and drove for mere seconds before he cursed and braked hard. He threw the car into reverse, backed off the road, and turned the wheel in the opposite direction, gravel and grass spraying as he hit the gas and took us back the way we had come.

Back toward Altman. And the Fae.

Are the militiamen coming after us? I asked.

"Not yet. But they saw us for sure. I thought the vampires had wiped them out. We passed a pickup flipped onto its roof and some bodies on the ground. But then there was another truck, and it shined a searchlight at us. I wasn't taking any chances."

We can't go back to Altman.

"The navigation screen shows a minor back road coming up that leads to a different county road that will get us to the state highway without getting any closer to Altman."

I continued lying paralyzed on my back, my hands pointed upward as if I were begging heaven for help. The windows showed only darkness, no street or traffic lights, not even welcoming lamps at the end of any driveways. At least being in such a rural area meant we were less likely to run into the Fae.

Why was Cory cursing and braking suddenly?

"There's a checkpoint," he said. "Armed, but they don't look like they're militiamen."

The car stopped. Cory lowered his window. I sensed Fae magic as someone reached the window.

"Can we pass?" Cory asked.

"What is your business?" asked a man with a slight accent you'd assume was European, but I knew otherwise.

"We're headed to San Marcos, but the road is blocked north of here by an accident. There's a detour up ahead I planned to take."

Though I couldn't see him, I felt the faerie's eyes upon me.

"What's wrong with the woman in your back seat?" he asked.

"She's fine. It's just a nervous condition."

"Wait here."

The faerie walked away from the car and spoke with an associate out of our earshot.

The rumbling of a truck engine grew louder behind us, and headlights flooded the car's interior.

Doors slammed. Boots crunched across the asphalt on either side of the car. Two flashlight beams raked the seats.

"Are you men with the militia?" asked the faerie.

"Yup. We're checking if these folks are supernatural," said a man with a Southern accent. "They were traveling right behind a bunch of vampires."

"The one in the back seat is a witch!" another man said with excitement. "I found her just now in the Monster Monitor app. I bet the others are witches, too."

"Well, well," said the first militiaman. "We bagged us three supernaturals. Three cash bounties. Secure the man and help me get them in the truck's bed."

"I'm sorry, gentlemen," said the faerie. "I've been ordered to dispose of them before they spread the word about us."

"They ain't spreading no word. We're locking 'em up."

"Gentlemen, please step aside."

34

"We deserve the bounties for them! We're taking them now."

I had no desire to feel the emotions of the antagonists outside the car, but the feelings were too strong to ignore: greed, anger, and the desire to kill.

The first shot was almost gentle-sounding, coming from a gun with a suppressor. Someone fell against the side of the car, rocking it.

The subsequent gunshots were deafening and went on and on and on, while I howled in horror through my immobile lips, wishing I could crawl onto the floor.

CHAPTER 5

SOPHIE

The gunshots finally ended, but a keening from inside the car continued.

Oh. It was me. Oops. I immediately stopped.

The car lurched forward and sped down the road. I inwardly cringed, expecting bullets to hit the car.

"Sophie, are you okay?" Cory asked.

"Uh-huh. Wha ha-hing?"

"Say what?"

What happened? My telepathy worked much better than my mouth.

"There were three Fae soldiers in human form and two militiamen. The first human was shot without warning. The second one took out all three faeries, but not without getting shot himself. They were all lying on the road, so I just took off."

Where are we going?

"We just passed the packing plant. We're finding a motel near Altman."

Are you crazy?

"I have no intention of bumping into more Fae checkpoints or militia, and it's too dangerous to travel in the dark. Darla is stirring, so hopefully the phytolucine spell is wearing off. If that's the case, the residents of Altman will soon be doing their usual routines, and we won't stand out."

Come to think of it, I did sense a weakening of the noxious magic that had permeated the area.

Okay, I agree with your plan. Check into a motel, then help me break the spell that paralyzed me.

Before long, streetlights whizzed past the window I was staring through from my vantage on my back. The question was, how much had the spell worn off in Altman?

The turn signal ticked as Cory made a turn, a gesture that seemed unnecessary in a ghost town. We pulled off the road and parked. A great deal of artificial light seeped into the car. *We must be in a parking lot.*

"The Sweet Dreams Lodge," Cory said. "I'm not sure if that name is adorable or sleazy."

He got out of the car, and I waited anxiously while Mom alternated between moaning and snoring in the front seat.

After an eternity, Cory returned and started the car. "I got us two rooms." He drove across the lot and parked again. "A desk clerk was working, though he was awfully groggy. A man in black sat on a stool watching him, obviously a faerie in human form. I wonder if their form of occupation is a Mafia-style protection racket."

He carefully picked up Mom and carried her from the car. When it was my turn, he brought me into a musty-smelling room where a single lamp glowed and deposited me on a bed.

"Let me get a little sleep," he said, "and I'll be back to work with you on the spell."

He turned off the light, and I lay there in the dark, completely disabled, with only my mind working.

And work it did. While Cory slept, I spent the hours studying the spell that bound me. It had signs of Baldric's handiwork and had been designed to attack any magician—human or Fae—who tampered with or broke it.

I couldn't help but suspect the magician he had in mind was me. He knew what side I was on in the struggle against the Faerie Queene and the Governor, and he wanted revenge for my besting him when he tried to control my mind.

Would I need to kill him? Somehow I knew my newfound emotional sensitivity as an empath wouldn't object too loudly if I rid the world of that treacherous faerie.

At some point I must have fallen asleep, because I had a nightmare – a horrific one that involved truckloads of supernaturals delivered to a basketball arena. Vampires, shifters, witches, trolls, and others were herded into the venue by faceless creatures brandishing weapons.

And I was with them. I took a seat in the uppermost row of the arena, next to Diego. Every seat was filled, and the floor was crowded by supernaturals forced to stand. The Jumbotron lit up with the face of the governor, reading us our death sentences. Then flames swept through the crowd.

I was whimpering when Cory shook me awake.

Bad dream, I said.

"Let's free you of this hex," he said. "I don't sense any ley lines nearby, so I can't harvest extra energy, but I'll transfer all my inherent energy to enhance yours."

Thank you. Please sit on the bed beside me.

He complied.

Place your left hand above my solar plexus . . . a little higher up on my belly. Okay. Now put your right hand on my forehead. Let me get my mind in gear and gather my own energies before I give you the word.

"Okay."

I prepared myself for spell casting, just as I normally would. I cast my deconstruction spell, which enabled me to visualize the structure of Baldric's spell. Then I let my empath powers kick in.

I wasn't trying to read his emotions; he wasn't here, after all. What I was doing was feeling for traces of his emotions in the spell he had cast. Its purpose was to seal the vampires inside the packing-house bathroom. But he hadn't avoided letting his hatred of me seep into it.

Hatred corrupts everything it touches. And sure enough, it had corrupted several strands of his spell's structure. It was as if they were coated with slime—the residue of his negative emotions. This residue didn't weaken the strands but made them stand out so I could sever them.

Ready, Cory? Give me the juice!

A surge of warm energy flowed from his hands into my belly and brain. It electrified and strengthened me. With this extra power, I set about breaking apart Baldric's spell on me.

It wasn't easy. He was an accomplished sorcerer, and his spell had been created to be as tamper-proof as possible. But never underestimate the strength of a witch who's been wronged.

One by one, I cut the strands of Fae energy that were the framework of the spell. They were strong and taut, breaking like piano wires with a twang that only I could hear.

The corrupted strands—the ones slimed with his hatred for me—were the toughest to break.

Can you give me more energy, Cory?

He grunted with the effort, and more warmth flowed into me. He was leaning over me now, and I saw the sweat on his skin and the strain on his face. I was struggling even more than he was, but it wouldn't be apparent in my paralyzed face.

Finally, a louder twang as a corrupted strand snapped apart. Then another and another.

The dark, dirty energy of Fae magic fled from my mind and body. It was akin to the feeling you get when blood returns after your leg has fallen asleep.

My ears buzzed and my fingers tingled. Warmth and contentment flowed through me. I lowered my arms from their zombie-like positions and sat up on the bed.

"You did it!" Cory said, beaming.

"I couldn't have done it without your energy. Thank you."

"Of course. But I need another nap now."

I got off the bed and helped him across the floor to his room, which adjoined mine. Mom sat on the bed, awake but pale and queasy-looking.

"How are you feeling, Mom?"

"Like the world's worst hangover after the world's seediest bachelorette party."

Cory and I filled her in on all the events that occurred after she had been overcome by the anti-human spell.

"Are we trapped here in Altman?" she asked.

"I don't know," I replied. "The Fae might not allow anyone to leave. And if we did, the militia might be outside the perimeter waiting to snatch supernaturals. In the meantime, I'm going to grab some food and bring it back."

"It's too dangerous," Mom said.

"I had no problem booking the rooms," Cory said. "I think the Fae are only interested in occupying the town."

"And I doubt there are any militiamen here. The shootout on the road proves there's some tension between the Fae and the militia," I added. "Don't know if it's territorial or testosterone. But it might be something we can use to our advantage later."

"There's a diner across the street from the motel," Cory said. "Bacon and egg sandwiches would be heavenly."

I told them I'd be right back and not to worry. In the back of the SUV were my sword and crossbow, not to mention the firearms we'd confiscated from the militiamen who were overcome by the Fae spell. But of course I couldn't take them with me. I had to behave like a clueless human, completely at the mercy of the occupying forces.

It was 8:15 a.m. on a weekday, but traffic was at a minimum as I crossed the street to the diner next to a used-car lot. I figured most of the residents were still trying to get ready for the day, suffering from "hangovers." The diner's parking lot held only a few cars. Notably, a UPP van was parked outside.

The diner was a charming old-school joint, spiced up by the aroma of coffee brewing and eggs on the griddle, with seating at the counter and at several tables and vinyl-covered booths. Only a few customers were there, hunched morosely over their food. From the windows in the rear, I got a glimpse of Lake Altman a few blocks away. Aside from the sparse crowd, it seemed like a normal day.

Only it wasn't. Sitting beside the cashier near the door was a handsome man dressed all in black. A faerie in human form. Was he planning to sit there all day, taking a cut of the proceeds? It seemed like a crude way of extorting money, but it was probably how the Fae were training the townspeople to fork over money to their new rulers.

The faerie gave me a piercing, suspicious stare, then lost interest and looked away.

At the far end of the counter was a sign for takeout orders. I walked over and waited until a woman about my age came out of the open kitchen behind the counter. She was pale and tired-looking, with bags beneath her eyes. Wisps of unruly blonde hair draped her forehead.

I ordered two bacon-egg-and-cheese sandwiches for Cory and Mom, a blueberry muffin for myself, and three coffees. The woman took the order to the kitchen, returning shortly afterward.

"Should be about twenty minutes," she said. "Our cook came in late, and we're running behind."

"I think there's a bug going around." I smiled.

Strong feelings of unease and anxiety were coming from her —not about me, but about the general situation in town. I also sensed honesty and compassion.

In a voice too low to be heard by the faerie on the other side of the room, I asked if the roads between here and San Marcos were blocked.

"We had a problem with that last night," I explained.

"No closures that I know of," she said. She glanced nervously at the faerie. "Unless you're on State Road 64. That's shut down near the state park. But there are more direct routes to get you to San Marcos."

"Why is it closed?" I sent trusting vibes to her, so she'd be honest with me.

"There's some secret government thing going on at the park. They don't want anyone going anywhere near the place."

"What kind of thing?"

She shrugged.

"Does it have anything to do with that guy by the cash register?"

"No. It started weeks ago." She leaned toward me and whispered, "I think it has to do with supernaturals."

42

"I see. Thank you." I had a bad feeling about this. "So, what's the deal with all these guys showing up in town last night?"

The server's eyes darted to the faerie and away. "I'm not sure. The owner of the diner said she was told it had something to do with efficiency."

"Huh?"

"They're some kind of consultants. From a big corporation with a state contract. They're here to make our town more efficient. And better. Or something like that. That's all I know."

"Sounds kind of scary."

"Yeah. It is."

Obviously, the Fae forces occupying Altman hadn't yet announced that the citizens were now ruled by the Faerie Queene. That kind of news would get too much attention and spread across the state. This lower-visibility takeover of the town would allow the Fae to do the same thing to more towns and cities before everyone in the state became alarmed.

I had a feeling this public-relations approach had been recommended by Governor Witlessin.

The server returned with my food in a paper bag. I thanked her and wished her good luck. When I paid the cashier, the faerie studied me and my body in the creepiest fashion.

I stepped outside and called Diego.

"The spell on you is broken!" he exclaimed. "Splendid! Where are you?"

"Altman."

"Why are you still there?"

I explained that we had followed the vampire convoy out of town but were separated when the militia attacked. I also described how the Fae method of taking over towns was to control them Mafia-style.

"We need to set up an early-warning system for supernaturals," I added. "To spread the word wherever the militia are active and whenever large numbers of delivery vans are spotted. There are a lot of small towns in this part of Florida. The Fae can easily take them with the strategy of using the militia to clear out supernaturals before enchanting the human residents with the phytolucine spell, then transporting faeries throughout the towns on the vans."

"I'm setting up a text-message string with the vampire guild leaders of other cities. I'll add the leaders of other guilds, as well as other prominent supernaturals. Trolls and ogres aren't fond of texting because of their enormous fingers, but they'll manage."

"Thank you. The Fae are obviously trying to avoid pitched battles, but we need to fight them every step of the way. Keep me updated if you hear of activity in other towns."

MOM LOOKED A LITTLE BETTER, THOUGH STILL GROGGY AND puffy-eyed. She slurped her coffee and devoured her egg sandwich without hesitation.

"It looks like your nausea is gone," I noted.

"What makes you say that?" she asked with a full mouth.

"What was it like at the diner?" Cory asked.

"The town is slowly waking up to the fact that they're occupied by a bunch of thugs who want to take a cut of their money. And I learned something interesting."

I mentioned to Cory and Mom that the server had told me the nearby state park was closed for secret reasons.

"I wonder if they're keeping supernatural prisoners there," I added.

Mom became animated and said something unintelligible.

"Weren't you the one who taught me not to talk with my mouth full?" I asked her.

"I said maybe Samson is there. We should investigate."

"The server said the park is closed, as well as the road that passes it. I'm sure it's guarded."

"How convenient that I have two witches in my family," Mom said with a mischievous grin. "I think we'll be able to at least discover what's going on there."

Normally, mothers are voices of prudence and reason. Not in my family.

"I can't speak for Cory," I said, "but I don't have any spells that can tell me what's going on there without taking great risks."

"Same here," said Cory.

I added, "But I know of someone who can easily find out what we need to know."

CHAPTER 6

SOPHIE

State Road 64 is the route we would have taken the previous night if the Fae checkpoint hadn't kept us from detouring on a back road to reach the two-lane highway. After we supervised a tow truck removing Mom's car from the ditch and taking it to the repair shop, I drove the three of us on 64 toward the state park.

Sure enough, we soon came upon signs warning the road was closed ahead. I saw an abandoned barbecue stand beside the road and pulled into its parking lot.

"Now it's time to use our reptilian drone," I said, turning off the engine and clearing my mind.

Ronnie, can you hear me? I asked telepathically. *It's Sophie. We need you to scout the Pine Hammock State Park. Can you help us?*

Yes, he replied in his Southern drawl. *As soon as I'm finished recounting my treasure hoard.*

We're on State Road 64, about six miles outside of Altman.

Be there soon.

We remained in the car and waited. And waited. Apparently,

a dragon who can live thousands of years has a different concept of "soon."

Dust swirled in the dirt parking lot. A loud drumming sound filled the air, and then, in a blink of an eye, a dragon landed behind the barbecue shack, hidden from the view of the rare passing car.

The only other time I'd seen a dragon was while visiting the In Between, and a sense of wonder filled me, making me smile with delight instead of the fear I'd felt last time.

Ronnie was enormous in dragon form. His body was twice the length of our SUV, and his tail was as long as his body. He crouched on four legs, his giant wings folded against his abdomen. A long, sinuous neck led to a massive head with jaws large enough to swallow a human whole. At the top of his skull was a crest that was missing a small section.

He was definitely one of the dragons I'd seen in the In Between.

Ronnie opened his mouth slightly, revealing rows of dagger-like teeth. A forked tongue darted out to sample the air. As he studied us in our vehicle, his fearsome mouth looked almost as if it were smiling.

Thank you for coming. But how did you get here? I asked. *I didn't see you coming.*

We have magic that tricks the eyes of humans and prey. Sometimes they're one and the same. Hee-hee. Sorry, bad joke. Anyway, with our magic, we appear to be ordinary birds in the sky. No one pays us any attention.

Good. We need you to fly over the state park and see what's going on there. We're wondering if they're using the property to hold prisoners.

Okay. No problem.

First I need to create a psychic connection with you. I have empath powers that will allow me to experience your emotions and the input from your senses.

Talk about invading someone's privacy!

It will only be temporary.

I got out of the car and approached him. Proximity made this process much easier. I moved close enough to his head to touch it, but didn't need to. Good thing, because my instinctive fear of the giant predator was hard to shake.

He smelled faintly of honey and leather. His psychic energies were immense. Curiosity was the dominant emotion I felt from him, along with a touch of wariness.

And, yes, bravery. Good thing, because courageous allies bring out the valor in all of us.

I sent my energies into his brain, making his emotions stronger as I became one with him.

Finally, it clicked. I saw through his eyes a pale, uncertain-looking woman standing before him. She carried no weapons and didn't look like a powerful witch. She simply looked tired and vulnerable.

Yep, that was me. I sat down in the dirt, amid the dust clouds swirling, as the giant wings unfolded and beat the air to lift the enormous creature against gravity.

Then, all I saw of him was the dark silhouette of a bird circling in the air—a kite or hawk. It disappeared toward the east, where the park lay.

Shutting down my senses, I put myself entirely inside Ronnie's mind and what his five senses were telling it.

The state park comprised hundreds of acres of oak and pine forest. The green blanket was broken up by a few small lakes and a large, grassy savanna in its center, far from the park's entrance on State Road 64. Ronnie swooped down to get a closer look at the savanna.

It was filled with an open-air prison camp.

A tall barbed-wire fence, about twenty feet from the wall of trees, surrounded the camp, forming a rectangle. Wooden guard towers rose at each corner. Scores of tents were pitched haphazardly around the camp, leaving an open area in the center.

Hundreds of people, male and female, milled about in the open area. Larger trolls and ogres stood out in the crowd. The humans were most likely shifters and indigenous faeries in human form, witches, psychics, and others with supernatural and paranormal qualities. In one corner of the camp was a wooden, windowless stockade where vampires were probably held.

As Ronnie flew lower and lower, an open area of land beyond the barbed wire came into view. It appeared to be a mass burial ground.

Ronnie's feelings of disgust and anger mixed with my own horror. I pushed my emotions aside to prevent my connection with Ronnie from weakening.

You told me you are searching for someone, Ronnie's voice said in my head. *What does your friend look like?*

I pictured Samson in my mind, focusing on my memory of his face. Ronnie seemed to understand. I lost myself again as I was absorbed into his consciousness.

Ronnie flew lower, over the mass of miserable people sitting on the trampled grass or pacing aimlessly. Some drank from plastic water bottles, while others rested their faces in their hands. Ronnie caught glimpses of people sleeping inside tents.

The heavily armed guards in the towers and those patrolling outside the fence looked like militiamen but wore uniforms I didn't recognize.

Where in the teeming mass of prisoners was Samson?

It seemed as if Ronnie was flying dangerously low, but he began to rise in altitude. And then he saw the man with a bandaged hand. The man's beard was large and unkempt, his hair dirty and unruly, his skin sunburned. He looked up at Ronnie, at what he believed was a bird, with a knowing expression. It was as if he knew the bird was supernatural.

It's him, I said.

Ronnie continued rising, buoyed by a thermal.

Some guards were looking at me suspiciously, he said. *Best to get out of here. Have you learned all you need to know?*

Yes, thank you so much. I was already feeling my connection with the dragon fading.

Then I will return to my sanctuary.

Thank you so much for your help. And don't be surprised if I ask for more. I hope that's not too presumptuous.

He laughed. *Humans are so cute and delicious. But sometimes exasperating! Until we meet again.*

My connection with him broke. I stood up, brushed off my pants, and returned to the SUV, where Mom and Cory sat in the air conditioning. Mom lowered her window.

"It's worse than we imagined," I said. "Samson is in the park. Along with hundreds of supernaturals surrounded by barbed wire in a prison camp."

Her face fell. "No."

"Yeah, and there's a burial site outside of the barbed wire. I don't know how those people died, but it looks bad."

"We need to rescue Samson."

"Mom, this place is impregnable. It's totally fenced in and there are dozens of guards, if not more."

"We can't just leave him there. He was taken extrajudicially. This camp is not part of the justice system – he was simply disappeared, and there's no one to advocate on his behalf except for us."

"Okay. How do we advocate?"

"By rescuing him."

My mind raced to find a scenario in which this would be possible. True, we had the militiamen's weapons in our trunk. But we had no training in using assault rifles and there were only three of us.

What about magic? Well, Cory and I both knew sleep spells to disable the guards. Then I could use my sword, Alfie, shooting purple lightning to cut through some of the barbed wire. But there were too many guards around, making it likely we would miss some of them with our spells. And they would shoot us.

"It's simply not feasible, Mom," I said.

"You could get gnomes to tunnel under the fence and into the camp. Like they did when you rescued me from the Faerie Queene's palace."

"I used up all my favors with the gnomes."

Mom grew agitated. "You're not taking this seriously."

"I am!"

"How are they keeping all of those supernaturals from escaping?" Cory asked from the driver's seat, leaning over Mom so I could hear him. "Are barbed-wire fences and guards with guns really sufficient to keep powerful creatures imprisoned? Shifters who can jump fences, vampires who are immune to bullets. Witches who have magic like ours."

"What are you implying?" Mom asked him.

"Fae magic must be involved. Like the spell that sealed the vampires in the packing house bathroom. If that's the case, we can't rescue anyone without breaking the spell that's keeping them there. And if we do break the spell, the supernaturals can use their own powers to escape. Are you up for breaking it, Sophie?"

"It didn't go so well for me last time I did that. But we can't let all those supernaturals rot in captivity. And the government might have even worse plans for them."

"How do you want to do this?" Cory asked.

Before I could think of a plan, a Florida Highway Patrol car pulled into the barbecue shack's parking lot. The burly state trooper got out of his car and approached us, coming around our car to the side where I was standing.

Suddenly I couldn't breathe. There was a warrant for my arrest after the governor had arranged a bogus charge against me when she found out I knew she was secretly a faerie. I had escaped from the sheriff's deputy who arrested me, but I assumed the warrant was still active. Good thing we were in Cory's SUV and not my car.

Please, don't let him ask for my ID, I prayed.

As if I wasn't panicking enough, I worried that he might have searched for the accused supernaturals on the Monster Monitor app. I was on there, listed as a witch.

All the blood drained from my head. I felt as if I were about to faint.

"What are you folks doing here?" he demanded. "The highway is closed just beyond here. Didn't you see the signs?"

"Yeah. We're figuring out an alternate route," I lied in a quavering voice.

"Don't you have a GPS to do that?"

"GPS? Do you see how old this SUV is?" *Jeez Louise, Sophie! Don't be a smart aleck!*

"You got a smartphone, don't you?"

"That's what I'm using."

He eyed me suspiciously. "Where are you going?"

"San Marcos."

"Head that way." He pointed in the direction from which we

had come. "Turn left on County Road 192 and take it to State Road 40, which will take you where you want to go."

"Thank you," I said, smiling so hard it hurt.

The trooper didn't leave. He stood there staring at me, waiting for us to leave.

Having no other choice, I got into the SUV, and Cory drove in the direction we were told. My heart was still racing.

"We'll have to come back at night," I said.

But just then, my phone buzzed. It was the text chain from Diego to the various supernatural leaders.

Heavy militia activity in Edgewood. Signs of an impending Fae invasion. Converge there immediately to stop the militia from arresting supernaturals.

I read the text to Mom and Cory. "We must go there right away."

"But what about the prison camp?" Mom asked. "We can't leave Samson there."

There was an anxiousness in Mom's voice that made Cory and me look closely at her. Sadness showed in Cory's face.

I wanted to tell him not to worry, Mom wasn't in love with Samson. Yet I wasn't entirely sure of that.

We rushed toward Edgewood and I braced for a fight. I needed a way to release all the anxiety that had been building in me.

CHAPTER 7

SOPHIE

Edgewood was on the other side of San Marcos, and since we were passing our hometown, we agreed to drop Mom off. She would be of no help to us in the upcoming battle if the Fae used the phytolucine spell. Besides, the inn needed supervision. Pinky, Roderick, and Archibald were technically in charge at the moment, but they didn't rule the place with an iron hand like Mom did.

"Be careful," she said before getting out of the SUV, concern in her eyes. "Let the shifters and vampires do the fighting. They can heal themselves."

"If you were there, you'd be on the front lines," Cory said. "I'm actually relieved that you're fully human and would fall asleep from the Fae magic."

Mom frowned. "Fully human but still oppressed for being a psychic, under the Supernatural Criminality Act. A law passed thanks to traitorous faeries who wanted to boost their political careers while helping the Faerie Queene conquer us."

"That's why we're fighting," I said, eager to get going.

Mom climbed out of the passenger seat. She was clearly showing her age. Years of supernatural entanglements, and an ancient goddess using her as a human vessel, had taken their toll. She blew us a kiss while I climbed into her seat with my sword and crossbow in my lap.

Cory glanced at my weapons. "You'd better hope we don't get pulled over."

"Then stay under the speed limit."

We headed for Edgewood, which used to be a farming village but turned into a suburb of San Marcos filled with expensive subdivisions. Located just off the interstate, north of the city, Edgewood had strategic importance. If the Fae took it, they would block our primary route of reinforcements or retreat, assuming the Fae attacked San Marcos from the south.

"Edgewood is just a bunch of gated communities with no downtown, only a single shopping center," I said. "How do you defend a town like that?"

"First, we need to take it back from the militia," Cory replied. "We'll worry about the Fae later. For now, we'll just drive around and look for suspicious pickup trucks."

We exited the interstate and went east on a main road. Up ahead was a traffic light and a shopping center to our right. Cory pulled into the center, anchored by a supermarket and hosting several small retailers in a long row. The parking lot was lightly filled with cars. The only pickups we saw were innocuous ones without occupants, parked here and there in the lot.

I began thinking out loud. "At the beginning of the Great Unmasking, the militia went after people in the Monster Monitor app, or they relied on informants who snitched on supernaturals. How could they show up in a town like this and find supernaturals without being tipped off?"

"I bet a lot of the folks they capture aren't even supernatural," Cory replied. "The militiamen just assume they're shifters or witches based on their looks. The obvious supernaturals—like trolls, ogres, or gnomes—wouldn't be out in public. They probably wouldn't even live here."

"They'd only find vampires during the day if they were directed to them by informants. And at night, a vampire would only be obvious if they were caught feeding on someone. Right? The militia has some secret way of finding them—it could be magic, informants, whatever. We have to stop it."

Cory glanced at me. "You've become super concerned about vampires. Is it because of Diego?"

My face grew warm, and I turned away before he saw me smile. "Could be."

I was spared further interrogation when we came upon a car riddled with bullet holes and its windows shattered. Shell casings were scattered across the surrounding asphalt.

"Looks like the militia's been here," Cory said. "Let's ask if anyone saw what happened."

We parked near the supermarket, but as we approached the entrance, we stopped. Yellow crime-scene tape stretched in front of the automatic doors. Handwritten signs were taped to the glass announcing the store was closed but would open in the morning. Two police cars were parked in the front. I would have expected more to be there. Just seeing the cars made my heart race.

"I hope no one in Edgewood gets the munchies today," I muttered.

We walked down the sidewalk that stretched along the length of the shopping center. A nail salon was closed, but the dry cleaners next door was open. The bell above the door rang when we entered. A dark-haired woman looked up nervously from behind the counter.

"Hi," I said. "Do you know what happened today? It looks like a battle took place out there."

I was afraid I'd awakened trauma in her because she looked like she was about to cry.

"A bunch of trucks were driving around the parking lot early this morning after we opened. It sounded like firecrackers were going off, but I looked out and saw they were shooting at a car. They pulled a gigantic man from the front seat. I think he was dead. Then they went into the supermarket, and I heard more gunshots."

"Wow. Then what happened?"

"I was afraid to leave my store, but I looked out the window and saw men in uniforms dragging three people from the supermarket. They put them in a van and drove away."

"Didn't the police try to stop them?" Cory asked.

"I called 911 and I'm sure lots of other people did. But it took the cops a half hour to show up. It was like they didn't care."

Or they were on the same side as the militia, I thought.

We thanked the woman and left.

"Now what do we do?" Cory asked. "The militia could be anywhere."

"I bet they're still around. It's Saturday, and supernaturals who commute to work are probably at home. The militia is surely looking for them. I don't sense any Fae magic nearby, so the militiamen still have time. Let's drive around and see if we find them."

The many gated communities that constituted Edgewood were mostly along the main road. We came upon a lushly landscaped entrance, complete with a fountain, beside a sign that said "Orange Blossom Estates." We pulled in and were met by a closed gate arm.

A uniformed guard in the gatehouse demanded to know who we were visiting.

"Uh, my brother, George," Cory said. He was a terrible liar.

"George who?"

"Smith."

The guard looked at a clipboard. "No one by that name lives here."

"Oh, I thought this was where he moved to." Cory's acting was much better when he played a befuddled middle-aged man.

"Try Tangerine Villas just east of here," the guard suggested.

Cory made a U-turn and headed east on the main road.

He didn't need to lie his way through the gate at Tangerine Villas. That was because the gate arm was snapped off and lying on the road. The guardhouse was covered with bullet holes.

"Looks like our friends have been here," I said.

"And they still might be. Start concentrating your energies in case we need to use battle magic."

Cory drove through the gate warily and continued to a fork in the road. He turned right, and we rolled past new cookie-cutter homes on small lots with minimal landscaping. Shorter streets that ended in cul-de-sacs branched off now and then to the right and left. The car's GPS showed the road we were on eventually circled back to the entrance. If the militia were still here, we would see them.

And we did. I just didn't expect them to come barreling up from behind us: six pickup trucks loaded with militiamen followed by two panel vans.

I froze with fear, but they didn't stop us. They flew by, then turned into a cul-de-sac, stopping in front of a home.

"They're going to specific addresses," Cory said. "They have a target list."

"Stop here and park perpendicular to block their way out," I said. "It's party time."

The militiamen didn't appear to notice us as they jumped from their trucks and ran to the home's front door. Two used a SWAT-style battering ram to bust through the door, and the rest swarmed inside.

There were at least twenty-four of them, not counting whoever was waiting in the vans. We were greatly outnumbered. Cory crouched behind the car, using the hood as cover. I stood behind the open passenger door like shooters do in action movies.

Cory and I each cast protection spells around each other. I couldn't speak for him, but I didn't make mine as strong as I could because I needed as much energy as possible for attacking. I wasn't sure how well the bubble would protect me from bullets.

Soon after, some militia goons exited the home dragging a man and woman.

I quickly learned that the militia's military intelligence wasn't as good as I'd thought, or perhaps they were simply non-intelligent. Because their captives were vampires who, once exposed to the daylight, didn't make it to the vans before they were destroyed by sun-scorching.

I turned away and grimaced. Then I finished conjuring my spell, sending amped-up energy from my body into Alfie. The sword crackled with purple electricity. I aimed it at the militiamen standing stupidly beside the piles of ashes that had been their captives.

Two, then three, then four of them went down when hit by my purple lightning.

That was when the rest of them noticed us and opened fire.

My body shook as bullets hit my protection bubble. Metallic pinging noises came from the car, especially from the door I stood behind. Most of the bullets seemed like they would have missed me, even without the spell. But I saw a hole in the inside of the door, directly facing my stomach. A bullet, probably from an assault rifle, had penetrated the entire door.

I gulped as I realized my protection spell had, in fact, saved me.

Fireballs the size of grapefruits whizzed over the car's hood and landed among the militia. Cory's attack magic was at work, and militiamen were dropping, engulfed in flames. The men on their feet still outnumbered us, but I hoped the magical pyrotechnics would scare them away.

No such luck. A group of them were charging right at us, firing as they came.

"Stay down," I called to Cory. "I'm going to draw them away from the car so you can pick them off from the side."

The door I crouched behind was crumbling from the onslaught of lead, so what I did next was not as foolish as it seemed. I dashed to my right, running around the SUV, out of the cul-de-sac, and right down the middle of the street that looped through the community. Alfie's scabbard slapped my back, and the crossbow jiggled in its sling, making my running awkward. But there was no way I'd leave my weapons behind.

Of course I kept my protection spell going, pumping more energy into it as the militiamen fired at me. Since they were running, their shots flew wide.

Screams came from behind me. I risked a backwards glance and saw Cory's fireballs taking them down like ducks in a shooting gallery.

Someone was peering out from a window of the house I was running past.

"Get on the floor!" I shouted. Would the resident take sides against the people shooting lightning and fireballs who were obviously supernatural?

The bullets hitting my protection bubble or whizzing harmlessly overhead ceased. I looked behind me. My pursuers had been felled, with others converging around Cory and the SUV. He was about to be surrounded.

I diverted some energy from my protection spell and added it to the reserves I pumped into Alfie. My lightning dropped two men before they reached Cory's rear. I sprinted back toward him.

One man lunged at Cory's back. He was stopped by Cory's protection barrier but fired at him at point-blank range. I shot lightning at him. It danced over the man's back but didn't drop him. A bullet that ricocheted off the protection bubble hit the man in the chest, to no effect. It occurred to me he was wearing body armor and a steel helmet. Yet another impediment to my powers.

The string of my crossbow was already cocked. I unslung the weapon and loaded a bolt. Crossbows were invented to pierce knights' armor, and that's exactly what it did to this militiaman's vest.

It was eerily quiet, except the moans of the wounded, and I realized Cory and I had won the battle. Just the two of us and our magic. I had expected police sirens at any moment, but none came. The local police had obviously known about the militia's plans and were instructed to stay out of the way.

"The vans!" Cory shouted. "They're escaping."

The two black panel vans with no logos bounced over the curb nearby as they drove through front lawns to get around the barrier our SUV created. My lightning blew out the front tires of the vehicle in front, which lost control and crashed into a house. The other van slammed into it.

I strode up to the vans and fired lightning at the drivers—just enough to knock them out but not kill them. Yeah, my empathy was waking up, and my appetite for destruction had disappeared.

Cory appeared at my side and helped me wrench open the rear doors of the first van. The cargo area was empty, but crosses and crucifixes hung from the walls. This was where the vampires were supposed to have been transported, if the militiamen hadn't stupidly destroyed them.

When we opened the other van, we had to duck as two wolves leaped over our heads and raced away between two houses. The werewolves must have shifted out of panic and desperation.

Left behind was an ogre sitting on his butt on the floor, hands resting on his knees. You would be forgiven for assuming he was a very large human, perhaps a defensive tackle with bulging muscles and no neck. But if you looked closely in the dim light of the cargo area, you'd notice the greenish cast to his skin and the pointy tips of his ears.

Ogres had modest supernatural powers, such as superhuman strength and senses, fantastic tracking abilities, and ways of masking their unusual appearances. Their population was small, and if they resisted the urge to eat people, they blended in well with society. This guy had not been so lucky.

"You're free to go," I told him. "We took care of the militiamen who captured you."

"I was minding my business, just stopping by the shopping center to grab someone for breakfast, when these nuts with all the firepower ambushed me," he said.

"Well, like I said, we took care of them. You can go." I was a bit nervous after he confessed he was not one of his species who had a human-free diet.

"No," he said, standing up, though he had to crouch because he was too tall. "I'm going with you guys. I'm tired of all this crap. It's time for supernaturals to fight back."

"We're happy to have you on our side," Cory said, though I wasn't so sure I felt the same way. Cory extended his hand and the ogre shook it, making Cory's hand look like a hamster's in comparison. "We're expecting the Fae to invade this town very soon. The militia was supposed to remove all the supernaturals, and the Fae have a spell to put the non-supernatural residents to sleep while the army takes over the town."

"We moved here because it was supposed to be a safe place to raise a family," the ogre said. "Who knew?"

"I'm Cory, and this is my stepdaughter, Sophie."

"I'm Greg. Nice to meet you. Let's go kick some butt."

Movement caught my eye. A wounded militiaman in the cab of the other van was raising a pistol at us.

"Watch out!" I yelled.

Before I could fire lightning at him, the militiaman dropped his pistol and sank onto the seat. The wounded scattered about on the street stopped moving. My skin tingled as a wave of Fae magic swept through the neighborhood like a fog.

The invasion was about to begin.

CHAPTER 8

DARLA

"**W**elcome back," Pinky said when I walked into the kitchen. She was at the island butcher block making finger sandwiches for afternoon tea. "How are you doing? I was worried about you."

"Much better, thanks." I gave her a kiss on the cheek and surveyed the food preparation, anxious to get back to the comforting mundane routine at the inn. I'd had my fill of the Fae and the evil machinations of politicians. "The scones smell like they're almost ready."

"I know. I'm using a timer."

Pinky, whose real name was Priscilla, was a rare skunk shifter. Her bushy black hair fit the part, and her nickname, Pinky, was christened by her friends when she was younger because it rhymed with stinky. As you would guess, that was a were-skunk's superpower.

She continued watching me inspect the food she was preparing. It was getting on my nerves.

"Why are you staring at me?" I asked.

"You seem so . . . okay. Sophie told me you were trapped in a town invaded by the Fae."

"I was, but not anymore. This is life during wartime, Pinky. You can't let the chaos and destruction affect your way of life."

"How can you say that? The inn was almost put out of business. Our only guests are supernaturals now, and we're operating illegally."

"That's exactly my point," I said, tapping my watch and nodding toward the oven. "You adapt and go on with things."

Pinky's smartphone timer chimed, and she quickly pulled the baking sheets of scones from the oven amid a moist blast of fragrant air.

"Perfect," I said, admiring the slightly browned exterior of the scones.

"You should know that someone has been watching the inn," Pinky said in a hushed tone.

"That's perfectly normal. Mothers Against Monsters are on the lookout for supernaturals. The police have been surveilling Sophie—though they could have arrested her by now if they really wanted to. And I wouldn't be surprised if the Fae were seeking me for one reason or another."

"And we're supposed to pretend everything is normal?"

"See, you're learning."

I left the kitchen and sat at the writing table in the foyer that served as the hotel's front desk. Opening the laptop, I checked the guest registry. The inn was only half full. It was better than being empty, of course, but with all the turmoil in Florida, few supernaturals felt safe taking vacations to San Marcos. Most of our guests were refugees fleeing the militia or the authorities. If the Fae took over more towns, we'd surely have more guests.

I knew one thing for certain: I needed to be more careful

when traveling to other towns to promote the inn. Going into Altman had been a terrible idea, even when Sophie told me that Samson might be in trouble. Why was I stupid enough to think I could help him if the militia had captured him?

I didn't think at all. That was the problem. I was concerned about Samson and instinctively raced to his house as if I didn't have a brain in my head.

Did that mean I still had feelings for him? Nah, no way. He was like a member of the family, that's all. A brother. A brother too handsome and stoic for his own good.

A hoot of laughter came from the courtyard. It wasn't likely that any of our current guests would be drinking by the pool in the middle of the afternoon. I headed down the hall past the kitchen, dining room, and living room, exiting into the courtyard.

The outdoor space was a large expanse of pavers enclosed by coquina-limestone walls built centuries ago. In the far corner to my left sat the small two-bedroom cottage where Cory and I lived. Built in the 1920s, it was comparatively brand new compared to the rest of the inn.

To the far right was a tiny pool, more of a soaking than a swimming pool. Between the cottage and the pool, against the wall opposite me, were planters filled with local foliage and a fountain spilling into a small pool where koi swam.

I should have known the laughter was coming from the fountain. Specifically, Jerry, the lion-faced gargoyle whose mouth was the waterspout, and Archibald, the demon-faced gargoyle perched on the wall beside him. The two supernatural creatures were an item, and Jerry frequently magically transported himself here from the Alhambra Hotel downtown.

"You two realize the inn is under constant surveillance, don't you?"

"We're behaving ever so respectably, love," Archibald said.

"Your loud voices and giggling could arouse suspicion," I replied.

"Any police on the street couldn't see us in here. They'd never know we're gargoyles. And we always get a warning when that dimwitted hotel inspector comes by."

"Guests could witness you. Even though they're all supernaturals now, there could be informants among them."

"Informants?!" Jerry exclaimed. "What kind of society have we become?"

"A cruel, paranoid one. Anyway, Pinky mentioned seeing someone surveilling the inn."

"Oh, you mean that elf fellow?" Archibald asked.

"Leighnel was here?"

"Yes. He came around looking for you when you went missing with your coupons." He said "coupons" with a sneer. "Then I saw him turn into a squirrel and climb a tree across the street to watch the inn."

"He must have tried to reach me telepathically when I was unconscious."

"Unconscious?"

"The Fae have a powerful spell that knocks out humans. I'm vulnerable to it."

"Oh dear. Yet another reason to pity you poor, weak humans."

"I have work to do," I said. "You two behave."

When I entered the main building, a tittering of laughter came from the courtyard.

I checked on Maria, who was doing laundry in the utility room. She was the new housekeeper, replacing Bella, who had quit because she no longer wanted to be associated with supernaturals and paranormals. Unlike Bella, Maria was one of us, a dryad who lived in an oak tree near the inn. She greeted me warmly, with none of the attitude Bella had displayed.

Afterward, I stepped into the parlor for some privacy and attempted to contact Leighnel. I say "attempted" because just as I was calling out to him telepathically, I was hijacked—what my family calls "freezing," and I prefer to describe as "going away."

Going away to the realm where the Goddess Danu dwelled.

This visit, however, was not to the primeval forest where I was usually sent. Instead, I stood on a mountain ledge, looking down at a valley obscured by mist. A howling wind buffeted me, and I clutched the roots of a dead tree that protruded from a cleft in the rock behind me. Above was the mountain peak, thrusting through dark, portentous clouds.

I was overcome by vertigo on this dangerous ledge, though I reminded myself I wasn't here physically. My brain wasn't buying it, though, because my body shivered in the chilly wind.

Danu appeared, strolling casually along a path that sloped down to me.

"You have an important task ahead of you," she said, her musical voice easily cutting through the howling wind.

"My plate is pretty full back on earth," I replied, shivering.

"You have no choice but to perform this task. The Elder God Yavevi is gathering strength and increasing his presence in the world. You must destroy him."

"I fought him once and made him retreat, but didn't come anywhere near destroying him, even using all my powers. I mean, your powers."

"My powers are becoming yours. Our transition is progressing quickly. Soon, you will be me."

"You know, this has been tons of fun, but I think I've had enough of being your human vessel. I'm too old and not up to the task. I think I'll just retire to my earthly pursuits."

"You have no choice." Her voice was angry. "This is not the time for your puerile complaints. The Elder God will destroy the earth if he is allowed to. Eventually, the entire universe as well. I am the only one who can stop him, and because I have not completed my return to the world, you must defeat him in my stead."

"But I—"

"Listen to me. For obvious reasons, he wants to prevent me from returning to the earth. His only means of doing that are to kill you and your daughter—even if you refuse to fight him."

"Why would he kill Sophie?"

"She is destined to be the leader of the Tuatha Dé Danann, the children of Danu. If you were killed, I would use her as my human vessel instead of you. So Yavevi must kill both of you. He would kill her first to make you suffer."

"That's so unfair—"

"Fairness is not a concept understood by deities. The Elder God will do what he wants, and you have no choice but to stop him. I cannot do it now, only you."

"But I couldn't destroy him when I fought him once before."

"I will ensure you have the use of all my powers. And you have an advantage this time: you know his name."

"What good is that?"

"Knowing and using his name gives you power over him."

"But how?"

"You mortals ask too many questions. You must learn to think for yourself."

Danu disappeared, but I remained shivering on the mountain ledge, clutching the tree roots for dear life.

"Danu, why haven't you sent me home?"

I know, I know. I ask too many questions.

As I stared at the swirling mist covering the valley thousands of feet below me, the thought came into my head: *You must let go.*

What a stupid idea. I was afraid of heights. There's no way I could allow myself to fall off this mountain.

You must let go.

Was that my thought, or was Danu putting it into my head? It seemed too trite for me to think of it. Then again, I reminded myself for the umpteenth time that I wasn't here physically; my body was waiting for me in the inn's parlor. I had come here through astral travel. It was almost like this was a dream.

My hands refused to loosen their grip on the roots. But I remembered Danu's warning. Yavevi would kill me and Sophie regardless of what I did. I would gladly give up my life to save Sophie, but I couldn't do it if I stayed on this mountain.

So I let go.

"She's finally back," said Archibald. He was in his usual place beneath the fireplace mantel.

"Good. It was rather awkward trying to speak with a human statue." The voice was Leighnel's.

I turned my head to find him sitting in a wingback chair, smiling at me.

"Howdy," I said, giving him a weak grin.

"Were you with the Goddess?" Leighnel asked.

"Unfortunately, yes. Now, are you here to demand something from me, too?"

"Actually, I have some information that could prove valuable." He studied me with concern in his eyes. "Are you all right?"

"I'll be fine. It was an abrupt transition from being on a mountain ledge to returning here."

I hadn't told Cory or anyone, but my astral visits to Danu were taking their toll on me, sucking up more of my energy than before. Taking away more of me.

I sat in the chair next to Leighnel's. "Are you going to share this information you have?"

"Your governor made a secret visit to our king," he replied. "The King wanted me to attend because I've become an expert of sorts on the Fae and faeries in general. He expected your governor to request help related to phytolucine. That wasn't at all what she was interested in." Leighnel arched his eyebrows.

"Will you get to the point?"

He laughed. "The governor said she had learned the Faerie Queene intended to attack the Elves, despite our peace treaty, after her army conquers Florida. The reasoning was the Fae would need our gold and other resources."

"I knew you couldn't trust them."

"The governor said she would be in a position to prevent this attack, and all she would need would be regular contributions of gold to her from the Elves."

"Sounds like extortion to me," I said.

"Indeed."

"Does the King know you're telling me this?"

"He directed me to tell you. He believes that if the Elves accept the governor's offer—or pretend to—she will be in a compromised position that you humans could use to your advantage."

"Maybe. She's made herself virtually untouchable, indulging

in all sorts of political and financial corruption right out in the open. Her opponents can't, or won't, do anything about it."

"When more towns fall, the human public will learn about the Fae. If they discover that she's supporting them, she'll be vulnerable. The Elves can help you take her down."

"What good will that be if we humans are conquered?"

"You're not fully understanding," he said. "The sooner you take her down, the less likely it is the Fae will conquer you."

I promised to pass the information on to Sophie. She had developed contacts among the media and the governor's opponents, hoping to spread the truth that the governor was secretly a faerie. But it hadn't worked, and the governor was reelected. Hopefully Leighnel was correct: once the public learned of the danger of the Fae army, they would be revolted by news that their governor was collaborating with them and extorting the Elves.

Unless it was too late for the truth to matter.

CHAPTER 9

SOPHIE

While the Fae magic rolled through the neighborhood like an invisible, chilling fog, I was relieved the spell didn't affect me like it did the militiamen. It seemed odd that simply inheriting the magic gene made me—in every other aspect a normal human—immune to the phytolucine magic, while Mom, filled with paranormal powers, would be knocked out by it.

I pulled out my phone and typed a message in the group chat about the Fae's imminent attack on Edgewood. Night was falling, which was when the Fae were most active.

"Don't you think we should get out of town while we still can?" Cory asked me.

I gave him a look that put the question to rest. He knew me better than that. I wasn't the type to run away from a fight. Well, I should add a disclaimer: if the supernatural guilds didn't send anyone to help us, we would be doomed unless we ran away like rabbits.

"How many supernaturals live in Edgewood?" I asked Greg.

"Do you think the militia captured them all, except for you and the two werewolves in the van?"

"There's only about twenty of us in town," he replied. "We all kept a low profile. Like I said, this is a bedroom community for raising families. My wife and kids are off visiting her parents. The rest of the supernaturals are shifters, except for a handful of vampires."

I told him what had happened to the vampire couple on this street.

Greg smacked his forehead. "What idiots the militiamen are! As far as I know, my neighbors and I were the only supernaturals those idiots bagged. And I'm not happy about it. I'm a taxpaying American citizen. The fact that I'm an ogre shouldn't make me lose my rights."

"I agree," I said. "But if you don't want to be persecuted, maybe you shouldn't eat people."

"Who said I do?"

"You did. You said you were at the shopping center to grab someone for breakfast."

"Figure of speech." He took on a haughty tone. "Humans are so literal."

"I'm only repeating what you said."

"Look, like every other supernatural, my family and I learned to adapt to fit into society. There are some quite delicious plant-based human-meat substitutes on the market nowadays."

"Sure."

"Really. I haven't killed a human in decades. I mean, not on purpose."

"I'm not here to judge you," I said in a calm voice, "but we supernaturals need to be above reproach. Even vampires have been minimizing preying on humans. Supernaturals shouldn't be oppressed like we are now. But we can't give humans any excuse to fear us."

"Humans fear rattlesnakes, but they don't try to wipe them off the face of the earth like they're doing with us."

"But they also don't allow rattlesnakes to roam freely in shopping centers."

"Point taken. I'll stick with the fake meat."

"You can always eat the proteins humans eat, like fish, or chicken, or whatever."

He shook his head sadly. "Nothing can ever substitute for the taste and texture of a fresh, not-too-old divorce lawyer."

"I don't care. You have no choice anymore."

"If we behave or not, it's really beside the point. Humans need someone to hate and they're going to make up stuff about us if they want to. Look at you—witches don't kill anyone. Only evil witches do, like evil humans. You guys cast spells to clear up acne or improve sex lives, yet the humans claim you sacrifice children to the devil. They just want to justify their hatred. When you think of all the atrocities humans have committed, they're the true monsters in my book."

While I had this frustrating conversation, my phone was blowing up with texts. Finally the guild leaders and others on the list were being roused to action. Unfortunately, they weren't of the same mind. Everyone had their own ideas of how we should face the Fae menace.

It doesn't matter that Edgewood is a nothing town, I texted to the naysayers. *It's strategically important. The Fae could cut off and surround San Marcos if they take Edgewood.*

They could be luring us away from San Marcos to attack the city by surprise, wrote Dr. Noordlun. I had my first regrets that we had elected him leader of the Executive Council. He was too cerebral and careful. I wished we had a leader who was brash and charismatic. Too bad Diego hadn't wanted to take the on the role.

The militia has already been here, I typed. *They destroyed at least two vampires. I don't know how many supernaturals remain. The Fae cast their spell to incapacitate humans minutes ago. Right now, our two witches and an ogre are the only ones here to fight the Fae.*

I will bring a detachment of vampires, Diego replied. *Rufus, can you send shifters?*

I'm coming with my family pack. There's no time to summon the others.

"What should we do before the others get here?" Cory asked me.

"Let's go to the interstate exit," I answered. "I'm expecting them to use delivery vans like they did in Altman."

Cory's SUV wouldn't start after being riddled with bullets, so we took the guns from it that we had confiscated in Altman. We pushed the unconscious militiamen from the cab of the van that still had intact tires, and Cory drove down the main road to the interstate highway overpass.

That Edgewood was a small community in a rural area made things simpler. The interstate had two off-ramps, one for northbound traffic and the other for southbound. I assumed the Fae would be northbound, and once they exited, their vehicles would turn right to head eastward into town.

We found a copse of trees just to the east of where the off-ramp joined the road into town and parked the van where it wouldn't be seen. Even if the Fae took the southbound exit, they would have to pass our position and be ambushed. Now, all we could do was crouch in the underbrush and wait.

"There are back roads into town," Greg said. "What if they don't take the interstate?"

"I'm betting they will. They have the perfect camouflage by

using branded delivery vans. And they don't know that anyone is waiting for them."

It felt as if we waited forever until headlights finally came down the off-ramp. This town really was Nowheresville. The lights belonged to a passenger car, though. It turned right at the traffic light onto the main road. Then it promptly coasted off the road and softly collided with a telephone pole.

I jogged over and looked inside the car. The driver was an elderly human who was slumped sideways in his seat. He looked uninjured. The impact had been gentle, and the airbag hadn't deployed. The human had simply been knocked out by the Fae's magic.

Cory whistled a warning, waving me back to the copse of trees. I sprinted to our hiding spot just as a long train of headlights exited the highway.

The Fae convoy had arrived.

"Wait until they come to the traffic light," I whispered.

The convoy was a mixture of vans from the familiar shipping companies—large box trucks along with smaller panel vans. They bunched up and slowed at the bottom of the off-ramp as they reached the traffic light, where they would turn right onto the main road.

Cory and I unleashed our attack magic. The purple lightning from my sword and Cory's fireballs hit the first truck and swept left, moving down the column of vehicles. Some caught fire while the others broke down, their electrical systems fried. The vehicles arriving in the tail of the convoy tried to get around the disabled vehicles in front. Until we blasted them, too.

The exit off-ramp was completely blocked. The first part of my strategy had worked like a dream, but the second part I hadn't quite figured out. That was the part about how to repel the hundreds of Fae escaping from the trucks. The ones charging toward us in human form, weapons in hand.

"Keep firing at them," I told Cory and Greg, who had armed himself with a confiscated assault rifle. "I'm going to work on a sleep spell."

In the past, my spell had been quite effective against humans, faeries, and other individuals in my line of sight. I couldn't cast a spell big enough to affect all the Fae, but I could enchant groups of them if they were close together.

The rattling of Greg's rifle disturbed my concentration, but I buckled down and blocked out all sounds, including the Fae bullets whizzing through the trees above our heads.

The magic burned inside me white hot. I sent it to the group of Fae nearest the copse of trees who were tightly bunched together. All five sank to their knees, then fell flat onto the ground.

But many more were approaching our hideout.

"I feel like my energy is running low," Cory said.

"Keep on fighting," I said. "When you can't cast any more fireballs, grab a gun."

My incomplete planning was freaking me out. Maybe we should have waited until the vampires and shifters arrived before we fought.

No, I thought. By the time our reinforcements arrived, the Fae would have been dispersed throughout the community. This was our best, and perhaps only, chance to keep them out of Edgewood.

The Fae were crawling toward us on their elbows, trying to avoid Cory's fireballs and Greg's bullets. We were in danger of being overrun soon. I cast another sleep spell and sent the nearest group into dreamland, but more were fanning out into the woods to our left, where I couldn't see them well.

A fireball barreled out of the woods toward me and hit a tree trunk right above my head. Jeez Louise, the Fae had a sorcerer with them. Our ambush, which had seemed like such a good idea, was quickly going sideways.

"Sorcerer!" Cory shouted.

"No kidding. He almost hit me. Fire back at him where his fireballs are coming from."

My phone buzzed in my pocket. *You've got to be kidding me*, I thought. *I'm kind of busy here.* I was going to ignore it so I could keep fighting—especially since handling a phone when using attack magic is a good way to fry the device. But if our rescuers were messaging me, I needed to know.

I pulled out my phone, which thankfully didn't explode.

We're en route to Edgewood now, Diego's text read. *Don't engage the Fae until we arrive.*

Too late, I replied. *We're fighting near the exit from the interstate.*

A faerie fireball whizzed past me. I pointed Alfie in the direction it came from, but I held my fire. I couldn't see anything in the dark forest and didn't want to waste my energy hitting tree trunks.

An age-old military technique would be to light up the forest with flares. So that's what I did. Except that my flares were magical, and instead of simply providing light, mine sought living creatures.

I pointed Alfie at an upward angle and sent purple globules up and over the trees. They looked like water balloons that emitted dazzling purple light. They were harmless, but smart. Once they were above the Fae soldiers, they looked more like giant fireflies buzzing in curvy patterns around the trees as they descended toward the forest floor.

And then they hovered over different faeries who were creeping toward us, spotlighting them like theater lights.

A faerie with a shaved head and a long robe froze in a circle of purple light. Cory's fireball hit the sorcerer before he could even think of ducking.

With the advancing Fae lit up like this, they took cover behind trees, and I could return my attention to the original thrust of the Fae attack coming along the road. They were almost upon us.

"I'm out of ammo," Greg said. "I have nothing left to use other than brute force, but that's my favorite weapon."

"You just got shot," Cory said to him. "Are you okay?"

"A couple of bullets won't kill an ogre."

As if in reply, the Fae soldiers fired a volley that sent tree branches tumbling down on us.

"That many bullets would do the job, though," Greg said.

I was taking cover behind a tree when a faerie appeared right next to me. He was just as surprised to see me as I was him. There was no time for anything other than plunging my sword into him. Though they believe they are a superior species, the Fae are just as mortal as humans are.

As he expired, an unwelcome jolt of empathy sent his emotions through my sword and into me. I experienced his pain, fear, and despair. But what struck me was his last thought, one filled with awe.

Translated from Faerie, it was: *The Goddess's Daughter*.

How had he known who I was? And why was his thought so full of reverence? I knew the Fae worshipped Danu under a different name, but it had never stopped them from attacking Mom and me in the past. Why was this guy so awed by me?

I pulled my attention back to the battle and impulsively fired off more magic flares so I could see how precarious our situation was. Also, I hoped the brilliant lights would make the Fae pause for a moment.

The flares revealed the worst possible scenario. We were completely surrounded by Fae soldiers creeping toward us from the off-ramp, the road, the forest, and from our rear. It was time to use my remaining energy for a protection spell around us.

But I had never known that faeries could fly when in human form. Why were the soldiers on the off-ramp launching into the air and landing on the pavement with splats?

Because the cavalry had arrived to save us. Vampires tore into the rear ranks of the Fae, taking them completely by surprise. The faeries emptied their weapons at their attackers to no effect. And believe me, it was nice to have the weapons not aimed at me for once.

Piercing howls rang out above the din of battle, and soon grey, white, and black wolves raced by in different directions, chasing down Fae soldiers one by one. There were only about a dozen wolves, but they were unstoppable, led by the giant white alpha who was Rufus.

The vampires worked their way through the faeries from their rear, moving closer to Cory, Greg, and me as we crouched in our copse of trees like General Custer on the tiny hill at the end of the Battle of Little Bighorn. Too bad for him that he didn't have vampires and werewolves as reinforcements.

The Fae were rarely known to surrender, but they weren't above retreating. Actually, the retreat was more like fleeing in panic. Their trucks had been destroyed at the front of the convoy, but others that were unharmed were parked in the back of the line of vehicles that stretched up the off-ramp to the interstate. The survivors fled to them.

The vampires fed on the wounded Fae, and I turned my head away in disgust. I could tell the act was not for sustenance, but a way to assert dominance. The wolves, just like normal wolves, couldn't resist chasing after the fleeing prey. From my vantage point, I could only see three or four trucks able to back up onto the highway and escape.

Diego approached me, his eyes blazing with adrenaline from the battle. I was relieved to see no trace of blood on his lips, meaning he hadn't fed on anyone.

He smiled jauntily. "Looks like we got here just in time."

"Thank you," I said. "They were about to overrun us."

Diego glanced at the battlefield. "Looks like you did pretty well, despite being so outnumbered."

"Magic is a force multiplier."

Helga, Eduardo, and Albert approached us. The first two were part of Diego's inner circle, and he trusted them completely. Helga was beautiful, with a shaved head and eyes in a blue shade I'd only seen in the undead. Eduardo, an ancient Spaniard, was tall with an angular face, making him resemble a royal from the paintings of Velazquez. Perhaps he'd actually been in some of the paintings.

Albert, with the strong, slender physique of a ballet dancer, had challenged Diego in the recent Crucible to determine who would be the new Duke of the Clan of the Eternal Night. Albert would have destroyed Diego had I not intervened with empath magic.

"What are your plans for Edgewood?" Eduardo asked Diego. "Will we hold it against further Fae incursions?"

"We can't spare vampires for mere garrison duty. There aren't enough of us to do that while protecting San Marcos. What is the status of the supernatural population here?"

"I don't think the militia rounded them all up," I said. "Very few militiamen came here."

"I sense resident vampires in the area," Albert said. "And other supernaturals I can't identify."

"The local supernaturals must protect their own town, then," said Diego.

Albert frowned. "We should protect them if the militia comes back."

"We can, if necessary, but they must be hyper-vigilant from now on."

"Frankly, I believe our focus should be wiping out the militia, not fighting the Fae. Protecting our fellow supernaturals should be our priority."

Everyone looked at Albert with shocked expressions.

"The Fae are the greatest threat of all," I said.

"To humans—normal and supernatural. Not to vampires. Existing under a Fae regime would be no different from what we endure with humans in control." Albert smiled, revealing his fangs. "And you must admit that Fae blood is sweeter and more potent than human blood. Must be the traces of magic in it."

Diego's face was stormy. "What a preposterous thing to say. The Fae are savage autocrats who would destroy any species powerful enough to be a threat to them. What we're experiencing with the Great Unmasking is child's play compared to what a Fae regime would do."

"You are the duke. I defer to you," Albert said with a fake expression of innocence. "I only thought that as supernaturals, we have more in common with the Fae than with humans."

"I agree with Diego," said Rufus, who had approached us. "The Fae would wipe out both our species."

"We will instruct the remaining supernaturals in Edgewood on how to protect their town," Diego ordered. "We will support them if necessary."

Diego turned away from us and shouted to the vampires scattered around the battlefield to return to the vans that had brought them.

Nearby, Cory was talking on the phone. I assumed it was with Mom, so I went and stood next to him. His face showed the strain of the fight we'd been through and the energy he'd used up for his magic. Then he heard something that made him alarmed.

"We need to get back to San Marcos," he said to me. "Darla told me tunnels have been found beneath the city. Fae tunnels for moving troops. The attack could come any moment now."

CHAPTER 10

DARLA

"As you can tell, the tunnel has been dug recently," Dr. Noordlun said.

We were at an excavated section of a street, looking down into a hole at a tunnel, the roof of which had been removed by the archeologists who had dug the hole.

"Yes," I replied. "You can tell it was made by the Fae and not by a freakishly large monster mole or coal miners who went way off course. The roof of the tunnel is a latticework of crystal that Fae sorcerers magically create from the soil."

Dr. Noordlun, chairman of the history department at San Marcos College, had come here, one of the many archeological digs that take place in the nation's oldest city, expecting to find early Spanish colonial pottery shards or relics from the Indigenous peoples. Instead, the graduate students working on the excavation showed him the tunnel they had stumbled upon.

"This tunnel is part of the Fae invasion plan?" he asked.

"Yes. They've probably dug miles of tunnels beneath us, allowing their soldiers to enter the city undetected. They'd be in their natural faerie forms, of course, which is why the tunnel is too small for humans. This means they're planning a much bigger invasion than what they did in Altman."

I explained how the Fae had slipped into Altman in innocuous-looking delivery vans and then set up a Mafia-like operation of extorting money from local businesses.

"Why wouldn't they do the same thing in San Marcos?"

"They surely plan to," I explained. "But there are many supernaturals here who will fight them. The militia didn't succeed in wiping us out, and hundreds of supernaturals have fled here from surrounding towns. The Fae probably also want a show of force in San Marcos with many troops to intimidate other, larger cities to surrender."

"Won't the National Guard or the U.S. Military get involved if we're invaded by a hostile foreign force?"

"My guess is Governor Witlessin will run interference for the Fae. She'll say they're not foreigners; they're a Florida militia that includes faeries among their ranks. She might even say she requested the militia's assistance in putting down an uprising of supernaturals. Or something like that."

"It sounds like we need an uprising to stop the governor and the Fae."

"That's what Sophie's been saying. Anyway, we should let the guilds know about the tunnel and the threat of imminent invasion. And maybe, just for the heck of it, report the tunnel to the public works department. The tunnel is a threat to the underground utility lines."

"It will take them weeks to do something about it."

I laughed. "So true. I'll ask Cory to destroy the tunnel. Thanks for showing it to me. Now, I have a favor to ask of you."

"How can I help you?"

"How far back do the historical archives of the Memory Guild go? Are there records from before humans existed?"

He smiled proudly. "Of course. That is why the guild has a stone-speaker and wood-speaker: to record non-human history. And the Tugara preserve some of the history of the universe before our planet and solar system existed."

"Good. I need to learn about the Elder Gods."

Dr. Noordlun's face fell. "Why would you want to do that?"

"Because one of them is trying to return to the universe. And I need to stop him."

THE ARCHIVES OF THE MEMORY GUILD MUST BE PROTECTED against any kind of cataclysm, imaginable or not. Therefore, they weren't kept on earth, but on an alternate plane of existence. To go there, one must use astral travel, in which your spirit and consciousness go on the journey, but your body remains on earth.

Diana, a member of the Memory Guild and an astral witch, arrived at Dr. Noordlun's office an hour later to use her magic to transport us.

"Darla!" the stout middle-aged woman exclaimed. "I haven't seen you for ages!"

I hugged her. "Yes, I've been neglecting my guild duties, but I've had so many crises lately."

"So I've heard."

"You haven't heard half of them."

"Diana, may we proceed now?" Dr. Noordlun asked.

The astral witch nodded and closed her eyes. I had no idea how she worked her magic, but she did it so quickly, it always took me by surprise. Before I could blink, I was standing between

Dr. Noordlun and Diana in the Hall of Records. We appeared as if we were in our normal bodies, but it was only an illusion.

The hall was a massive space seemingly built with marble, in which thick square columns rose to a towering ceiling. The shiny marble reflected what appeared to be sunlight streaming in from skylights high above us.

There were thirteen rectangular bookcases placed at regular intervals across the floor. Each was about forty feet long, twenty feet wide, and two stories tall, packed with what appeared to be the spines of leather-bound books. There were no gaps at all from missing volumes.

The bookcases had no ladders or walkways to provide access to the shelves higher than a human could reach. I drifted through the rows dreamily, admiring the historical library feel and how the roundish surfaces looked so much like old-fashioned leather book spines, shiny and scored in intricate patterns. The bookcases exuded a rich smell, but not quite like leather. There was no trace of dust or mildew in the scent.

The first time I had come here, I was baffled by the fact that the books were not marked with titles or numbers. I had wondered how in the world you could find the book you were looking for.

Then I had learned that these were not books at all, and that I was not standing between giant bookcases. The "bookcases" were alive. They were immortal creatures called the Tugara, who were literally living memories. They contained all the history and memories of the universe, biological computers that constantly updated and added to the data they held.

I placed my hand on the nearest one and felt the gentle stirring of life. The Tugara were believed to be distant relatives of dragons but also had some plant-like characteristics. Though the

docile creatures lived indefinitely, they could be killed. Fortunately, they produced a single offspring every century or so.
There were once twelve of them, and I was honored to have
witnessed a new one join the family.

I wished I could use my psychic abilities—psychometry and
telepathy—to communicate with the Tugara. But I couldn't. Not
even under the influence of Danu, because these creatures were
not from earth, having existed before our planet was born.
Where they came from, no one knew.

Only Dr. Noordlun could communicate with the Tugara, a
paranormal gift bestowed upon him by the creatures themselves
who recognized that our guild's mission was the same as theirs.
If Dr. Noordlun were ever to pass away, the Tugara would anoint
another guild member with this power.

I stepped away from the creatures as Dr. Noordlun
approached the one furthest from where we had appeared in the
hall. The nearest one was the youngest, and they were positioned in order of their age. The oldest one gave few signs of its
greater age, though at first glance you'd think the book-like
patterns of its hide appeared dustier and faded.

Dr. Noordlun murmured something I couldn't hear and
rested his forehead upon one end of the oldest creature. I'd
guess that was its head—if it even had one—though it looked no
different from its opposite end. I hoped Dr. Noordlun wasn't
attempting to communicate with its butt.

The professor stood silent and unmoving. I glanced at Diana,
who wore a serene smile as she watched him.

"The Elder Gods, as you call them, are not as old as they
seem," Dr. Noordlun said in a distant voice, as if he were in a
trance. "There were other pre-religious gods before them who
have long faded away."

He was silent for a long time, making me worry he had fallen asleep.

"The Elder Gods are not, in fact, gods," he continued. "They are extraterrestrial beings who fooled the first humanoid species on earth into believing that they were gods. Yavevi visited this planet many times back then until humans developed their own religions. So why is he returning now?"

Good question. Diana and I waited patiently for the answer. It seemed to take forever, Dr. Noordlun standing silent and immobile with his forehead resting against the massive Tugara.

He suddenly broke the silence. "These so-called Elder Gods, especially Yavevi, are attracted to strife. Wherever these beings come from, in deep space—even from that far away—they can sense when wars, famines, natural disasters, and other causes of great suffering occur on inhabited planets. Yavevi has returned to earth because he feels the dark energy of hatred that is increasing around the world. He also knows that we earthlings are killing our planet. He feeds upon that dark energy of hatred, strife, and destruction."

"What do we—" I cut off my words when I saw Diana give me a glare and make the "zip it up" gesture. She was justified; my words would have broken Dr. Noordlun's trance and connection with the Tugara.

"If Yavevi comes here to stay," the professor continued, "he will hasten the destruction of all life on this planet, feed upon the chaos, and become stronger than ever. Other Elder Gods may join him until earth is nothing but a dead, uninhabited planet. He must be stopped."

He went silent again. We waited until he broke contact with the Tugara, taking a deep breath and coming out of his trance. He walked past the rows of creatures and joined Diana and me, his forehead lined with concern.

"How do we stop Yavevi?" I asked, though I suspected what his answer would be.

"You will find a way, my dear," he said to me with a forced smile. "You, as Danu, after fully becoming her. Only Danu can banish him and heal the earth. And she can do that only when she has completely returned."

"But what will become of *me*, Darla?"

"You will be Danu," he said wistfully. "I pray Darla will still be recognizable in the Goddess, though."

"But what if I have to die to become her?"

A tear formed in the corner of his eye. "It wouldn't be a true death, then, would it?"

AFTER DIANA ENABLED OUR ASTRAL TRAVEL BACK TO THE REAL world and our bodies we'd left behind, I found several voicemails on my phone. Two were scam calls, which were comforting in a way, because while the world seemed to be barreling into Armageddon, fraudsters were still confidently plugging away with their crimes.

The other messages were from Cory and Sophie. They wanted to meet at the inn later to discuss the defense of San Marcos and asked me to invite Dr. Noordlun. But I had to take care of some unfinished business first.

Namely, freeing Samson from the prison camp.

CHAPTER 11

DARLA

I returned to the inn in the middle of afternoon tea. At first glance, you'd think it was a typical tea from the old days when we had normal human guests. Now, running as an unlicensed establishment catering to supernaturals, the crowd was anything but normal. Shifters and faeries sat at the tables, appearing to be human but radiating the supernatural vibe. The two gnomes and the ogre sipping tea at Table Three betrayed the normality.

Pinky was on her own today, because Sophie and Cory hadn't returned yet from Edgewood, but she had it completely under control. She'd made the scones and finger sandwiches to my high standards and was bustling about the dining room, serving food and pouring hot water into teapots, her jet-black hair bobbing as she smiled and made jokes.

It was both reassuring and sad to see her doing such a good job. She was taking a big load off my back but also made it apparent that I was no longer so critical to the functioning of the inn. It wasn't all my show with my family and Pinky as mere supporting characters anymore.

Was my world learning to continue on without me so that I could take up my duties as the Goddess? Did I even have a say in this?

I went into the kitchen and munched on egg-salad finger sandwiches. A vine had forced itself inside through a gap in the windowsill, and seedlings of some sort appeared in the caulking of our farmhouse sink. Welcome to my world as the human vessel of a nature goddess.

A world into which she was increasingly thrusting herself, trying to make my world—and my life—hers.

"So, love, what's all this about Fae tunnels?" Archibald asked, suddenly looking down at me from the wall above the sink.

"How do you know about that?"

"I know everything that goes on inside this inn and with its innkeepers. Gargoyles are silent and unmoving, but ever watchful."

"I only wish you were silent."

"Do the tunnels mean a Fae attack is imminent?"

I sighed. "I suppose. We'll destroy the tunnel we found, but the Fae are surely coming. And there's no one to stop them other than the supernaturals. I'm sure the governor will order the police to stand down, but even if she doesn't, they'll be incapacitated by the Fae magic."

"Do not worry, Darla. San Marcos is filled to the brim with supernaturals right now. We won't let the Fae take the city. 'We shall fight on the beaches,'" he said in a convincing Winston Churchill impression, "'we shall fight on the landing grounds, we shall fight in the fields and in the streets—'"

"I'm not in the mood right now. Detective Samson is in a

prison camp with other supernaturals, and I need to rescue him."

"You must rescue all of them so that they can join the fight against the Fae."

"I think rescuing one person will be difficult enough, thank you."

"Nonsense!" Archibald had returned to his rumbling Winston Churchill voice. "Those supernaturals are being held there with no legal rights. They must be freed!"

"By you and what army? Go recruit some supernaturals to help me. I have research to do."

I left the kitchen and went to the cottage, settling down with my laptop in the second bedroom we used as an office. By all appearances, the prison camp seemed to be kept secret from the public, but I wanted to learn who was running it. Any information I could learn would be helpful if I was really going to break Samson out.

Yeah, as if any of this was rational.

I searched the internet for news stories about supernatural prison camps. No surprise, I found nothing. Next, I visited the websites of various law enforcement agencies, beginning with the Altman Police Department, since the town was nearest the camp. Nada. A search of the county sheriff's office website came up empty too.

This was not unexpected. Although the Supernatural Criminality Act had been passed in Florida, it didn't appear that detained supernaturals were being charged under the new law or were going through the normal legal system at all.

While doing random searches regarding Florida and prison camps, I finally struck gold. A news article mentioned that the state had recently awarded a lucrative contract to a private prison company based in South Florida. The purpose of the contract was vague. It was to accommodate any overflow of inmates in the state corrections system.

The thing was, there was no mention of any overflow, nor a reason there would be one. I believed it was safe to deduce that the true purpose of contracting with the company was to imprison supernaturals who weren't processed through the state's legal system.

The website of the private prison company didn't mention detention of supernaturals under its menu of services, but I found a page full of press releases and combed through them. One bragged about the company's contract with the state, but it used the same vague language the news article had.

Under "Investor Information," I finally found what I was looking for. A quote from a financial analyst predicted a massive boost in revenue, and resulting stock price, thanks to the Supernatural Criminality Act.

Private prisons were notorious for their low pay, so it was a good possibility the guards at the camp were poorly trained. It gave me the slightest glimmer of hope that we could overcome them.

Archibald appeared, perched on the wall above the filing cabinet, where there was concrete-block construction beneath the drywall. He never attached himself to mere drywall and studs; he seemed to require stone of some sort. Not surprising for a stone-speaker.

He shook his demon-like head sadly. "No takers on your requests for recruits, except for Gorkee. The gnomes she commanded, however, said no. So did everyone else I spoke to. The entire supernatural community is preparing to fight the Fae. They don't want to be distracted by your raid."

"Everyone turned you down?" I asked, disappointed. "You weren't gone long enough to speak to many people."

"Oh, I get around this city quickly, my dear."

I was pleased that Gorkee, the ever-loyal indigenous faerie, would help me. But even with the magical help of Sophie and Cory, a brute-force assault on the prison camp would fail with so few fighters. A more secretive jailbreak would be required. Tunneling beneath the fence, though, was out of the question without the gnomes.

"Perhaps your goddess powers will be of some assistance," Archibald said.

"You read my mind. I just don't know yet how the Goddess can help."

"You'll figure it out. Cheerio!" Archibald disappeared from the wall to leave me alone with my thoughts. Too bad he couldn't join me on the mission. A gargoyle, anchored to stone, was an excellent guard for your building, but was of little help when you were out in the wilderness.

While I was using the bathroom, a seedling sprouted from the caulking in the shower. It grew before my eyes, like a stop-motion video on a nature show.

The Goddess was strong in me today. Would she be strong enough to enable me to free Samson?

Weariness suddenly overcame me, and I stumbled to the bedroom, lying on my back on the bed. I closed my eyes but didn't fall asleep. Something was happening in my body that wasn't painful or unpleasant but was completely unfamiliar.

It felt as if an organism was growing inside me, like the seedling in the shower. A physical presence somewhere in my head. Did it involve the benign cyst the MRI had found in my brain? Was the cyst turning malignant? I didn't think so. In fact, the presence I sensed radiated benevolence, making me happy.

I realized it was the seed of divinity from the Goddess.

As her human vessel, I had experienced her powers flowing

into me temporarily, then ebbing. I would feel the warmth of her healing powers and hear the music of her songs that calmed people and erased aggression. On rare occasions, her warmth in my gut would burn and I would be her angel of war, destroying creatures that were harmful to our world.

This was the first time I had sensed something physical in me. I called it a seed, but I truly didn't know how else to describe it. I just knew it was a sign that she was taking me over physically.

I was excited by the Goddess's presence in me but also frightened. My human sense of self still dominated, and it didn't want to loosen its hold on me. I couldn't blame it. I was me, Darla, and until this point, I was Darla enhanced by Danu.

What I, and my sense of self, feared was that Danu would completely take over and Darla would cease to exist. I might die, even.

A jolt of the Goddess's power surged through me like adrenaline. I felt ecstatic, full of love and strength—as if I could cure any illness in any creature and turn the world verdant again. Yes, this was a drug I could easily get used to.

But my attention was shattered by the roar of engines on Cadiz Street, on the other side of the courtyard wall. The threatening growl of large-engine pickup trucks, just like those that had hunted me down in Altman. The sound continued as truck after truck drove past the inn.

The militiamen were back in town, and there were lots of them. They must have come to get rid of the supernaturals, so the Fae could disable the human population with their phytolucine magic and there would be no one to fight back.

"Are you awake?" asked Archibald, who had appeared on the wall above my bed.

"Get the word out that the militia is here!"

"I've already told all the gargoyles and grotesques. They're spreading the word to all the supernaturals. What worries me is that the sun hasn't set yet, and the vampires will be vulnerable."

"All the nests should have human guards now, after the Great Unmasking. You must warn them."

"My messengers are doing that, love."

"Hopefully the militia won't be able to find the vampire nests. And what about the inn? Have any militiamen stopped here?"

"No, they haven't," Archibald said in a calming voice. "As far as the state knows, this inn is no longer operating and we supernaturals have moved out."

I didn't have his confidence that the militia would leave us alone.

"Tell our guests to hunker down as if a hurricane were coming. Stay inside, keep curtains and blinds closed, don't turn on any lights. No loud noises. We'll feed them here tonight, so they don't need to go anywhere."

Roderick had been in charge of procuring whole blood to feed our vampire guests. It was quite a clever scam: he posed as a blood-bank technologist for a hospital and ordered pints in bulk from the blood banks. Our vampire guests were refugees from nests in nearby towns, so no one would know they were here. I prayed they would be safe.

"The militia is in town," I said to Cory when he answered the phone. "When are you guys coming home?"

"We're on our way," he said. "Stay inside."

"No kidding. Watch out for ambushes."

I told him I loved him, and he said the same to me. These days, you could never assume those dear to you would be safe.

Archibald disappeared from the wall. I went into the bathroom to splash water on my face, and when I looked in the mirror a familiar face appeared in it, as if she were standing behind me.

It was Birog, the Druid ghost. Her face was painted white and adorned with runes I didn't recognize. A huge mane of unruly red hair, partly braided with small flowers, covered her forehead and flowed around her shoulders and neck like a flooded river.

"I haven't seen you for a while," I said, not exactly in a welcoming tone.

"I've visited yer daughter, I have," she said in her thick brogue. "The daughter of Danu will have her work cut out for her, to be sure. And so do ye. The survival of the planet depends upon ye. But first, ye've got to protect yer city from invasion and yer people from tyranny."

"Isn't that a bit much to ask of one woman?"

"It's not too much to expect from a goddess. The time is nigh." She cackled with pleasure before fading from the mirror.

Distant gunfire startled me. The face I saw in the mirror was mine, not the Goddess's. How the heck was Darla supposed to save the day?

CHAPTER 12

SOPHIE

"Drop me off at Valencia Street," I told Cory as we drove into San Marcos.

"Why?"

"Diego's nest is there. It's still daylight, and I'm worried about them. Mom said the militia is back in town."

"I thought Diego lived above his restaurant."

"Not since he became duke of their guild. He moved into a mansion with his inner circle for his safety. And because vampire leaders never live alone."

Cory turned onto Valencia Street. "Shouldn't you be at the inn for your own safety?"

"If the militia is ordered to capture me again, the inn is where they'll go. Right?"

"It's safer for you there than running around town. You know, there's still a warrant out for your arrest."

"No kidding, though I'm more in danger from some random vigilante who recognizes me from the Monster Monitor app. Or from Baldric, if I get him angry by manipulating him with the spell in his brain. But I don't intend to do that. I just want him to crawl into a hole somewhere and leave me alone. That's the house up there on the right."

Cory whistled. "Not bad." He pulled up in front of the three-story 19th-century brownstone.

"Yeah. Diego's loaded. That's what you get from centuries of investing."

Cory touched my arm as I was opening the passenger-side door. "You don't have to do this."

I turned and saw the concern on his face. "Yes, I do."

"Dr. Noordlun is the leader of the guilds now. If there's a general in this war, it should be him."

"I'm just doing what I feel I must." I got out of the SUV. "Tell Mom not to worry. I'll be home later."

Cory waited to drive away until I waved to him after climbing the front steps. I was met by the guard in a black sport coat. His hair was cut short, and he had the strong, impassive face of an ex-cop or military guy. I turned on my empathy to sense if he was loyal and not an undercover militiaman.

"You're Sophie, right?" he asked in a neutral voice.

"How did you know?"

"Diego described you. The only human he said was allowed to visit during daylight. What's in the duffel bag?"

"My sword and crossbow. I'm a witch. I don't need a gun."

I felt the affection and loyalty the man felt for Diego, which made me relieved I could trust him. He trusted me, too, despite my weapons. Vampires are extremely selective when hiring human guards, as you would expect. However, Diego's associate, Billy, had been captured by the militia thanks to a treacherous guard.

"Are you aware the militia is in town?" I asked.

"Yes. We're hoping they won't know a nest is here. Diego and his friends moved in only last week."

"Just in case, are there additional guards?"

"There's someone watching the rear."

"That's not enough to stop a militia."

He smiled grimly. "There are very few of us in my field in San Marcos. There wasn't a need for more until now." He looked at his watch. "The vampires should wake up soon. If any bad guys get inside, they'll have hungry vampires to deal with."

He opened the door for me, and I went inside. The tall, arched foyer had a narrow table against the wall with a small lamp emitting a dim light. I turned right into a parlor that was dark except for the light from the foyer. The windows were covered by heavy drapes and probably blackout shades as well. Placing my duffel bag on the floor, I sat on a leather couch and waited.

Despite what you've seen in old movies, vampires don't sleep like the dead until night falls. They're often awake for a small portion of the day, especially during the long days of summer, as long as they stay out of the sun.

The house was silent, save for the ticking of an antique clock on the fireplace mantel. I sensed the supernatural energies of the vampires upstairs, but didn't hear any of them moving about. Just sitting here waiting was driving me nuts, so I pulled out my phone. The group text among the guild leaders was full of warnings about the militia, but no status updates. I needed to talk to someone.

"Yes?" Rufus's voice was unfriendly. He probably didn't recognize my number.

"It's Sophie. Do you have any intel on the militia?"

"A small detachment already attacked a shifter family in Old

Town. It didn't go well for the militia. We're calling all the shifters to come to the compound where my family pack lives. Safety in numbers, you know."

"What about the other supernaturals in town? Do you know how they're faring?"

"No. And their leaders haven't texted anything. You know, we've all worked hard to assimilate ourselves into society while keeping our true identities secret. Before the Great Unmasking, it worked out fine. But aside from our compound and the vampire nests, most supernaturals live alone or with their families. They're scattered all over town and vulnerable to heavily armed crazies."

"Yeah," I said. "How are we going to protect everyone?"

"I bet the militia is going to mass their forces and attack our compound and the vampire nests first before they fan out through the town to round up individuals. We need to kick their butts so they can't do that."

A gunshot rang out in front of the mansion, followed by several more.

"Gotta go," I said. "The crazies are here."

THE MILITIA DIDN'T BOTHER TO USE CLEVER TACTICS; THEY just drove up in their pickup trucks and opened fire without even getting out of their vehicles. Bullets peppered the front door and the windows of the parlor. The windows must have had bulletproof glass, so I ventured a quick look through one.

The guard who had let me in lay wounded on the front stoop, while the one stationed at the rear of the house was firing at the militia from the alley, taking cover behind the corner of the building. He wouldn't last long, because a rental truck pulled up and disgorged more militiamen.

I ran up the stairs and shouted for everyone to wake up. But even the undead can't sleep through volleys of gunfire. Diego, Helga, and Eduardo were already out of their bedrooms.

"How do I get onto the roof?" I asked, panting for breath.

"There's a stairwell on the third floor," Diego said. "Be careful."

"You too. The militiamen will enter the house any moment now."

I reached the third floor, where two male vampires I didn't know were standing on the landing, looking down. In the corner, a narrower staircase ascended to darkness. I went up it, slid open the bolt on the door at the top, and stepped out onto a flat roof covered in slate. A waist-high wall surrounded the roof with four chimneys rising above it.

Peering over the wall in the front, I saw a mass of olive-drab uniforms moving from the vehicles toward the front door. The shooting had stopped; the second guard must have fallen or retreated.

It took me only seconds to prepare my battle magic. Anger is very helpful in moments like these. I pointed Alfie down at the sidewalk and sent forth a torrent of purple lightning. Several men went down, and I jumped backward away from the wall right before the bullets hit it or whizzed over my head.

I cast a protection spell around myself and ventured back to the wall, but at a different location. The great thing about my spell was while it didn't allow anything to penetrate it, I could attack outwards through it. When I fired down on the militia again, their return fire came much quicker, and I felt the impact of a bullet on my protection bubble.

There were too many of them and only one witch. I needed to try a different weapon. None of the spells I knew could defeat the militia, only make a few of them fall asleep. I wished I could create magical vats of boiling oil to pour down on them like in a medieval siege. My best bet would be to return downstairs and use my protection spell to seal the doors and windows for as long as my energy lasted.

Could my empath magic achieve any results? There were so many men, and they were all highly focused and disciplined. Emotion played no part in their actions.

Or did it? Their shared goal was to defeat the enemy, and they were highly motivated to do so. As I had learned, my empath magic worked best when I convinced people to do what they already wanted to do and was in their best interest.

Well, the vampires weren't harming them now. The witch was. I was their greatest threat for the time being. So, I set about creating magic to convince them I was the enemy they wanted to defeat. I would make them feel that instead of neutralizing me after they broke into the house and attacked the vampires, they would have to take me out first.

I clutched the amulet hanging from my neck that Orlena had given me to increase the power of my empath magic. When my energy peaked, I transmitted thoughts and urges to them, focusing especially on a tall guy strutting around in a cowboy hat who appeared to be their leader.

Get the evil witch. She's our greatest threat. She's killed and wounded our brothers and will murder the rest of us with her diabolical magic unless we kill her first. After we waste her, the vampires will be easy pickings.

And just to be safe, I added:

This is an expensive mansion with a sprinkler system. We can't burn it down. We must fill the witch with lead and stake the bloodsuckers. It will be easy and righteous.

Was I crazy, you ask? Not really. I'd observed that these guys only carried small arms—not mortars, rocket-propelled grenades, or anything like that to blow me off the roof. If they wanted to take me out before they fought the vampires, they would have to come up and get me.

And I had a plan, you see. Of course, I had no idea if it would work. I'd used my empath magic on groups of people before, like the crowd at Marge Moosebacher's hate rally and kids playing soccer outside their school. But this time I was giving specific instructions to violent morons. I couldn't be certain that every one of them would obey me. But it was worth trying. After all, I was simply reinforcing what they already wanted to do: kill me.

I ran downstairs and shouted to the vampires, "Go inside your bedrooms and stay there until all the militiamen are inside the house."

"You want us to cower in our rooms and let those thugs take over our home?" Eduardo asked from the second-floor landing.

"They'll come to the roof to kill me," I explained. "You'll attack them from behind."

"You can't sacrifice yourself like that," Diego said. His agonized expression pleased me.

"I have no intention of sacrificing myself."

Just then the front door burst open, and the thudding of combat boots echoed in the foyer below us.

"Follow the plan!" I shouted as I raced upstairs to the roof. Vampires didn't much like taking orders from humans, but they'd better do so if they wanted to survive.

When I returned to the roof, I looked over the wall. A handful of militiamen were positioned outside the house. I sent more empath magic at them, goading them into wanting to destroy me. Then I shot my lightning at them, knocking one to the ground, which sent the others storming into the house, enraged.

It wasn't long before the door at the top of the stairs crashed open. An overweight militiaman stood there, holding an assault rifle, blinking in the glare of the setting sun, looking for me.

I aimed my sword at him, and the bolt of purple lightning knocked him backwards into the stairwell. Curses and thudding bodies came from the stairs as he knocked down the soldiers behind him like bowling pins.

That felt really good, I had to say.

I couldn't savor my triumph, though. More men came up the stairs. My advantage rested on the fact that the stairs were narrow, and the militiamen had to climb them in single file.

I blasted the next man exiting the stairs and the one behind him. But those in the rear pushed those in front of them and knocked the fallen to the side. I kept shooting my attack magic, and the militiamen kept coming, swarming from the door like ants.

I retreated to a far corner of the roof as bodies piled up, but my foes advanced toward me. Once they were away from the doorway they had room to fire their weapons, and bullets slammed into my protection bubble.

In between lightning bolts, a man with crazy eyes sprinted toward me, spreading his arms for a tackle. I dodged him, swung Alfie into his back, and sent him flying over the wall to the ground.

My energy was weakening. I was using too much by maintaining a protection spell strong enough to stop bullets while simultaneously shooting my lightning.

Weren't the vampires attacking yet? The sun hadn't fully set, but the vampires were safe from it if they remained inside.

Diego, I'm about to be overwhelmed up here, I called with my mind despite knowing he wouldn't hear me. *Please attack now.*

A bullet penetrated my bubble, though my magic slowed the projectile enough that it dropped harmlessly to the roof. This was a bad sign. I slipped Alfie into its scabbard on my back and grabbed my crossbow from my duffel bag. Jumping on top of the wall, I took cover behind a chimney, forcing myself not to look down at the ground below.

I had only ten bolts in the quiver clipped to the crossbow's stock. Each of them found its target. After I used the last one, I noticed the flow of men out of the stairwell had slowed.

Shouting came from the stairs, and the men turned around and went back down. Then came the gunfire and horrified screams.

Finally, the vampires were attacking.

I felt safe enough to leave my position behind the chimney, so I jumped down from the wall, returned the crossbow to the bag, and unsheathed Alfie. I crept cautiously toward the open door to the stairs.

A militiaman flew into the air from the door as if launched from a cannon, soaring across the roof and over the wall.

Yep, the vampires were attacking.

I waited until the gunfire petered out. More haunting screams echoed from below, making me cringe. I approached the doorway, pointing my sword forward, but paused as footsteps came up the stairs.

Diego walked out onto the roof. Relief filled his face when he saw me. "Thank goodness you're safe," he said, smiling.

"Same with you." I wanted to kiss him, but the blood

smeared all around his mouth—human blood, no doubt—ruined the urge.

"We took some prisoners," he said. "Perhaps you can use your empath powers to convince them to talk. I want to know how they found our nest and the homes of so many other supernaturals. We'll be wiped out if this continues."

"I'll try my best."

CHAPTER 13

SOPHIE

Three captured militiamen were in the kitchen, tied to wooden chairs in the breakfast nook. They wore combat fatigues with patches indicating the different extremist militias that had come together to form this private army under the governor's command.

One was thin with bugged-out eyes and a swastika tattooed on his forehead. Beside him a large, bearded man sat, grimacing in pain, his left hand bandaged. On the end to my right was a guy who looked strangely familiar, though I struggled to place him. All three looked up at me with hostility when I approached.

The vampire Eduardo leaned against a nearby wine refrigerator. "I believe Albert is the traitor who is giving up the names and locations of our people," he said to Diego, who sat atop the island counter. Helga stood beside him. "Give me an hour with these humans and I'll get them to confirm my theory."

"That means nothing," Diego replied. "They'll tell you anything you want if it stops the pain."

Eduardo smiled. "Who says I will stop the pain? These barbarians destroyed Billy and countless other vampires."

"Sophie," Diego said, "perhaps you have better methods of getting them to reveal what they know. If they even know who the informant is."

I had already begun reaching out with my empathy, reading their emotions as if I were assessing weather data, but with my gut instead of my brain. What hit me the strongest was fear and hatred—two emotions that often go together—the former causing the latter. Since the days of our primate ancestors, humans were frightened and wary of those who were different from us. And so we hated them.

Becoming civilized required recognizing those primitive responses and managing them to avoid our societies being constantly at war.

The prisoners were afraid of the vampires. I couldn't blame them. Undead predators with preternatural abilities who want to sink their fangs into humans are scary. I knew that firsthand. Many years ago, when I was a girl going through drug rehab, I was held captive by vampires who wanted me to be their milk cow. I was rescued, but the trauma stayed with me.

I taught myself not to tarnish all vampires with my past fears. Getting to know vampires, and looking past their monstrous natures, allowed me to see them as people—humans who had transitioned into a different form of existence with unique needs. For example, I never thought of doddering old Roderick as a vampire, but more like an uncle.

And Diego had simply been Mom's fellow member of the Memory Guild who became a friend of my family. Until he stirred something inside me that was unlike anything I'd ever felt with a human guy, despite the trauma from my past.

"You're a witch," said the prisoner on my right—the one who seemed familiar.

"What makes you say that?" I replied.

His nostrils flared as if he were sniffing me. "I just know." He was a homely-looking guy with light-brown hair, a large nose, and sagging jowls.

Finally I remembered who he was. The dream-scenter who had picked the lock on the inn's main door before the militia raided the place, then shifted into a bloodhound and sniffed my bed and pillows. Mom had told me about him and showed me the security video of him in human form at the front door.

We assumed he had read my dreams and confirmed to Baldric that I knew the governor was secretly a faerie, putting my life in danger.

"You're a dream-scenter," I said to the militiaman.

"What makes you say that?" He wore a sly smile.

"I just know. Do you work for Baldric?"

"I don't know that name."

It was time to use my empath magic to get him to talk. When you have a secret, it's draining. You must constantly be on guard to not let it slip out in conversation or say anything that contradicts the web of lies you've built to conceal the truth.

Having secrets is a burden. Most people want to be relieved of such burdens. They wish to tell the truth, even if it's shameful or incriminating, but they won't because they fear being punished or judged negatively.

My empath magic sought to convince this man that he wanted to unburden himself and tell the truth.

His emotions told me he was conflicted about being in the militia. He felt guilty about hurting innocent supernaturals, even though he loathed them. Especially faeries. I discovered his name was Wilfred.

Why did I ever agree to help that freaking faerie Baldric? I hate that slimy jerk and our lying governor, he thought.

"Wilfred, admit you've used your dream-scenting abilities to help Baldric," I commanded. Then I let loose a blast of magic into his head along with these thoughts:

I want to tell the witch the truth about Baldric. It's time to reveal everything. I'll feel much better when I'm finished with that slimy jerk.

His shoulders sagged, and his tense posture melted away. He took a deep breath. "Yeah. I helped him." He shrugged and spread his hands. "He ordered me to. I should have gotten paid for my services, but because I joined the militia, I had to obey his orders. The governor put our brigade under his command. So, I found out what the witch knew about . . . the governor. You're that witch, aren't you?"

"Yep. I know the governor is a faerie, and she's helping the Fae invade our cities and make us all her slaves."

"Well, it's worth it if we get rid of you supernatural monsters."

"Faeries are supernaturals too," I said. "So are you."

"We're not as bad as vampires." He glared at Eduardo, Diego, and Helga. Eduardo hissed at him and the glare turned to fear.

There was something he wasn't telling me. I sent more magic into him.

"Wilfred, Baldric had access to the membership rolls of the supernatural guilds of this city," I said. "Did he share that information with the militia?"

Wilfred appeared to struggle with his impulse to divulge what he knew but finally succumbed. "Yeah. He gave us names and addresses."

Diego growled. "I bought this house too recently for the address to be in the rolls, but Baldric must have found out about it."

"He gave us the address," Wilfried said. "He told us it would be an easy mission."

Diego laughed. "It wasn't the only thing he got wrong. His visions of a future with power and wealth are about to be dashed."

"Weren't the membership rolls taken from him when he resigned as president of the council?" Eduardo asked.

"He made a copy of them, obviously," I said. "I had worried about this. I'm warning Dr. Noordlun. He'll pass it on to the guild leaders, who will notify their members that they're in danger."

While I made my phone call, I hurried to follow Diego as he strode through his house and out the front door. Night had fallen, and all was quiet.

The street was littered with shell casings and fallen militiamen. A number of them had apparently survived and escaped the vampire counterattack, but several trucks remained, belonging to those who hadn't.

"Where are the police?" I asked, even though I knew the answer. They had been ordered to stand down and allow the militia's attack to proceed.

Diego's car was parked a half block away. I got into the passenger seat without being invited.

"Are you certain you want to witness this?" he asked as he started the engine.

"Baldric's expecting someone to find out about his betrayal. You don't want to walk into the lair of a Fae sorcerer without some backup."

"I'm perfectly capable of dealing with him."

"And I'm the only one who can control his own spell that's lodged in his brain." I didn't mention to Diego that I had magically assisted him the previous time he and Baldric had fought to a draw. And Baldric would have won if I hadn't been there.

"His brain will be of no use after I'm finished with him."

Jeez Louise, even a 500-year-old can't resist trying to be a tough guy.

"Shouldn't we have a strategy before we confront him?" I asked.

We stopped at a red light. Diego glanced at me. "The strategy is, I will kill the slimy bastard."

"That's not a strategy. It's a goal."

Diego chuckled. "You humans are so silly."

"You were a human once."

"But I wasn't silly. I served the King of Spain, and he sent me to the isolated armpit of the world known as San Marcos, where we rarely had enough to eat and constantly fought the French, the English, and the pirates. There was only one vampire here at the time and he turned me. I never had the luxury of being silly."

"I'm just saying, Baldric is crafty. Having a basic plan of attack isn't too much to ask. Right?"

"My plan is to confront him and pop his head off like a cork." He placed his hand atop mine. His skin was cool, but it made my skin hot. "I realize I sound full of foolish swagger, but I'm furious at his treachery and wish to kill him immediately. I'll devise my tactics as I go."

There was no reasoning with him, so I remained silent until we arrived at Baldric's auto repair shop. It was closed for the night, but he was often there after hours. Sure enough, a light burned in his office window, and his personal Maserati was parked near the entrance.

I got out of the car, crossbow in hand. I had spent my normal bolts in the battle with the militia, but there were three bolts made of ash wood that I wouldn't waste on humans. Ash wood not only kills vampires when you shoot them in the heart, it is also effective against faeries, capable of penetrating a sorcerer's protection spell.

Diego loaded a fresh clip into his handgun. Bullets will kill faeries, but not sorcerers using protection spells. See, he should have thought ahead before rushing into a fight with a powerful sorcerer.

The door of the shop was locked, of course, but I quickly opened it with a spell. We walked into the darkened customer service area, and Baldric's voice came from the repair bays.

"We're closed right now, except for pitiful creatures seeking revenge." His voice was insufferably cocky. He had, as I feared, expected us.

"I hope you're devising tactics," I whispered to Diego. He ignored me and walked to the door that led to the bays. I was right behind him, conjuring a protection spell for us.

"I sense magic. I don't want to be protected by your magic."

"Okay, Mr. Macho," I replied as I completed a protection bubble around myself.

While Diego had refused to devise a strategy and tactics, I had a plan. It was the most obvious one: use the spell in Baldric's head to convince him to run away. I simply wouldn't bring myself to use empath magic to convince Baldric to enable his own death. I didn't know if I even could. He had originally created the spell to make me do his bidding against my will, and I had successfully hijacked it, forcing him to resign from the Executive Council. Making someone bring about their own death was too tall an order. However, getting him to retreat and save his skin was very doable.

When we walked into the large, open working space, the overhead lights came on and revealed Baldric standing atop an elevated hydraulic lift.

"I'm so happy you survived the militia raid, Diego," he said in an exaggerated stage voice. "I'll appreciate the pleasure of destroying you myself. And you, Sophie, will be taken care of at the same time."

A half dozen sharpened wooden stakes flew from the pit beneath the bay Baldric stood above. The projectiles flew in an arc, raining down upon Diego. The vampire batted them away so quickly it was a blur to my human eyes.

But then another volley of stakes flew from the pit—dozens this time. I doubted Diego could deflect all of them, and I pushed myself against him, letting him into my protection bubble. The stakes bounced off it harmlessly.

"I told you I don't want your magic," Diego shouted at me. He fired his gun at Baldric, but the Fae sorcerer had his own protection spell that blocked the bullets.

"Really?" Baldric said mockingly. "A vampire with a gun?"

Diego stepped out of my bubble and walked toward Baldric. "Why don't you fight me without the crutch of your magic? Stop being a coward. If you want to best me, do it with your bare hands. You can even use a weapon if you want."

Diego was attempting to mesmerize Baldric and control him, sort of like what I was trying to do with the spell in the faerie's brain. Problem was, if you were of sharp mind and strong resolve, you could avoid being mesmerized, as long as you realized early enough that it was happening.

Baldric jumped down from the raised lift and grabbed wooden stakes from the floor, one in each hand. "Okay, vampire, let's go."

I had thought a fight mano a mano between a vampire and a faerie would be short, and deadly for the latter. But Baldric used a type of Fae martial arts that put Diego on the defensive. The faerie leaped and spun, thrusting the stakes savagely.

Diego batted them away, but couldn't land any blows on Baldric.

I frantically probed Baldric's brain, searching for his magic that was inside it like a cyst—that he had put there accidentally when trying to insert it into me. I found the pocket of energy and connected with it.

I want to flee so I can fight another day, my empath magic transmitted to him. *It's what I want, what I had planned all along. Lure them here, humiliate them, and then escape.*

Amid his lightning-fast moves, Baldric smiled at me. The desire I had pushed into him had been received, but he resisted it.

"I know what you're doing, Sophie," he said, panting. "My plan was to lure you two here and humiliate you."

Good, I thought, *it's working after all.*

"And that is what I shall do."

My vision went dark, air whooshed from my lungs, and I was immersed in liquid.

Then, I was gone.

CHAPTER 14

SOPHIE

"Sophie, are you okay?" asked Diego. I couldn't see him. I couldn't see anything. But I sensed he was beside me.

I gasped, and thankfully I could breathe. My starving lungs filled with air that had the electric taste of magic that was foreign to me. Fae magic. It was cold enough to make me shiver.

"Can you hear me?" My voice was faint and echoey.

"Yes. How do we get you out of this thing?"

"What thing?"

"It's like a giant glass vial. Baldric created it magically. I don't know how he could do it while fighting me, but he did. And while I was distracted, trying to help you, he fled."

I realized I couldn't see because my eyes were closed. It felt as if my eyelids were glued. I cast a variation of my unlocking spell, and my eyelids fluttered open. Diego peered at me with worry. We were still in the repair bays. The sharpened wooden stakes littered the floor. And Baldric was nowhere to be seen.

The magical construction that confined me did appear to be glass, or some crystalline substance, tinted slightly red, which was the color of Fae magic. I tapped it with my knuckles. It was rigid and strong, cold as ice, but I knew it wasn't actually frozen.

Did the material have the molecular structure of ice? I cast a spell that generated warmth around me, adding energy to it until it was as hot as I could bear. The glass-like material wasn't melting at all. I sent a burst of heat out of my fingers as they touched my enclosure, and the heat still had no effect.

At least I wasn't shivering anymore.

"I hit the vial with a wrench and a hammer, to no effect," Diego said. With a vampire's preternatural strength, that was saying something.

"Step back," I said. "I'm going to try my attack magic."

The confines were too tight to allow me to remove Alfie from the scabbard on my back, so I sent the purple lightning directly from my hands. It bounced off the enclosure and struck me.

Yikes, that hurt! I felt bad for all the people I'd attacked with this power, and I was glad I hadn't used the full strength.

"Bear with me for a while," I said. "I'm going to figure out the structure of the spell Baldric used and see if I can take it apart."

"I'm not going anywhere without you."

I cast my deconstruction spell and went into a trance. Soon, the structure of the magic that confined me came into view. I expected it to be like the sealing spell that had trapped the vampires in the bathroom of the packing house in Altman, but I saw no yarn-like strands. In fact, it didn't resemble any Fae magic I was familiar with.

I poured my energy into studying the structure. It was made with transparent building blocks that I was very familiar with, because it resembled human magic. Then it dawned on me: this was my own freaking magic.

Baldric had created the vial that confined me by using my protection spell that was around me during his fight with Diego. He'd used my magic against me, altering it into his own creation.

Well, that should be easy to break, right? Even though I could sense that the protection spell I had created before the fight wasn't active anymore, I went through the process of breaking it.

Nope. No luck. I had no connection with, or control over, this spell.

Baldric had basically stolen my spell, tinkered with it, and made it his own before using it against me. It was his revenge for my using his magic against him. He obviously knew I had broken the sealing spell he had engineered to transfer from the packing house to me. He must have wanted to use magic that I couldn't break this time.

But why would he assume I couldn't break my own spell, even if it had been altered? Because the irony of life is that we often know ourselves less than we believe. Baldric had bet I wasn't self-aware enough to control my spell.

Maybe he was right.

I continued to work with the deconstruction spell, trying to take apart the altered version of my protection spell. But the protection spell was too darned good, especially with Baldric's alteration. I needed to stop denying the fact that some deep introspection was the only thing that could get me out of this mess.

So, I released the deconstruction spell and stood there asking tough questions about myself. What was my true goal in life—to be a powerful witch or a normal person doing a normal job? Even as a powerful witch, I needed an income. Would I be content with the paltry salary I got working at the Esperanza

Inn, which may or may not remain in business? Could I find a way of making money with my magic?

No, pondering my career options was a waste of time. I needed to unlock a secret I was keeping from myself if I wanted to be self-aware enough to break this spell. Right? But how could I even identify this secret if it was a secret?

Well, I was an empath. It was time to use my power on myself. I poked around in my memories and explored my subconscious. I took a close, painful look at the weaknesses that led to my drug use in my youth, the lies I'd told throughout my life, and the times I had inflicted emotional pain on others.

I forced myself to be honest about whether my attraction to Diego was truly budding love or was merely a physical attraction. I admitted that his exotic nature, being immortal and all, was a big part of my fascination with him. Still, I couldn't deny the feelings of true love.

I had to go deeper and more painfully. The only way was to distance myself and neutralize my ego, allowing my empath powers to read this person who was me. I studied myself as if I were a stranger.

And I finally found the painful truth I'd been seeking:

Killing people was too easy for me.

I had thought it was my anger issues that had led me to becoming an enforcer for the guilds. But I realized it was also because I didn't have a problem carrying out the rare orders to assassinate someone. Killing wasn't the taboo it should have been.

When my psychic powers of empathy developed, I couldn't work as an enforcer anymore because I saw things from my intended victims' perspective. That made me feel guilt and shame for the killings I had done. Mind you, there were only a handful of victims, but every single one was an anathema.

If I hadn't become an empath, I might have continued being an enforcer. I obviously hadn't been born with enough empathy for me to be a decent person. How ironic that it took a psychic power to give me the empathy I should have had. Actually, an overabundance of empathy.

I felt wiser now, but pretty rotten about myself. However, having faced the brutal truth, I now saw the world in a different light. When I cast the deconstruction spell again, I perceived details that had eluded me before. The differences in the magical handiwork of Baldric versus my protection spell were obvious now.

In a few minutes, I altered the magic that bound me and made it similar enough to my original protection spell. Then I broke it. Easy peasy. Yeah, right.

Diego smiled with delight when I stepped toward him. Then his smile faded. "Why do you look so glum?" he asked. "You've freed yourself."

"Because I have to go kill Baldric now."

EVER VAIN, BALDRIC KEPT A HAIRBRUSH IN HIS OFFICE FROM which I took strands of the beautiful black hair that covered his head in both his natural and human forms. I used the hair for a locator spell that told me he was still in San Marcos. He undoubtedly assumed I wouldn't be able to free myself from his spell, but he should have feared that Diego would come after him. I guessed Baldric had remained in town because he was confident he could destroy the vampire.

The spell provided me with a visual of the house he was in and its neighborhood. Diego insisted on driving me there, but I ordered him to remain in the car. This was a task I had to perform. If Baldric saw Diego, it would start a fight again.

We drove to a neighborhood far enough from the historical center of town to consist of newer-built homes, if you considered homes from the 1950s to be newer. In 500-year-old San Marcos, they were. We drove along winding streets beneath stately live oak trees and parked in front of a two-story brick colonial that matched the visual from my spell. Baldric's car was sitting in the driveway beneath an exterior light attached to the garage, the only light that was on at the house.

I saw the house number on the mailbox and searched for it on the property appraiser's website. Oh boy, the home belonged to Marge Moosebacher, the president of Mothers Against Monsters and yet another secret faerie who was a traitor to the supernatural community.

This would be awkward. Were Baldric and Marge in a relationship? Given the late hour, that seemed likely. I didn't see a second car and hoped that hers wasn't in the garage. Maybe he was house-sitting for her. I would hate to have to fight two faeries at the same time.

I rang the doorbell. What kind of assassin would ring the bell and knowingly end up on the doorbell camera? One who didn't have any f's to give.

Baldric opened the door in human form, wearing a bathrobe. He was shocked to see me.

"You?" he mumbled.

"Who is it?" came Marge's voice from upstairs.

"Work related," Baldric called to her. "What do you want?" he asked me in a low voice.

"I have unfinished business." I gave him a steely stare into his gorgeous green eyes.

"It was quite clever of you to have escaped from my spell. I thought using your own spell against you would stump you."

"Yeah, I'm pretty clever."

"But not as much as I. I'm far more experienced in magic than you." He was being so arrogant that it would make my job much easier. "You tricked me before and put my spell into my own brain instead of yours. But I easily overcame it. You can't control me with it anymore."

"That is true."

"Haven't you had enough of this rivalry between us? You simply can't beat me. I suppose I'll have to kill you, because this is getting tiresome."

"There's one thing you forgot," I said. "You overcame the spell that's in your brain, but its structure is still there. I still have a connection to it."

His eyes narrowed with suspicion.

"I can't make you follow my will," I continued, "but I can do something much more substantial."

"What?"

"Give you the same kind of brain bleed you caused in Orlena when you tried to kill her."

My empath magic connected me with the spell in his brain, and I poured all my energy into it as well as all my hate and anger.

Yeah, I wasn't as good a person as I had thought I was, and I didn't have a problem killing someone if I could get around my newfound empathy.

And that's what I successfully did. Baldric's eyeballs rotated upwards, and blood tricked from his ears and nostrils. He collapsed facedown onto the bricks of his front porch.

He didn't appear to be breathing. I touched the carotid artery on his neck. No pulse.

Another murder that I must carry to my reckoning. But it had to be done. The traitor needed to be taken out. I wasn't trying to justify my deed; we were at war now, and Baldric was the enemy.

Emphasis on past tense.

I returned to Diego's car, and he studied my face.

"Baldric is dead. Please take me back to my car so I can go home and sleep."

"You can stay at my house."

"Where a battle just took place?"

"Yes," he said, touching my hand. "A safe place even a heavily armed militia can't take."

Yep, stay at his house was what I did. But don't jump to conclusions. A crew of human workers bustled about cleaning up the detritus of the violence and repairing damaged doors and windows. It was unclear if they knew the clients who had hired them were vampires. Speaking of whom, the undead residents were gathered in the library debating strategy.

Diego kindly sat with me in the kitchen while I sipped a cup of hot chocolate. Why vampires would have chocolate in the house was beyond me, unless Diego had known that it was the key to my heart.

"Don't be so hard on yourself," he said, sitting across from me in the breakfast nook. "Ever since I first knew you, when your mother joined the Memory Guild, I considered you a caring, compassionate person."

"Who had anger issues and lacked empathy," I replied, sulking.

"You most certainly had empathy. You've always had it. Natural empathy beyond your empath powers."

"I worked as an enforcer. Though I didn't know it would involve assassinations when I took the job."

"You were a soldier. Soldiers kill because they must, not because they want to. Most are morally good."

"I don't know. . ."

He stood and reached across the small table, placing his hands on my cheeks. Then he leaned forward and gave me a quick kiss on the lips. After drawing back, he moved in for another kiss but stopped himself.

My racing heart skipped a beat and slowed when Diego sat down. I reached across the table and put my hand on his large, ebony-skinned hand.

"My apologies," he said, slightly out of breath. "I shouldn't lead you on like that."

"Don't apologize. But what do you mean by lead me on?"

"I told you once before that I cannot give my heart to a mortal human. I did it once and was devastated by her death. Call me weak and cowardly, but I cannot go through that again."

My pleasure at his admitting he was falling for me was ruined by the disappointment of his fighting it.

"I understand." I didn't know what else to say. Arguing that I still had several good years ahead of me wouldn't be very convincing to a centuries-old immortal. And no, I would never try to use empath magic on him to sway his heart.

"And I respect you too much to get involved in only a temporary relationship," he added.

"How thoughtful of you." I couldn't hide the sarcasm in my voice.

He laughed and gave me a devilish smile that offered me the tiniest bit of hope.

Then, the mood was destroyed when Mom's urgent text message appeared on my phone.

CHAPTER 15

DARLA

"Um, don't you think we should have more people to help us?" Cory whispered to me as we crouched behind bushes in the dark woods outside of the private prison camp for supernaturals.

"We've already discussed this." My voice was stern. "This is going to be a surgical strike to whisk Samson out of there. It's not a battle. There are too many guards with guns."

"That's exactly what concerns me."

"Cory, this is not the storming of the Bastille. It's a jailbreak. You distract the guards. Greg helps me cut the wire, and we run like heck. I've sent a telepathic message to Samson to wait as close to the fence as he can, right over there." I pointed at the spot. "We've gone over the plans countless times. Let's do this. As soon as Greg gets back, go to your position a hundred yards to the right and let loose with the fireballs."

To be honest, I was a little nervous about Greg and me being able to cut the wires quickly enough, but we had two strong bolt cutters with handles covered in rubber in case any of the barbed wire was electrified. While the guards investigated Cory's pyrotechnics, we would clip-clip-clip and, as I'd said, run like heck out of there to the SUV parked as close to the camp as we could get it.

A scuffling in the underbrush heading this way made me tense up, but it was only Greg. The large ogre crawled behind the bushes to us. His greenish visage caught a ray of moonlight, revealing a frown, but maybe that was his resting ogre face.

"I was sniffing for magic." He pointed to his gigantic nostrils. "Just as I feared, there's magic in the camp—Fae magic. They must have a sorcerer helping them. I don't understand how these private-prison thugs get their tiny minds around working with a supernatural creature."

"What's the magic for?" I asked.

"I think it's some kind of baffle to restrict the magic the prisoners have. To keep the witches from casting spells and the shifters from shifting."

"I was wondering how they kept the shifters from jumping over the fence," said Cory.

"That's a freaking tall fence. No wolf or leopard could get over it."

"We only need to help a certain wolf get through it," I said.

"That's going to be a problem." Greg shook his head. "I don't think Cory will be able to shoot fireballs this close to the fence because of the baffle."

"I can move further away," Cory said.

"Even if that works, your fireballs won't make it over the fence," Greg replied. "Sure, they'll be a distraction, but not as big as we were hoping for."

"There was a Fae sorcerer at Edgewood. Why didn't he use a baffle against us?"

"A baffle is anchored to a specific location, and it probably takes a long time to set it up. The sorcerer can't carry it around with him."

"Sophie is good at breaking other people's spells," I said to Cory. "Do you think she could disable this baffle?"

"I don't know. Maybe. But she's probably still busy helping the vampires."

"I can't believe you allowed her to go there, knowing the militia was attacking them."

"When has she ever listened to me?" he complained.

I pulled out my phone. "I'm going to text her."

"Your phone is in silent mode, right?" Greg asked.

I ignored him and typed: *I hope you and the vampires are safe. We desperately need your help.*

Surprisingly, she answered right away. *We kicked the militia's butt. Turns out Baldric gave them Diego's address. Baldric is no longer a concern.*

That's nice, dear, I typed. *Now can you meet us at the prison camp for supernaturals? We need your magical assistance.*

I have to go all the way out there?

Yes. We can't rescue Samson without you. We're near the spot where we spied on the camp before.

I'll be there in 40 minutes.

"She'll be here soon," I said to my crew.

Greg shushed me and pointed toward the camp. Dark silhouettes of men were visible through the leaves of the bushes to our right. It was a patrol headed in our direction, just outside of the fence. We'd seen a previous patrol when we were reconnoitering the place, and the men stayed close to the perimeter of the camp, far from where we were hiding. I hoped that would be the case with this patrol.

Were we far enough from the baffle for Cory's magic to work? His fireballs would be crucial if the men found us. We had firearms, but Greg was the only one of us who could shoot straight.

We sat listening as the crunching of twigs and old pinecones came closer. I feared the rattling of my heart was loud enough to give our location away. But the patrol kept moving without stopping. They passed to our left and soon were gone.

"Give them time to circle the entire camp, and then we can get busy," Greg whispered.

"When is Sophie going to get here?" Cory asked.

I looked at my watch. "Any time now."

"What if her magic can't help us?" Greg asked. "We should alter our plan. Cory, like I said, your fireballs won't be as effective because of the baffle. To better distract these dimwits, can you create sound effects that sound like explosions?"

"Um, I haven't done that before. I could probably figure it out."

My phone vibrated. Cory and Greg looked like they wanted to strangle me, but at least my ringer was turned off. It was a text from Sophie.

I just drove past the SUV. A group of prison guards are around it. I'll have to park far away.

"Guards found the SUV," I said to the others. "The patrol that passed us must have detoured from the perimeter. Or it's a different patrol."

"They know we're here," Greg said.

"They might think the SUV belongs to campers, even though the park is closed," I suggested.

"Doesn't matter. They'll look for the campsite to chase the campers away. And they'll find us. We must start the operation now or abort it."

All my tension mixed with surging frustration made me lightheaded. Buzzing filled my ears. But instead of passing out, I felt energized. The familiar warmth began in my solar plexus and spread throughout me. The buzzing in my ears turned into ancient music. I forgot about the problematic details of our plan and all my worries. Power surged inside me, and I jumped to my feet, startling my companions.

I wasn't me anymore. I was the Goddess. And I had the entire forest at my command—the trees, the creatures, the underground springs, and even the wind.

"What the...?" Greg mumbled.

"She's not Darla, she's Danu," Cory said, gazing at me with wonder.

"Danu?"

"The ancient Celtic mother nature goddess. She's returning to earth, and my wife is her human vessel."

"Maybe you should have told me this before we went on a risky rescue mission, huh?"

"Oh, don't worry. Danu is much better than wire cutters and distraction spells."

Their voices were inconsequential squeaking that didn't concern me. I walked slowly from behind the bushes, past the trunks of pine trees, toward the barbed wire and wooden posts of the fence. The squeaking creatures begged me to stop, but I walked onward. And as I did, my trees walked with me.

Ripping and roaring sounds filled the night as thick roots popped from the earth and trees moved toward the fence like humans walking through heavy snow. More squeaking voices came from inside the fence, but they were lost beneath the noise of topsoil torn asunder.

When the trees reached the fence, they plowed into the wire, pushing it into the camp. Wires snapped, and those that didn't yanked the support posts from the ground. On my order, the trees stopped moving and settled into their new homes, having retaken some of the land back from the humans.

Supernatural creatures, most in human form, were streaming out of their enclosure, stepping over the fallen wires, and running past me into the forest. Gunfire came from humans in wooden towers. I had no fear of their puny weapons, but the fleeing supernaturals were being harmed.

All the waters of the earth are my children—those that fall from the sky, that dwell upon the surface, and that travel in the crevices below ground. I commanded those that were nearby to help the fleeing innocents. There were freshwater springs below this forest that gushed through the sponge-like limestone, always eating away at the rock. I increased the water pressure to ever higher levels.

Rock crumbled deep beneath me, underground pockets collapsed, and sinkholes opened in the ground like gaping, hungry mouths. Sinkholes aren't uncommon in Florida. But a guard tower tumbling into one of them, then a second tower sucked into the earth—that was certainly uncommon.

Meet the Goddess, bitches!

To help disorient the evil humans a little more, I called upon the waters of the skies. The moon was eclipsed by dark, heavy clouds, and the heavens disgorged a monsoon amid hurricane-force winds. The third guard tower was knocked down, and the tents formerly occupied by the prisoners whipped away like plastic shopping bags in the wind. In this torrential rain, the guards stopped shooting because they simply couldn't see anything to shoot at.

I couldn't ensure the safety of every prisoner who fled, but at least I gave them all a fighting chance. And somehow, a bedraggled man in tattered clothing and a shaggy beard showed up in front of me.

"Darla, is that you?" Samson asked. "I feel that it's you, but it doesn't look like you. I walked straight ahead from the prearranged spot, but all these trees aren't supposed to be here, and I'm disoriented."

Something about his voice brought me back to myself. Or perhaps Danu had finished her job and decided it was time to leave me. That, and the fact that Cory and Greg had caught up to me and were staring at me in the pouring rain, made me self-conscious. Which made me fully Darla again.

"It *is* you! Darla!" Samson hugged me.

I felt guilty about Cory watching, so my return hug was circumspect.

"Thank goodness you're free. But let's all get the heck out of here before you're shot or recaptured."

"Or we're all shot," Cory said, coming up to stand beside me.

"Thank you, too, Cory," Samson said.

"My pleasure. And this is Greg, who escaped from the militia in Edgewood."

"Nice to meet you, bro," Greg said. "And Cory, I don't smell the baffle anymore. The sorcerer must have been put out of action. You might want to crank up your magic in case we need your fireballs to take out any bad guys."

"I'm working on it."

I was unsteady after all the goddess action, so I let Greg lead us back to the SUV. With the trees in different positions, we relied on the ogre's sense of smell to find the way.

A bearded man in a drenched private prison uniform stepped out from behind a saw palmetto tree. "Are you monsters?" he shouted, aiming his assault rifle at us.

Two of Cory's fireballs engulfed the man half a second later, and he collapsed to the ground.

"Yes," Cory said. "We are."

An occasional gunshot rang out behind us as we made our way toward the road, but I believed the guards had been soundly beaten. My phone buzzed.

What happened? Sophie texted. *It sounded like an earthquake and then I heard gunfire. Someone just walked past me who had the supernatural in her.*

I replied, *We rescued Samson and freed everyone else.*

Did Danu have a hand in this?

She did.

That explains a lot, Sophie typed. *Can you ask her to stop this rain?*

The rain petered out of its own accord, and we found Sophie waiting at the SUV. A male gnome stood beside her.

After she hugged Samson, she asked if we could give the escaped supernatural a ride back to San Marcos.

"I'm driving my car with counterfeit plates," Sophie explained. "If I get pulled over, I don't want the little guy to get arrested with me."

"No problem," I replied. "Are you returning to the inn?"

"I'm going to Diego's house. It will be dawn soon, and I want to be sure their new security guards show up and are legit. His regular ones are in the hospital, thanks to the militia."

Hmm, I thought. *She's becoming very attached to Diego. Should I be concerned?*

After Sophie left, and everyone except me piled into the SUV, a familiar voice spoke to me from the shadows.

"I knew I sensed Danu was here tonight," Leighnel said. The tall, slender elf stepped into the moonlight that was breaking through the clearing clouds. "We were alerted to a great disturbance in the forest, and I was sent to check it out because the royal council believed it might be related to the Fae and phytolucine."

"It wasn't," I said. "We were helping a friend, a shifter, escape from a prison camp. Danu took over the operation and destroyed the camp."

"Impressive." He smiled with admiration.

"I'm grateful to her. The camp needed to be destroyed. It was filled with supernaturals captured by the governor's private militia and imprisoned here by a private corporation that probably bribed the governor for the business. These poor detainees here received no due process, and Lord knows what would have happened to them. Leighnel, it's time the Elves joined the fight against the governor and the Faerie Queene. Your people are supernaturals too."

"Of course. But you know that we avoid being pulled into human affairs, and we have a peace treaty with the Fae."

"This isn't a human affair," I insisted. "Yes, the militia had been persecuting us, but the entire affair was engineered by the indigenous faeries to help the Fae of the Unseelie Court conquer Florida and other states. Your people will end up being ruled by them. Our governor told you the Fae would attack the Elves."

"That is what she claimed in her attempt to extort gold from us. If it's true, I cannot say. For now, the King wishes to honor the treaty, and I must not question his wisdom."

"You can make sure he has all the facts and beg him to reconsider. If not, the Fae will come for the Elves next, even if he pays the extortion to our governor. She won't be able to stop the Faerie Queene from attacking you, if that's what the Queene wants."

Leighnel's eyes widened as he finally realized the seriousness of the danger. Obviously the Elves didn't care about what could happen to humans. Nor did they care what the Fae were up to, as long as the Fae didn't harm the forests. The Elves needed to realize that their comfy existence of living apart and unbothered would soon end if the Fae became the dominant species.

"I will request an audience with His Majesty," Leighnel said, "but I cannot promise he will listen. Have you not used the information of your governor's extortion to damage her politically?"

"Sophie is working on that."

He disappeared into the forest, and I got into the SUV. During the drive back to San Marcos, thinking about our victory that night made me hope for more victories to come.

Until I got the text from Sophie telling me to keep Roderick safe. Apparently, something bad was going down among the vampires of San Marcos.

CHAPTER 16

SOPHIE

The moment I arrived at Diego's mansion, I sensed something was wrong. The night-shift guards weren't there, which wasn't as concerning during the night when the vampires were active and able to defend themselves. Yet, with Diego being the leader of their guild, and the militia having just attacked the place, you'd expect to find guards posted at the doors.

The front door wasn't even locked. When I went inside, I found a home that had lights on everywhere but was completely silent. My uneasiness kept me from calling out. I simply wandered from room to room. No one was home.

When I reached the third floor, I found a pile of discarded clothing and a pair of men's shoes in the hallway. These vampires were much too meticulous to drop their clothes on the floor like teenagers. I approached the pile warily, and my heart sank.

Brown dust was mixed in with the clothes. The dust of an instantly decayed vampire who had been destroyed. This was a murder scene.

My first thought was to make sure they weren't clothes I recognized as Diego's. They weren't. They didn't look like anything Eduardo would wear, so they had probably belonged to one of the vampires living here that I hadn't met.

Who had destroyed this vampire? A militiaman? A crazed vigilante? The police? In the current climate of fear among supernaturals, I didn't immediately wonder if a vampire had done this, but it was certainly possible. And where were the rest of the vampires who lived there?

I called and texted Diego. Of course he didn't answer, both enraging and scaring me. Next, I texted Mom to let her know about the possible vampire catastrophe.

I took the stairs to the second floor and checked for anything amiss in Diego's bedroom. I'd never been in there before. Unlike his bedroom in the apartment above his restaurant, this one didn't have a bed from the sixteenth century. It was an ordinary, contemporary design. In fact, all the furniture in the room looked generic, like it had been rented or purchased en masse.

There were no signs of a struggle. But something caught my eye and almost stopped my heart.

Diego's phone lay on the floor against the wall just inside the bedroom door. He was not the careless type who would simply drop a phone without noticing. I picked it up and saw notifications of my unread texts. His psychic energy lingered on the device, but not enough to use for a locator spell. I entered the bathroom, looking in vain for a discarded hair to use. Either Diego's housekeeper was impeccably clean, or vampires don't shed hair.

"I thought I'd find you here."

Yikes! I nearly jumped out of my shoes. The vampire Albert

stood in the bathroom doorway, his tall, lithe body tense and ready to spring.

"What happened to Diego?" I asked, trying to sound braver than I felt.

"My confederates took him and his inner circle to the fortress. It's time for a reckoning. He cheated when he beat me in the Crucible. I was told he had magical help." He looked at me with a knowing smile, exuding hatred, resentment, and jealousy. But I also sensed ruthless ambition and deceit.

"According to the rules of the Crucible, spectators can pitch in," I said. "Like the vampire who tossed you the sharpened stake."

"What matters is that I would have won were it not for you. We ended up with a foolish duke who has led us poorly. It's time for new leadership. We should not be involved in the war against the Fae. Come with me."

I recoiled in disgust and fear when he grabbed me around the waist and slung me over his shoulder. My upper body hung upside down, my face in the small of his back. His ponytail danced and smacked my cheek as he descended the stairs. He held me so tightly with both his arms that I couldn't even attempt to squirm out of his grip.

Yeah, I punched the back of his legs. And what good did that do? Nothing. I cast my sleep spell, but it didn't work. It was never a given that magic would work on a vampire, and my immobility spell didn't work either. I'd probably been sloppy in my spellcraft, but Jeez Louise, I was upside down.

He exited through a back door, and I expected to be thrown into a car. But instead he ran along darkened, deserted streets eastward toward the bay. A vampire can run faster than the local speed limit. It was disorienting, speeding through the night with my head upside down and seeing only cobblestones passing in a blur. It was impossible to concentrate enough to cast an effective spell.

He jumped over a fence, and his landing almost knocked the wind out of me. When he crossed a wooden bridge over an empty moat, I realized we were at the Castillo, the fortress built beginning in the 1600s to defend San Marcos from invaders. How ironic that he would come here during my city's present circumstances.

Albert climbed the stone stairs and then dropped me. I landed hard on the floor of the battlements. An unfamiliar vampire bound my hands and feet with rope as I took in my surroundings. Diego, Helga, Eduardo, and two other vampires were tied up with metal cables. Guards holding wooden spears stood at the ready. Behind them, beyond the ancient Spanish cannons poking through the parapets, the bay shined darkly in the moonlight.

In the center courtyard of the fortress beneath the battlements, a throng of vampires had assembled, a smaller number than had attended the Crucible. These were all the remaining undead, not destroyed by the militia, from San Marcos and surrounding towns.

"What are you doing?" I asked Albert.

"We are going to acknowledge that I am the new Duke of the Clan of the Eternal Night. And this pretender—" He pointed at Diego—"will be executed with his cronies by sun-scorching."

The blood drained from my head, and I slumped to the stone floor.

MY FAINTING SPELL WAS BRIEF. ALBERT WAS ADDRESSING THE crowd as I struggled to sit upright again.

". . . and continue to resist and avoid the militia until the Fae have conquered San Marcos," he said in a booming voice. "The Fae will have no more use for the militia, which will leave the city. In fact, I suspect the Fae might even slaughter them."

The crowd murmured its approval.

"Once the Fae rule the city, our existence will return to normal. We will thrive during the night and prey upon the Fae, just like we've always done with humans. But Fae blood is so much sweeter!" He gave a hearty laugh.

Many of the vampires in the courtyard laughed as well. I concentrated and opened my senses to feel for their emotions. Sometimes it was difficult for me to read vampire emotions, especially when they were in a large crowd. Several of them had affection for Albert, but most were wary of the coup that was taking place, and they feared for Diego and his circle. They also had great anxiety about the militia and especially Albert. They simply didn't trust him.

I looked at Diego. His face was dark with anger and humiliation.

We can turn the vampires against Albert, I said to him telepathically. He looked at me sharply, so I knew I'd gotten through this time. *Speak to the crowd. I will amplify their positive feelings about you and what you say.*

He nodded. *I will.*

"This is not the right path forward!" Diego shouted. He sat on the floor, bound like I was, but he was near the inner edge of the battlements, allowing him to be seen by the crowd below.

One of Albert's goons smacked Diego in the head with a spear.

"Allow me to speak," Diego implored Albert. "I am their

leader, and you're about to execute me. If you want them to follow you, you must respect their will and mine."

"There's only an hour before dawn and your destruction," Albert replied with a sneer. "So go ahead and yap at them like a small dog on a leash."

I wondered where the vampires would secure shelter from the sun with so little time left to find it. But I remembered today was Monday, when the Castillo was closed. They could seek darkness in the bowels of the fortress.

"Fellow members of the Clan of the Eternal Night," Diego said in a booming voice, "we are facing the greatest threat our kind has seen since the Spanish Inquisition. We have been revealed to humans and have been mercilessly hunted by them. And now we have a foreign invader, the Fae of the Unseelie Court, who want to rule us. Who believe we are inferior creatures to them. Who will treat us as such. Most likely, they will persecute and destroy us like the humans are doing."

Angry grumbling rose from the crowd. Borrowing power from the amulet Orlena had given me, I used my empath magic to coax more anger from them focused on the Fae.

"That's nonsense," Albert said. I revved up the crowd's skepticism of him.

"The only way we vampires can survive is to defeat those who persecute us—who fear and hate us," Diego continued. "In a world dominated by mortals, we can't change their fear and hatred. But we can prevent them from hunting and harming us. We can blend into the shadows of society like we did for centuries until the Great Unmasking. We can be safe again and enjoy eternity with the pleasures only vampires can appreciate. Once more, we will be the masters of the night and deniers of mortality. We are vampires and we are great!"

The crowd cheered, and I sent them magic that enhanced the inspiration and hope that Diego gave them.

"How do we become safe again?" He leaned over the edge of the battlement. "We defeat the Fae. We wipe out the militia. And we take down the politicians who have been using their constituents' fear and hatred to increase their own power."

The crowd gave a lusty roar.

"And we do that by being united. Each species of supernaturals is small compared to humans and the Fae. We must band together, all of us—vampires, shifters, trolls, ogres, elves, and the rest. We must bring the local faeries back into our camp. Together, we'll form a front that will be as strong as or stronger than those who want to enslave us."

The excitement coming from the crowd was intense, and I magnified it.

"And when I speak of unity, what is the most important union of all? The Clan of the Eternal Night. Our guild of vampires that helps us protect ourselves and maintain our sublime existence. We can no longer fight with each other. Or stab other vampires in the back. We especially can't stage a coup to disrupt our leadership in the middle of our greatest crisis ever. Do not allow the traitor, Albert, to destroy me!"

The crowd surged toward the stairs on either side of them and up to the battlements. Albert and his guards panicked.

"Stake them now," Albert ordered.

I cast a protection spell covering Diego and the captive vampires. The guards were shocked when they thrust their spears only to have them blocked by an invisible wall. They kept trying futilely. The first vampires from the crowd reached the battlement and were running toward them.

"The witch is doing this!" Albert screamed, pointing at me. "Kill her."

Well, I can only maintain one protection spell at a time. I couldn't cast one for myself, nor could I take refuge in the one I had created because I couldn't get past Albert's henchmen.

The first member of the crowd was staked by a spearman guarding Albert. The nearest guard thrust his spear at me. I dodged the spear, but I couldn't stand up to run and I had no time to try a different defensive spell. He lunged again.

I rolled across the floor and fell from the ledge of the battlement, directly onto the seething mob of vampires below.

The vampires of San Marcos had strict rules governing their feeding and predation. In our modern society, they needed to show restraint and good judgement. But still, a human dropping into a crowd of excited vampires was like tossing fish chunks into a shark tank.

Two vampires caught me before I hit the ground. Others crowded around me like I was a plate of Sophie Tartare.

"Hey guys," I shouted, "you need to go upstairs and free Diego before he's staked."

The eyes of the vampires around me said they wanted to feed, but their better angels made them find enough self-restraint to spare me. I was carried along with the tide of bodies toward the stairs and upwards, to the fight ensuing atop the battlements.

Albert's guards were the only armed combatants there tonight. But they were vastly outnumbered by the crowd. Several crowd members were impaled and destroyed by the spears, but the weight of their onslaught soon overcame the guards.

I wasn't close enough to see the details, but a body skewered by two spears was thrust up above the throng. It was Albert, who soon dissolved in a cloud of dust.

Someone found the bolt cutters the guards had used when binding Diego and his aides. The metal cables were cut and the vampires freed. Diego pushed through the crowd now surrounding him, shaking hands, slapping backs, and hugging. When he found me, I got a hug. Glad it wasn't a backslap, right?

"I'm grateful for the effect your magic had on everyone," he said.

"It was your words that turned the tide. My magic merely added extra sugar to the cookie dough."

The blank look on his face told me I'd used the wrong metaphor. Even though Diego was a restauranteur, vampires don't think about food the way humans do.

"Where do we go from here?" Diego asked.

"Dr. Noordlun is a capable president of the Executive Committee," I said, "but he's not an inspiring leader for a war. You must take more of a leadership role in this fight. The vampires and the shifters will be on the vanguard, and I'll help you recruit other supernaturals to the cause."

"We need to get humans to stop fighting the supernaturals who have always lived among them. The humans' true enemy is the foreign invader."

My phone buzzed. Diego patted his pockets. I handed him his phone, which I still had from his bedroom.

It was the group text of the supernatural leaders: reports of militia in Luttvale Beach, as well as more delivery vans than normal.

"They're attacking our nearest suburb," Diego said. "I don't believe we're ready for this."

"Ready or not, we have to fight."

CHAPTER 17

DARLA

"Your people have been such loyal allies in our war against the Fae," I said to the wizened old gnome guest during breakfast at the inn.

"We have. And, frankly, we're tired of sacrificing warriors to save your butts," he replied in creaky, squeaky English.

"Would you like another scone fresh from the oven?" I handed him one with tongs.

The gnome, Chieftain Skeetch, looked at the scone with desiring eyes, his beard sprinkled with scone crumbs. He appeared to be trying to resist but succumbed to temptation. "Yes, I'll have one more. But don't think you can bribe me with scones."

"Would you like me to make you eggs to order?"

"I'm quite satisfied with the buffet. Again, I am not suscep-tible to bribery." He spread clotted cream and jam on his scone and devoured it.

The Gnome people don't have a monarch and live in scat-tered family clans. The local clan had indeed saved our butts on more than one occasion when battling the Fae, taking heavy casualties. I didn't blame them for being reluctant to continue fighting, but San Marcos was their home too. All of us, of all species, must band together to save our city.

"Oh, could you spare one more scone?" he asked coyly.

"My pleasure." I placed one on his plate and—

Ended up standing beside the waterfall in a familiar primeval forest. The Goddess had summoned me again. She emerged from behind a waterfall, wading through the waist-deep water of the pool beneath it.

"Danu, thank you for helping us rescue my friend last night," I said. "Along with the other prisoners. I didn't even ask you for help."

"I did not help you. I *was* you, and you were me. *We* rescued them. We make a great team, girl." She grinned.

I cocked my head. That wasn't the kind of language she normally used.

"Your strong desire to save them, and your fear of being stopped, brought me into you unbidden," she continued. "I care nothing about your war. I only want to stop evil and prevent the Fae from harming the earth. But you care greatly, resulting in my assisting you. Do you understand what this means?"

"No." Actually, I was beginning to understand, and it frightened me.

"Our transformation is nearly complete."

"But I don't want to transform," I whined. "I admire you. You could say I worship you. But I don't want to become you. I want to remain who I am with the life I've built."

"You don't enjoy my powers of fertility, healing, and stimulating life itself? My ability to control nature? I'm really awesome, aren't I?" There she went again with the non-goddess-like language.

"Well, I've got to admit those powers are pretty cool. But your powers of destruction are scary."

"And you have used them often."

She had me there.

"Why did you choose me?" I asked.

"I've already told you why. You are the reincarnation of my son, the Dagda. With you as my human vessel, my son's spirit rejoins me, like the reverse of giving birth to him. To return to earth is a process of rebirth, of starting anew. Not just for me, but for the earth."

"Yeah, but—"

"A rebirth for you, too. That body you inhabit is frail and mortal. It will eventually dry up like a husk of wheat and blow away into the wind. Becoming me will bring you immortality and the sublime existence of a deity."

"I was kind of looking forward to getting older, retiring, and having grandchildren. Puttering around in the garden. Exploring new recipes. Playing bingo."

The Goddess laughed. "You find that more pleasant than healing the earth?"

"Yes. Especially the bingo."

"You are ignoring the vicissitudes of growing older: declining health, pain, frailty, and loneliness."

"I'll have my family."

"If they do not precede you in death."

That was a low blow. But I supposed goddesses don't say cruel things merely to hurt you.

"Your daughter will be the rebirth of the demigod race who were my children," Danu said. "She will be the leader of the Tuatha Dé Danann."

"Don't be so sure. Sophie has a mind of her own."

"Her destiny will choose her, not the other way around."

"I don't want to leave her. I don't want to leave my husband, either."

"Your human mortality makes that inevitable. But as a goddess, you will have options."

"What do you mean?"

She smiled. "You shall see."

"I'm still not sure about this. I need to more time to consider it."

"You have no choice. You must make a sacrifice."

"Why?"

"Sacrifice is necessary for the rebirth of a deity. You have used my powers many times. There is a price for that."

"I must sacrifice my life?"

"Come. Join me in the water."

I obeyed, wading naked into the stream and then into the deeper pool. I hadn't realized I was naked, but visiting the Goddess was like dreaming, except with real consequences.

When I was an arm's length away from her, I was overcome with her power and beauty. Her long tresses of black hair were silky and shiny with youth. Her face was stunningly beautiful, with sharp angles that made it unlike the actors and fashion models of today who represent our notion of beauty. A wreath of woven flowers covered her full breasts.

Most of all, she beamed with benevolent powers. I'm good at sensing the supernatural in people. What I sensed in her was different. It was the pure radiance of divinity, which you never encounter in real life.

"Come with me behind the waterfall, into the cave."

My natural, stubborn will to live, that all mortals possess, wouldn't allow me to obey her. Despite being intellectually intrigued by her proposal, my instinct was to resist it in order to survive. Would the transformation kill me outright? Would it be like my episodes of "going away," leaving my catatonic body behind? Or would I walk out of that cave in the same body, with the only difference being my goddess status?

"Come," the Goddess demanded.

"I'm sorry, but I can't just yet. I'm not ready."

"There isn't much time. You must defeat the Elder God. Only a goddess can do that."

"Why don't you?" I asked. She frowned. "With all due respect," I added.

"I have not returned to the earth yet. The Elder God is there trying to destroy the planet. That is why your war with the Fae is inconsequential to me. Come. You have much work to do."

An urge to fulfill my duty filled me. I'd never imagined having a duty to save my planet before, but I began wading through the pool toward the waterfall. Danu smiled and led the way through the cascade that pounded my head and shoulders in an invigorating way.

When I emerged from the waterfall we were in a dark grotto, enclosed by the cliff above and by the waterfall. I faced the opening of the cave, where faint orange light spilled out. Danu waded up to it and beckoned for me to follow. She bent slightly because of the low ceiling and disappeared inside.

My legs automatically followed her, but just before I entered the cave, I hesitated. My instincts as a living creature warned me of serious consequences if I went in there. I placed my hands against the cliff face to stop myself from going through the opening.

And that's when I was back in the dining room, standing beside Skeetch, the gnome. He chewed vigorously on a sausage link, looking up at me when my consciousness returned. His eyes narrowed with concern.

"You were frozen for a while there," he said. "I feared you'd had a stroke."

"No, no. Just a mild form of seizure I occasionally have," I said with a forced smile. "Nothing to worry about."

"We'll see about that."

The scone I had served him before I "went away" was still on his plate with only one bite missing.

"I'll bring out another batch of scones. Would you like one?"

He patted his belly. "As lovely as they are, I'm a wee bit full."

"Well, have a nice day. And please speak to your clan about joining the fight against the Fae."

"I'll see what I can do."

I found Pinky in the kitchen and asked her to cover me for the remainder of breakfast service while I went to my room to nurse a migraine.

"I didn't know you got migraines," she said.

"Neither did I." I couldn't bring myself to tell the truth that my head was spinning from a debate with a goddess.

When I returned to the cottage, Cory was still there, sitting at the dining table with his coffee and laptop. He looked at me with concern.

"I'm going to lie down for a bit," I said.

"What's wrong? You look like you've seen a ghost."

"I see ghosts here all the time. I saw the Goddess. She's pressuring me to complete our transition."

"Oh no," Cory said, upset. "Why won't she leave you alone?"

"She's very determined." I kissed the top of his head and went into the bedroom, plopping on my back into the bed.

Cory followed me into the room. "I—I don't want to lose you. Is that what's going to happen? Has she explained what exactly will happen to you when you become her?"

"She was very vague about it. I'm hoping I'll still be me, but with goddess powers." I didn't sound very convincing.

Cory lay down on his back beside me. "You mean the same body? But your personality would be different, right?"

"I don't know about my body. And the Goddess doesn't have much of a personality, really. She just acts, well, divine. I have noticed she's a little quirkier now. Could that be my influence? Does that mean we're melding together?"

"I don't want to think about that. What did she talk to you about?"

"She said she doesn't care about the governor and the Fae. She's worried about the Elder God who wants to destroy the planet, and only I can stop him. But I need to be transitioned into her to defeat him."

"Man, this is so messed up. Did she say anything else?"

I debated mentioning this but went ahead. "She said I must make a sacrifice."

Cory was silent.

"She didn't specify what kind of sacrifice," I added.

"That worries me," Cory said in a low voice. "So many religions have stories of death and renewal. Is she going to kill you?"

"I wouldn't put it like that." I didn't mention the Goddess's words about my body becoming like a dried husk. "At the end, she wanted me to enter a cave behind the waterfall where I often visit her. I didn't go into the cave. I was afraid I wouldn't come out."

"Darla, baby, I don't want to lose you."

"You won't." I kissed his cheek. "If I become a goddess, I can do whatever I want. And what I want is to be with you always."

A tear appeared in his eye. I kissed him again, this time on the lips. He hugged me desperately, and I crawled on top of him. Our kissing grew frenzied, savage, as if we weren't simply loving each other but fighting fate and destiny, resisting the wills of all those who wanted to tear us apart and harm us to further their own agendas.

Soon, our clothes came off, and we made love with an intensity we hadn't had since our early marriage, trying to forget about aging and loss. When we had finished, we lay on our sides, spooning, my back against his chest, his arms around me. I listened to his breathing and emptied my mind of all my worries and all the complexities of life.

But after a while, I got that feeling in my head again, as if the cyst in my brain was a goddess seed. And it was germinating.

CHAPTER 18

SOPHIE

Driving through town on my way to Luttvale Beach, I stopped at a supermarket for some supplies to sustain myself for a while in case there was going to be a battle. I filled my cart with granola bars, fruit, water, and those little snack packs kids love. I also gathered copious amounts of chocolate, because you can't win a battle without it. Right?

I was deep in thought about what percentage of cocoa I wanted in my gourmet chocolate bars when someone stopped behind me.

"You!" a woman said. "Was it you?"

I turned to find my archnemesis, Marge Moosebacher, glaring at me.

"Hi," I said.

"Did you kill Baldric with your magic?"

"Baldric's dead?" I asked with all the fake innocence I could muster.

She frowned even more. "Yes. A cerebral hemorrhage."

"Why would you think I did it?"

"Someone came to my house that night, and Baldric answered the door. I found him dead on the front porch. I know that you two have been antagonists, to say the least."

"I don't think it's possible to give another person a cerebral hemorrhage."

"You're a witch. You did it with your magic."

"I'm not a witch," I lied. "I'm just into New Age stuff like crystals and incense. Your Monster Monitor app is wrong to call me a witch. I should sue—"

"Witch!" she shrieked. "Don't lie to me!"

"Faerie!" I shouted back at her. Yeah, I know. Not very mature. I needed to de-escalate and get out of there.

"She's a witch!" Marge screamed, pointing at me. "A dangerous, murderous witch!"

Another woman who had been approaching the candy section scampered away, while curious faces peered at us from both ends of the aisle. Marge's behavior wasn't just embarrassing for me; it was potentially fatal. In these times after the Great Unmasking, accused supernaturals were threatened by random vigilantes, as well as the militia and the police.

"Leave me alone, faerie!" Maybe if I accused her, too, our accusations would cancel each other out, and onlookers would think we were both crazy. "Let me pay for my food and get on with my business."

She blocked my cart with hers. I rammed it. Previous encounters with her had taught me that my sleep spell and the like didn't work on this indigenous faerie. She had once successfully broken into the inn before retreating. Later I discovered my empath magic worked on her. In fact, I had convinced her to reveal her true faerie form in front of the crowd at a rally.

I cast my spell, clutching my amulet to enhance the magic,

while she pushed my cart with hers. It was a shopping cart demolition derby.

This woman can reveal my true nature, I telepathically sent to her. *It's too dangerous to confront her this way in public.*

I broadcast to her the fear of being revealed and arrested, along with sympathy for me. *Even if she is a witch, she's a harmless one. I have no proof that she killed Baldric. His hemorrhage was probably natural.*

She actually snarled at me like an animal, struggling with herself as her emotions changed and tamped down her initial urge for confrontation.

I can attack her another time if I want. It's too dangerous for me to do it here and now.

She looked confused by her conflicting emotions, as the ones I sent her won out. Her shoulders slumped with exhaustion.

"Excuse me," I said, maneuvering my cart around hers. "Have a nice day."

Several sets of eyes bored into the back of my head as I headed for the checkout lines. I jerked my head to meet the eyes of those staring at me. Some people were fearful; others were cruel and judgmental. Most were simply curious. I send a cloud of calming emotions billowing from me that trailed me as I went. The cashier avoided eye contact, and I escaped from the store with my water and snacks.

Out of the frying pan and into the fire, I thought as I drove from San Marcos toward the conflict that awaited in Luttvale Beach.

AS ITS NAME IMPLIED, LUTTVALE BEACH WAS A BEACH TOWN south of San Marcos. My hometown extended to the coast and had its own beach. Luttvale Beach, though, was solely on the

barrier island that ran along the coast, separated from the mainland by the Intracoastal Waterway. Keeping control of the town
was critical to prevent the Fae army from advancing up the coast
to San Marcos's beach and then attacking the city from the east
as well as from the south, eventually encircling the city.

Luttvale Beach had a funky surfer vibe, with small artsy
shops, mom-and-pop motels, and seafood restaurants with
outdoor seating. It didn't look like a potential battlefield, and
there were no obvious places for defensive lines. Of course, this
hadn't been a conventional war anyway.

I met Cory at the public beach parking lot. He had arrived in
his SUV with Greg and two additional witches from the Magic
Guild, Jocelyn and Bert. Jocelyn was a mage and was the oldest
and most experienced of the witches here. Tall and slender, with
long, straight silver hair and dressed in black, she was what you'd
imagine a bad-ass witch to look like—very risky for her after the
Great Unmasking. She was who I'd put my money on for
replacing the ailing Orlena as Arch Mage of the guild.

"Mom is safe at home, right?" I asked Cory.

"Yes. No more battles for her. She's been freezing too much
lately."

"Have you guys seen any militiamen around?" I asked him
and the others.

"Not yet," Cory replied. "We've only been here twenty
minutes or so."

"I got a call from a witch friend of mine who lives here,"
Jocelyn said. "The supernatural community in this town is small,
mostly witches and a few shifters. Two families of beach trolls.
No vampires—not a surprise in a beach town. My friend saw
militiamen in their pickup trucks drive up and down the main
road yesterday, but she hasn't heard of any supernaturals
abducted by them."

"Is your friend in hiding?" I asked.

"Yes. The witches and shifters have congregated in a few homes just off the beach, and they put the hurricane shutters up to make the homes look like they belong to snowbirds who left for the season."

"Good." After we discovered Baldric was giving the militia the addresses of guild members, we'd all been ordered to move to temporary quarters. I guessed that I, too, should stay away from the inn, especially now that I was back on Marge Moosebacher's radar.

Simply milling about in the parking lot was not useful or safe. "I wish the shifters from San Marcos would show up," I said. "I'm expecting the vampires will arrive tonight. In the meantime, we should split up and watch the road south of town, and the bridge from the mainland, for any suspicious vehicles."

Everyone agreed. But before anyone left, a car pulled up. The driver was the faerie Gorkee, in human form. With her was an elderly gnome I recognized as a guest at the Esperanza Inn. I leaned into the open driver's side window and shared what little information we had.

"Your name is Skeetch, right?" I asked the gnome.

He nodded. "Your mother—she's such a cute lady—she said my people were needed in this war. Alas, I begged our clan for volunteer fighters to serve under Gorkee, but they refused."

"They lost too many fighters in the raid on the Faerie Queene's winter palace," Gorkee explained with sadness. "I was their leader, and I failed them."

I felt guilty about that, too, because the main purpose of the raid was to rescue Mom and, later, me.

"You did not fail them, Gorkee. The mission was a success." And to Skeetch, I added, "I understand, and I appreciate the sacrifice of your clan members. But no one can be neutral in this war."

"Then where are the blasted Elves?" he asked.

"Exactly. They falsely believe they can sit out the war on the sidelines. Boy, will they be shocked when the Faerie Queene forces them to chop down their own forests."

An EV pulled up nearby, and Dr. Noordlun emerged. He wore a baseball cap with the logo of San Marcos College and an overabundance of sunscreen on the parts of his face not covered by his large white beard. For some reason he wore a tweed sport coat on this hot, sunny day at the beach.

"Ah, our general has finally arrived," Jocelyn said with sarcasm.

I rarely thought of Dr. Noordlun as a supernatural, but he did have some psychic abilities. He was an energy-speaker, possessing a rare ability to read the various forms of energy that run through the earth and are used in magic.

As the head of the Memory Guild, Dr. Noordlun used his abilities to communicate, in a manner of speaking, with energy and learn its history—its surges in power and its use by witches and wizards. This was akin to scientists learning about the history of the earth by measuring the carbon dioxide in glacial ice or by studying tree rings.

He could also sense when the energy field had been disrupted by aberrant magical activity. Even more impressive, he could locate ley lines and manipulate their powerful currents of energy. Normally, only the rare witch, like Cory, could locate ley lines and siphon their energy.

With his psychic abilities being so esoteric, Dr. Noordlun shouldn't have been a victim of the Great Unmasking. But he was, thanks to his name being on the rolls of guild members.

The professor wandered over to our group standing near our

vehicles. "Good morning. Sorry I'm late. I was completing a paper I'm submitting to a history journal. Please bring me up to date. We're here because the Fae army is coming?"

Everyone exchanged worried glances.

"The militia was spotted nearby earlier," I replied. "They come to towns to remove supernaturals before Fae forces capture the towns. We got here before the Fae arrived to stop them."

"Ah, I see. Quite reasonable. Now, are you the only forces we have here?"

"We're assuming shifters will show up, but we don't know when. The vampires will probably come after the sun sets, but we're not sure."

"Hmm, we're not well coordinated, are we?" Dr. Noordlun asked. "That is a failing on my part."

No kidding, Captain Obvious, I thought, but did not say it out loud. We had to cut the professor some slack, though. As the president of the Executive Council, he was the administrative head of the guilds, but technically not our general. The guilds had never had a general before because they hadn't needed one. That was how we ended up fighting the militia and the Fae haphazardly, with various groups taking the initiative. We couldn't rely on that formula anymore.

"We've decided to split up and monitor A1A south of here and the traffic coming over the bridge from the west to look for an increase in delivery vehicles," I told Dr. Noordlun. "But since the shifters haven't arrived yet, I propose we send only two scouts. The rest of us should remain in town in case we have to fight to defend it."

"Quite reasonable," the professor replied. "Who wants to be the scouts?"

Gorkee and Skeetch volunteered. I gave them my phone

number to notify me if danger was approaching. Then I called Rufus.

"Where are you guys?" I asked him.

"We're in Ossway."

"What the heck are you doing there?"

"Fighting the militia. A small detachment was raiding a trailer park where shifters live. We chased them away."

"But we were supposed to meet in Luttvale Beach. The militia has already been here, and we're expecting Fae to come at any moment."

"My pack demanded we protect the shifters who live in Ossway. The militiamen showing up in Luttvale Beach could have been a feint."

"So could the ones in Ossway." I tried to hide my anger. "This is no way to fight a war."

"We need a real general—not a professor. I'll volunteer to serve."

I didn't respond. I'd secretly wanted Diego to be our general. Aside from my feelings for him, I could vouch for his intelligence and valor. But his vampire aversion to sunlight was a bit of a problem.

"Thank you, Rufus. I—wait a sec, I'm getting incoming calls from our scouts. I'll call you back. But please, please, come to Luttvale Beach now."

"Will do."

I answered the calls from Gorkee and Skeetch. They both reported long convoys of delivery trucks coming north on A1A and eastward, over the bridge from the mainland.

The Fae were moving in.

"Dr. Noordlun," I shouted. "The Fae are coming right now."

"Well, my powerful and talented magicians," he said, "we are the only ones who can stop the Fae. Gather your energies—I can help you with that if you wish. And prepare your spells. We're about to have a fight on our hands."

Cory, Jocelyn, and Bert walked through the parking lot to the shoulder of A1A. They moved away from each other, so their magic would not conflict. Greg pulled an assault rifle from the car and walked brazenly across the street to an outdoor bar, where the patrons stared at him nervously.

Me? I got back on the phone. "Rufus, two convoys of delivery vehicles are about to arrive. We need your help *now*."

"We're coming. The problem is that the bridge we need to take is clogged with those delivery vehicles. We're stuck behind them. We'll attack them before they dismount to attack you. But we'll be hitting them from the rear, so we can't reach the trucks in the front of the convoy."

"Sure. Whatever you say, Rufus." I ended the call.

And that's when the pickup truck pulled into the beach parking lot and stopped beside our gathering. Two militiamen were in the cab grinning at us while two in the truck's bed aimed their assault rifles at us.

"Looky here," the driver said through his open window. "This looks like a group of supernaturals to me. What do you think they are, Tommy, witches?"

"Witches, for sure," said the man in the passenger seat.

"Gentlemen," I said, "for once in your ignorant lives, you are correct."

The men aiming their weapons at us lowered them before slumping to the floor of the bed, thanks to my sleep spell. Before I could cast it on the cocky guys in the cab, I felt a blast of magic shoot past me, and the men stiffened, remaining frozen like statues.

Jocelyn smiled at the results of her spell. "Perfect," she said. "Look at the stupid expressions on their faces."

Greg jumped into the bed of the truck and gathered weaponry.

"Why is the militia still here if the Fae are about to arrive?" Cory asked.

"Probably poor communication," I said. "Just like what's happening with our side."

"Wait," Bert said. "Do you feel what I'm feeling?"

I sensed Fae magic in the air, growing steadily stronger. "Yeah, the anti-human spell laced with phytolucine. The Fae are here."

The people in the restaurants and the beach parking lot staggered about drunkenly, eventually lying down on the ground. They would be fine when the spell wore off, except for some cases of sunburn.

The thump of a body hitting a car made me wheel around to see Dr. Noordlun going down, unconscious. Just like Mom, having psychic genes didn't save him from the spell, unlike supernatural species and humans like me with magic in my blood.

"Another reason we need a new general," I muttered.

We had no time to prepare before the first delivery van rolled down the street, followed by several others. The van stopped at the tiny town hall at the beginning of the business district. The others continued in our direction, undoubtedly to drop off Fae soldiers to occupy the restaurants and shops.

"Let's open fire from here," I said to Greg and the witches. "Use the pickup truck as cover."

I drew Alfie from its scabbard and primed the sword with energy. Cory's fireballs were already hitting the trucks and vans when my purple lightning arced from my blade and engulfed the faeries pouring from the nearest truck that had pulled up beside a cafe. Jocelyn shot streams of flames from each hand as if she were using a flamethrower. Bert sent fireballs, similar to Cory's but larger.

The delivery truck next in line was swallowed in an inferno. The vehicles behind it attempted to pass in the oncoming lane, but the first one exploded. Thanks to our magic, the convoy was completely blocked. Not bad for a mere four witches.

The Fae soldiers finally realized where all the destruction was coming from and charged on foot away from the convoy toward the beach parking lot, firing as they went. Bullets thudded into the pickup truck that we hid behind. I believed they would stop shooting at the truck, realizing that militiamen were inside. But they didn't care. The inside of the windshield was covered with blood.

I hoped the militia would find out that their members had been killed, without hesitation, by the Fae. Maybe then the militia would take the side of the humans, their own species, instead of the creatures who wanted to enslave them.

There we were, an ogre with a semi-automatic rifle and four witches armed with attack spells. We fired at the Fae soldiers without stopping.

But they kept coming.

CHAPTER 19

SOPHIE

"We need to get out of here!" Bert screamed.

"I'm putting a strong protection spell around all of us," Jocelyn said. "I'm pouring all my energy into it, so I'll be unable to fight while the spell is active."

Our steady torrent of fire and lightning was inflicting serious losses on the Fae, but they were spreading out and trying to outflank us along the beach to our left.

"We're going to be overrun!" A panicked Bert raced toward Cory's SUV parked behind us, leaving Jocelyn's protection spell. Gunfire dropped him before he made it.

A faerie appeared in the parking lot to our right, raising his weapon. My lightning danced over his body, and he went down to the sandy ground. He shifted into his natural faerie form as he died.

Red fireballs soared over the parking lot and landed nearby. A Fae sorcerer had arrived at the front lines. This was bad, very bad. In this battle, like in Edgewood, the Fae used human weapons, mainly pistols and rifles. They didn't have artillery, rockets, or grenades—probably because heavier armaments were difficult for a secretive supernatural species to buy. Instead, sorcerers shooting fireballs were their cannons, and phytolucine-laced magic was their chemical warfare.

I called Rufus, my hand shaking so much I almost dropped the phone. Sharp, echoing pops came from bullets deflected by the protection spell. "We need you now! We stopped the convoy, but the soldiers are about to overrun us."

"We crossed the south bridge and are attacking the rear of the convoy," Rufus said, gunfire in the background. "I'll send some of my shifters up around the convoy toward your end."

At last the sun was close to setting, but we needed the vampires faster than that. I hoped they were already in town, waiting in heavily tinted vehicles or windowless trucks to emerge and fight. I called Diego.

"Yes, of course, we've already been on the move," he answered, irritated by my question. "Unfortunately, the militia blocked the north bridge before we got across. We must wait until sunset to eliminate them."

I cursed. The north bridge was too far away for the anti-human spell to knock out the militia. We had no choice but to wait for the vampires to break through the roadblock and drive here.

"We need a spell that will stop the Fae long enough to allow us to escape to the north," I said to our small and shrinking team. "They won't be able to chase us in their vehicles with the road blocked by all this wreckage. After the sun sets, the vampires will cross the north bridge and link up with us."

My heart filled with hope when I saw four wolves racing along the tops of the sand dunes toward us. But they were fired on by the Fae trying to outflank us on the beach, and the wolves descended to the beach to destroy them. These shifters would help our overall situation, but it wouldn't stop the onslaught we faced from the street.

"Remember the bunker-busting spell you used to destroy the underground Fae laboratory?" I asked Cory. "Can you use it now?"

"I don't have enough energy after creating so many fireballs."

"You can siphon energy from me."

Cory shook his head. "I took energy from a ley line before casting that bomb spell. I'd have to drain you of everything, and even that might not be enough."

"You can take all I have."

"If I do, you'll be powerless for hours or more."

Jocelyn fixed me with intense eyes and nodded. "I'll have your back."

Cory and I stopped fighting to preserve energy. Only Greg was left using conventional ammo to slow the Fae advance. Bullets bounced off the protection spell, but it wouldn't save us forever.

I knelt beside Cory. "Let me go into a trance, then do what you've got to do."

After closing my eyes, I forced my mind to shut out the cacophony of battle noises. I focused on my inner energies and went into a meditative state. I drew my energies together and enhanced them with the elemental powers from the nearby ocean. Like Cory, my energies had been depleted by my attack magic. But I managed to accrue a concentrated mass of power in my solar plexus.

Cory placed his left hand on my stomach and his right hand on my head. Soon, I felt a tingling sensation on my scalp as he made a connection with my energy. I pushed it out toward him as he drew it from me. Heat surged through me to his hands. My skin burned where he touched me, but not so much as to be unbearable.

I grew weaker as my energy flowed from me, giving me an empty feeling. My magical faculties remained, but they were like a car that wouldn't start because of an empty gas tank. Even my normal physical energy seemed to leave me, and my body sagged.

"I got it." Cory removed his hands. "I feel bad draining you like that."

"Do you have enough for the spell?" My words were slurred as if I were half asleep.

"We'll see."

I opened my eyes to the terrifying sight of faeries slipping past the cars near ours in the parking lot. Cory chanted and made esoteric motions with his hand while bullets rattled against the protection bubble.

A dark mist swirled above the heads of the approaching faeries and spread over the rest of the Fae forces. It expanded and thickened, becoming like the scariest thunder cloud you've ever seen.

"Bombs away!" Cory called.

The cloud disappeared as an invisible explosion rocked the area. The boom was deafening, and the blast knocked us to the ground, even within the protection bubble. Cars rocked, windshields shattered, and car alarms went off. My ears were ringing.

Not a single faerie soldier remained on their feet. I didn't know how many of them had been killed or only knocked unconscious. This was our only chance to escape.

"Good job, Cory," I said. "Let's all get out of here."

Cory looked exhausted. I was too weak to get off the ground until Jocelyn helped me up. We headed to the SUV. When we came to Bert on the ground, Jocelyn checked his pulse, then shook her head sadly.

"Help me get Dr. Noordlun." I approached him, still slumped against the door of his car after the Fae spell overcame him. My heart plummeted when I saw the bullet wounds. "My God." He had no pulse.

Jocelyn put her arm around me and led me to the SUV. "We must leave now." She got behind the wheel.

"We can't leave him here," I begged.

"We'll come back for him after the battle is over."

Greg strode over and picked up the body, placing it in the SUV's cargo area. He put Bert in there, too. Greg must have sensed that we wouldn't have the chance to come back and get them.

Just as we pulled out of our parking spot, the four wolves bounded over the dunes and attacked the few faeries who were getting back to their feet after the spell bomb. I turned away to avoid watching what happened to them.

"Your spell really messed up those faeries," Jocelyn said to Cory as we exited the lot just past the where the road was blocked by destroyed vehicles. We drove north along A1A. "Unfortunately, I see more trucks arriving with reinforcements."

"It was just a delaying tactic," he replied. "And it wiped me out."

I leaned against the backseat window, too weak to sit up straight, looking at Luttvale Beach in the dusk. We passed cars that had gone off the road when their drivers passed out, and several pedestrians sleeping on the sidewalk. Leaving the commercial district, we saw fewer pedestrians and the occasional resident unconscious on their front porch.

My stomach was in a knot. I worried that the Fae in pursuit would clear away the wreckage and catch us. But I relaxed a bit when I saw the north bridge coming up, rising high above the

Intracoastal Waterway, its streetlamps revealing no roadblocks and cars moving across it freely.

We stopped at a traffic light, waiting to turn left and head over the bridge. A motorcade of passenger vans and limousines with tinted windows passed through the intersection after crossing the bridge, turning south toward Luttvale Beach.

It was the vampires! The light changed, and we turned left. The road inclined as it led to the bridge, and a convoy of delivery trucks coming across the bridge from the west passed us. I turned around and saw they were turning south at the inter-section.

I pulled out my phone and called Diego. "There's another Fae convoy coming behind you! They followed you over the bridge, heading toward Luttvale Beach."

"How could that be?" he asked, angry. "We have scouts all over the area south of San Marcos. There were no reports of convoys."

"Your information was old, I guess." He hung up on me. "Turn around, please," I said to Jocelyn. "I want to make sure the vampires don't get trapped."

"There's nothing we can do to help them."

"I wouldn't mind shooting a few more faeries," Greg said.

"Well, I'm the only witch who can fight now," Jocelyn said, making me feel ashamed.

"Let's just observe the battle," I said. "We can join the fight if the vampires need help."

"We'll observe from a distance. Let's do it from here." Jocelyn pulled over. "I see a pair of binoculars on the floor beside Cory."

Cory handed them to me and I left the vehicle, walking unsteadily across the traffic lanes to the south-facing side of the bridge. We were high above the water, near the crest of the bridge, and I had a mostly unobstructed view of A1A running south to my left beneath the streetlamps.

Not far from the intersection, the vampire vehicles had parked sideways across the road and shoulders, blocking all passage. The new convoy of delivery trucks had stopped just short of the roadblock. The sound of gunfire floated up to me. I peered through the binoculars and saw a whirlwind of acrobatic vampires tearing apart the units of Fae soldiers.

I found Diego in front of the vampires, fighting with more fury than any of them. His shirt had been torn nearly off, and even viewing through binoculars, I saw his muscles rippling beneath glistening skin, with a yellowish cast from the streetlamps.

The Fae convoy was much smaller than the one that had attacked Luttvale Beach from the south. I wondered if these vehicles had broken off from the earlier convoy and driven north on the mainland to trap our witchy resistance force before we escaped.

The vampires advanced, pushing the Fae backwards to their trucks. I didn't know how many bullets a vampire could endure before being destroyed, but I heard a lot of shooting, and the vampires appeared to be winning.

Or so I thought. Movement in the right edge of the lenses turned out to be the headlights of more delivery trucks coming from the south—from the main force in Luttvale Beach that we witches had fought. The vampires were getting squeezed from the front and the rear. The Fae sorcerer had apparently survived, because fireballs arced toward the vampires, setting two of them on fire—one of the few ways to kill vampires. I hurried back to the SUV.

"Jocelyn, we need to get off this bridge and help the vampires." I was panting, still incredibly weak. "Fae have come from the south and the vampires are trapped. The ones that attacked from the north have been decimated by the vampires, and if you and Greg attack them from behind, I bet the vampires can break through them and escape over the bridge."

"Are you serious?" she replied.

"Hell yeah."

"Get in." She rammed the shifter into reverse, burned rubber, and took us backward down the bridge incline. We stopped just behind the Fae trucks.

Through my open window, I sensed the anti-human Fae magic spreading through the air from the sorcerer. But humans were the least of their worries.

Greg leaped out of the SUV and low-crawled toward the delivery trucks, looking for targets. He had grabbed extra clips of ammunition from the militia pickup truck in the beach parking lot and was eager to pick off faeries. Jocelyn followed him.

The trucks and vans at the rear of the convoy had been emptied of troops. The witch and the ogre slipped past these vehicles until they neared the faeries hiding among the trucks in the front as they shot at the vampires. Greg opened fire and Jocelyn unleashed her stream of flames. Faeries screamed.

I couldn't just sit there and watch. There must something I could do despite my weakened state. I loaded my crossbow and followed my comrades past the empty trucks, ignoring Cory's calls to stay by the SUV.

As I neared the battle, I had a better view of what was going on. The vampires were completely on the defensive, taking cover among their vehicles from the sorcerer's fireballs and unable to use their lethal strength to kill the faeries in hand-to-hand fighting. I crept closer, past my comrades.

"Sophie! What are you doing?" Jocelyn gestured at me to return. "You're too exposed."

A bullet whizzed by my ear like an angry hornet. "You're right," I replied.

I climbed onto the roof of a panel van and, lying on my stomach, searched the Fae forces from the south, beyond the vampires, until I saw him: the sorcerer. No one shot at me up there; they either didn't see me or thought I was a Fae soldier of the convoy from the north. I loaded an ash-wood quarrel, tipped with iron, into the crossbow. Then I aimed while holding my breath and pulled the trigger.

The sorcerer dropped to the ground and changed to his diminutive natural form as he died. I silently praised the magical benefits of ash wood for penetrating the faerie's protection spell and being toxic to the species.

When the fireballs ceased, the vampires went back on the offensive. Because the Fae force from the south was larger, the vampires directed their wrath at the smaller force from the north. They clearly realized they needed to retreat, and the only direction they could go was north.

Jeez Louise, I thought. *How are they going to maneuver past all the delivery trucks blocking the road?*

I climbed down from the roof and looked into the van's cab. No keys or key fobs inside, so I couldn't drive it out of the way. There was nothing I could do to help because I lacked enough energy for magic.

There was access to the beach half a block away. Perhaps I could remedy the situation. I walked past homes on the short sandy street, over the dune ramp, and across the beach until my boots were immersed in the wash of the surf. Putting my mind into magic mode, I gathered my depleted internal energies and drew upon the vast elemental energy of water from the mighty ocean at my feet, sparkling in the moonlight.

You see, among all my complicated relationships with the supernatural and paranormal, I was a water witch at heart. Of the five elements—water, air, fire, earth, and spirit—water was the one with which I had a natural affinity.

I chanted a mantra that helped me connect with the water's elemental energy. It wasn't a spell per se, but a way to focus my brain and open my magical sensibility to most effectively channel the power from the sea. I was pressed for time, but I pushed away the thought, forcing myself to relax. The invigorating warmth poured into me, heating my solar plexus.

Soon, I had harvested as much energy as I could. I turned and ran back to the battle.

With Jocelyn and Greg having attacked from their rear, and the vampires savaging them frontally, the Fae convoy from the north was defeated. Many of the vampires were in their vehicles trying to escape but were blocked by the abandoned delivery trucks. Other vampires, backed by Jocelyn and Greg, tried to hold the larger Fae force from the south at bay. But they couldn't do so much longer.

I hopped into the nearest vehicle, a large box truck. Of course the stupid keys weren't there—most likely in the pocket of a dead faerie. But I had a trick up my sleeve.

With my refreshed energy, I cast a relatively simple spell that ignited the spark plugs and turned on the engine. I drove the truck off the street into the driveway of an antique shop. Then, I turned on the engines of the other trucks that blocked the street. I moved a second one while a couple of vampires took care of the others.

"Jocelyn, Greg!" I shouted. "Let's get our supernatural butts out of here!"

We raced to the SUV and I got in, joining Cory, who had moved to the driver's seat. Jocelyn and Greg continued to fire at the faeries, giving the vampires some cover as they drove at top speed away from the battle.

"Get in!" I told them. They did so and we shot away, up and over the bridge, mixed in with the vampire convoy. A limousine roared past us, Diego's face in an open rear window. What a relief to know he had survived.

I got a text from Rufus. The shifters had been unable to defeat the Fae and had retreated to the mainland.

Not until that moment did I remember that I had left my car behind in the beach parking lot where the battle had begun. The Fae now occupied Luttvale Beach, so I would not be seeing my car again for a long time, if ever.

Others had sacrificed so much more, so I couldn't dare complain. Two of them lay in our SUV's cargo area.

"Sophie, brilliant work taking out the sorcerer and starting the trucks," Jocelyn said.

I merely nodded in acknowledgment.

"What do we do now?" Greg asked.

"Appoint a new general," I replied. "Before we suffer total defeat."

CHAPTER 20

DARLA

I was still awake, watching TV in the cottage's living room, when Cory and Sophie returned from the battle. They both came to the cottage to see me.

"I was worried to death about you," I said. "I wish you would have called and updated me more often."

"We were too busy trying to stay alive," Sophie said.

Cory gave her an exasperated look. "We were fine. But busy. I'm glad you stayed home and I didn't have to worry about you."

"On your last call, you said the Fae captured Luttvale Beach. Is that definite?" I asked.

The two nodded, looking ashamed.

"You did the best you could," I said. "You're not professional soldiers."

"There's something we have to tell you," Cory said. He put an arm around me. "Dr. Noordlun was killed."

I gasped in surprise. "Why was he even there?"

"Because he was the president of the executive committee,

he thought he was our general. The Fae's phytolucine spell knocked him out, and the Fae shot him."

I remained quiet for a while. I'd never been close to the professor, but his death made my heart ache. It was so unnecessary. All of this was unnecessary. The supernatural community had lived among humans for centuries with no major problems. And now people were dying, simply because of fear, ignorance, and hatred. Oh, and because of the political ambitions of evil people.

"I saw a TV interview with Marge Moosebacher and Governor Witlessin," I said, trying to change the subject.

"Yuck," Sophie said, making a face.

"That horrible Moosebacher woman was boasting about how the community has truly come together to fight for public safety. In other words, hate their supernatural neighbors."

"I bumped into her before the battle," Sophie said. "I'm afraid I need to move out of the inn again, in case she sends someone after me."

"I understand and want you to be safe. The governor was bragging about how many supernaturals have been rounded up or 'eliminated.' That was the word she used, like they were cockroaches. We need to take that corrupt woman down. Have you pursued the story Leighnel told me about the governor extorting the Elves?"

"Not exactly. I've been busy. And I guess I'm pessimistic that spreading the news will do anything to harm the governor. The story that she's a secret faerie didn't stop her from being reelected."

"People simply couldn't believe it," I said. "They will easily believe a politician is corrupt, though."

"Yeah, but our state legislature wouldn't impeach her. She would never resign. So, what's the point?"

"We must get the truth out. It's just one of the many ways we should fight her."

"Okay, okay. I'll contact Joe Romesco, the guy who used to work for the governor's opponent. I hope he can get the info to a receptive media outlet. But for this to work, we need Leighnel to introduce himself to the public."

I shook my head. "The Elves have never been revealed to modern humans. They're the only species that hasn't been outed in the Great Unmasking. Maybe that's the reason the Elven king doesn't want to break their peace treaty with the Fae."

"Why did he tell you this information if he won't back it up?" Sophie asked.

"He only wanted to help. He doesn't understand the human media ecosystem."

"He's not the only one who doesn't."

AFTER THE ESPERANZA INN BEGAN CATERING SOLELY TO THE supernatural crowd, I was accustomed to seeing all sorts of unusual characters walking in through the main entrance. In the old days, they would include gaudily dressed tourist couples from, say, Topeka. Nowadays, I'd see a wendigo or even a centaur.

That morning, it was an angel. Literally. The archangel Raphael disguised as a human, his wings hidden. He wore a white suit with a white tie and his blond hair was so brilliant it appeared to form a halo with reflected light. No, not a literal halo. His smile was so dazzling I had to squint.

"Raphael!" I wanted to give him a hug, but knew it was forbidden. "How fantastic to see you again."

"I'm happy to see you as well." He stopped a few feet from

me, his celestial power making my skin tingle. Or maybe it was his hotness that caused the tingling.

"Have you come seeking a favor from Danu?"

"No, from you, Darla. The only mortal human I can trust. I need your help to find an archangel who is missing here on earth. In San Marcos, I believe. It's Michael, a guardian angel of so many souls. He was investigating this bloody inquisition you humans are waging against the supernatural creatures."

"Not *we* humans. Certain despicable humans, in collaboration with the Fae."

"I am not at all surprised the Fae are involved with this, nor that there are humans depraved enough to harm an angel."

"Do you think Michael was killed?"

Raphael laughed, a delightful sound. "Angels cannot be killed. But I fear he might have been captured. People armed with the power of evil can capture an angel during a moment of inattention. Exactly how he would be constrained, I do not know. Perhaps Fae magic was involved."

"But why would anyone—human or Fae—want to capture an angel?"

"Illogical fear. Warped conspiracy theories. A display of power. There are many possible reasons, and all are evil. Can you help me find Michael?"

"I'll try."

"Try your best. Please." With that, Raphael turned and walked out. There were no indications of his wings beneath the white suit coat.

At first, I was surprised that Raphael sought my help in this, even though he had once enlisted me, with the help of Danu, to repair a tear in the Veil that protects our world from the creatures of the underworld. In this new case, I would have thought

OF VALOR AND VAMPIRES

angels would be best at locating and rescuing one of their own kind.

After mulling it over, I realized Raphael wanted a human's help because who else would better understand the demented minds of humans and the evil we're capable of? He was probably correct in believing the disappearance had something to do with the Great Unmasking.

Since Marge Moosebacher had become the face of anti-supernatural pogroms, I conducted a deep search of her social media feeds. What a dark, soul-crushing journey that was. I avoided the countless videos of her monologues describing the catastrophic threats supernaturals represented for humans— especially the God-fearing ones in wealthy neighborhoods with adorable children who were constantly at the mercy of savage monsters.

She also collected videos of monsters created by other people. A lot of these were low-quality fakes that had the production value of B movies from the 1950s. Others were apparently made with AI. A few of them might have been authentic.

Finally, I came upon the video I was looking for. It was authentic and bone-chilling. A young woman speaking to the camera claimed she had been praying, and an angel visited her. He was beautiful and had giant white wings, but the woman feared he was actually a fallen angel—a monster in service of the Devil. She claimed she shot it with a gun she kept beside her Bible.

Normally, she would have lost me. Who would shoot an angel? Even so, surely that would have no effect on the celestial being. But the next video footage showed a very realistic-looking angel lying stunned on the grass in someone's yard. And guess

181

who was also there? Yes, Marge Moosebacher. Marge spoke to the camera.

"A devout friend of mine was attacked by a fallen angel. Fallen angels live in hell and serve Satan, and they come up to the earth to torment virgins. You can't kill these monsters, but you can trap them for eternity."

I gasped as the next shot showed a cement truck backing up into the yard and a couple of militiamen pouring concrete onto the angel, completely covering him. Then the video cut back to Marge.

"When the concrete cures, we're gonna hide this monster somewhere. And when Jesus finally returns to earth in the Second Coming, he's gonna slay the monster."

This video was ridiculous. Who could take it seriously?

Well, I did after Raphael told me Michael was missing.

Just the other day, I had said to a guest at the inn, "Some supernaturals are not exactly angels, but they're no worse than many humans and don't deserve to be persecuted like this." Well, look how low we'd come. They were not just going after witches, werewolves, and vampires. They even harmed an actual angel.

I wanted to believe the video was fake, yet I had to find out where the concrete sarcophagus was hidden, just in case Michael was really in there. How the heck could I find it? I'm no witch, but even Sophie couldn't find it. Her locator spells require physical items associated with the missing person. We didn't have anything physical from Michael because he was celestial.

What was I supposed to do? Capture and torture Marge until she gave up the location? I considered other, less violent, tactics, but came up with nothing. Until I realized that I lived with an expert whom I could consult.

"Archibald?" I called out as I entered the parlor. The gargoyle was at his usual perch beneath the fireplace mantel, frozen in stony slumber. "Archibald, I need your expertise with stone to help us find a missing angel."

Normally, when I would attempt to summon him, he would usually ignore me until I lost patience. This time, he animated into a living creature almost immediately. My request must have sparked his interest.

"What's this?" He peered intently at me. "An angel?"

"Yes. The archangel Michael. A woman shot him, which stunned him so much he remained in human form. He was then encased in a concrete sarcophagus where he'll be trapped forever."

"She *shot* him? Humans never fail to dismay me."

"As a stone-speaker, you can read history by communicating with stone. Can you locate stone with your powers?" My voice was desperate.

"Potentially. We gargoyles and grotesques have a mental catalog of all forms of stone in and around San Marcos. The natural formations above and below ground, and everything from the bricks and concrete manufactured by humans to the limestone, marble, and other materials they've quarried."

"You can locate concrete?"

"When there's a large construction project, we certainly know about it. Not when an individual human pours concrete for a mailbox post. But that doesn't mean we can't find it. Let me put out word to the others of my kind."

"I would appreciate it. How long would it take to find the sarcophagus?"

"It could take some time. Don't worry, love, the angel can exist like that indefinitely."

Archibald disappeared from the mantel to spread the word among the other creatures of his species. I knelt in a corner of the room and prayed to Raphael, hoping to convey what I'd learned.

I sensed his presence in the room, though he did not appear in a visual sense, and I repeated the story of Michael's capture.

"How could he have been shot and trapped like that?" I asked.

Your theory is correct. When we angels appear before humans, we take on various degrees of physicality. Sometimes as just a voice in your mind, like I am right now. Other times, we manifest more materially. When Michael visited the woman who was praying to him, he would be fully physical if she had a powerful belief in angels. Her shooting him probably shocked him so much that he could not recover and transform from his physical form. To my knowledge, humans have never attacked angels before.

"Welcome to America," I said. "I'll try my best to find him."

CHAPTER 21

SOPHIE

"Someone needs to go on mute," Orlena said at the beginning of the video meeting. "Your monkey familiar is making a racket."

Being practitioners of an ancient craft, members of the Magic Guild were decidedly old school. We didn't have an email newsletter. Jeez Louise, could you imagine that? No, our newsletter was printed on magic parchment paper that self-destructed after it was read. And for our monthly assemblies, we rented out a meeting room in an old museum.

But times being what they were, we decided it was too dangerous to have all the witches, wizards, and mages together in one place. The militia would salivate at that prospect. So, we put aside our old-school ways and began having our meetings via video conference.

I sat with my laptop on the bed of my rundown motel room, having returned to my nomadic life of hiding from Marge Moosebacher, the militia, and Lord knows how many other villains who were hoping to kill me. I chose this motel because it had good Wi-Fi. And was next to the best donut shop ever.

Orlena presided over the video call. Our Arch Mage—the title of our leader—suffered from complications from the brain bleed caused by Baldric that she had miraculously survived, perhaps with the aid of magic. It was painful watching Orlena struggle to speak, and she was confined to a wheelchair. I'd heard she had difficulty casting spells.

She read a list of the guild members from San Marcos and surrounding towns who had been captured by the militia and sent to prison camps. That was depressing, even after hearing that five of them had escaped when Mom rescued Samson. She mentioned three witches who were missing, with no witnesses to what had happened to them. Finally, there was a moment of silence for Bert, who died in Luttvale Beach.

"It's time for our shout-outs," Orlena said in her slurred voice. "Lori's campaign to raise money for the Witches' Legal Fund met its goal again this month. Thank all of you for your generosity." She paused while the membership applauded, represented by three screens of our faces in rows of little squares. When I scrolled through, I saw Cory. "Federico used a novel repellent spell to drive away a group of street-punk vigilantes who were about to attack him and his mother." More applause. "And I wish to bring special attention to Sophie for her amazing valor."

Oh boy. My face reddened with embarrassment.

"Sophie has been instrumental in our fight against the persecution of supernaturals," Orlena continued, "as well as the invasion of the Fae." More perfunctory clapping. "Many of you don't realize how much damage she's inflicted upon our enemies, and how much courage and tactical brilliance she has shown."

I wasn't used to Orlena being so complimentary about anyone, let alone me.

"Just yesterday, Sophie was part of a tiny group of witches, including poor Bert, who fended off the Fae for hours before they were forced to retreat in the face of the enemy's superior numbers. The shifters couldn't stop them. Neither could the vampires. Sophie's resourcefulness saved the vampires from being wiped out when they were surrounded and enabled their escape."

There was another round of applause, a little more enthusiastic this time.

Orlena paused to contain her emotions. "As you know, my injury has left me partially disabled. I'm finding it extremely difficult to serve as your Arch Mage. Even if I were one hundred percent, I would not be a good wartime leader of our guild. We've experienced hard times, and I'm afraid it will get worse. We need a leader who will fight for us and alongside us—and who has the best chance of helping us win. That is why I'm regretfully announcing that I shall step down from my role, and why I'm enthusiastically endorsing Sophie to take my place."

No one said anything. I cleared my throat, which made my face fill the screen. "Me?"

"Absolutely," Orlena replied.

"But I'm not a mage."

"Arch Mage is a ceremonial title. I checked the guild bylaws, and the role may be filled by a witch, wizard, or mage. A novice is ineligible, of course, but you're a quite experienced and powerful witch."

"I second the motion," said Bob, a former Arch Mage. He had been forced to resign when he was turned into a vampire against his will. However, he could continue to be in the guild as a regular member.

There were surely several members who were against me becoming the leader, because they wanted the role themselves or were skeptical of my leadership qualities. If I wanted this job, I would need to win them over. I didn't want to use my empath magic to change any opinions, though. It would feel like cheating.

But did I want this job?

"Isn't it true, Sophie, that you worked as an enforcer for the Executive Council?" asked a young witch named Nan.

"Yes, and I regret it. Especially after I became an empath."

"Her skills as an enforcer make her the perfect leader for this moment," Orlena said.

No one could argue that a killer instinct wasn't valuable when we had ruthless enemies.

"Hey, I'm a pacifist, a healer," said an elderly witch named Saul. "I don't want to turn our guild into an army. Why can't we just go underground until it's safe to come out?"

"Because hiding won't guarantee your safety," I replied, surprised by the passion in my voice. "Look around—the militia is picking us off every day. Right? And if the Fae conquer our state, it will never be safe to come out. They consider humans and witches to be inferior. They will enslave us or finish the job the militia is doing. If you don't want to be on the front lines, that's fine. We need healers. But we must fight back."

Murmurs of assent came from my computer's speakers.

"We're in such a dangerous position because our state government sold us out," I continued. "The governor is a secret faerie—a truth that no one seemed to believe before her reelection. She made a pact with the Faerie Queene to give Florida to the Fae by eliminating the most effective opposition to the invasion. And that is the supernaturals. The Fae have a spell that basically makes humans unconscious, but it doesn't affect us. That's why we're being eliminated."

"It's not just about prejudice?" someone asked.

"That's part of the reason the governor and her allies chose this strategy. By stoking hatred and fear, they grew stronger politically. The thing is, I'm pretty sure the legislators up in Tallahassee don't know about the governor's secret pact. They believe they're going to have total power forever, with no idea they'll end up subservient to their Fae overlords. The governor, though, will be rewarded by ruling our state in the Faerie Queene's name."

"She's our authoritarian ruler right now," Jocelyn said. "Why would she want to serve the Faerie Queene?"

"Because Florida is still subject to the laws of the United States. If the Fae conquer us, we'll be part of the Land of Faerie, where a despotic ruler can get away with anything. Also, remember, the governor is a faerie herself."

It seemed most of my audience was looking down, probably sending private messages to each other.

"History shows that the only way to overcome a tyrant—when you don't have foreign allies and their armies helping you out—is for all the people to band together, even if they have different beliefs and agendas. Witches don't always agree with, say, shifters. But we all have in common the desire to be free of tyranny. That's why we must all fight, whether it's on the battlefield or behind the scenes. If we don't have courage, we don't deserve to be free."

"Hear, hear!" Orlena said, clapping.

"Who will fight with me?" I shouted. Lots of raised-hand emojis popped up on my screen. I hadn't been sure I wanted this position, but I think I talked myself into it.

"Why is it necessary that we magic practitioners not only

survive these terrible times but go on to flourish? Because there is so much unexplored potential in magic. Our craft used to be portrayed as old crones stirring potions in cauldrons, casting spells to remove warts or make someone fall in love. Today, we are discovering new ways to heal people, to repair the environment, to improve crop yields. I've used my empath powers, mixed with magic, to persuade people—not bend them to my will, but get them to do what's good for them and for others. Perhaps someday, magic can be a force for peace in the world.

"We can achieve new, great advancements in magic only by collaborating. A healthy community of magic practitioners working together. And the only way to make this happen is to work together to ensure our survival. To defeat the governor and her militia, to repel the Fae, and eventually overturn the Supernatural Criminality Act."

My computer speakers crackled with applause.

"We will hold the vote now," Orlena said. "Do you agree with my nomination of Sophie for Arch Mage? Vote aye or nay in the comments box."

I watched the ayes fill the comments section, peppered with a few nays.

"Sophie has won the majority of the vote," announced the guild secretary.

"Congratulations, Sophie!" Orlena said. "I pass the wand virtually to you."

MY ACHIEVEMENT WAS BITTERSWEET. AFTER THE CALL, I stared at the drab painting of a seagull on the wall of the dreary motel room. Already I missed being at home. Before I had checked in, I stopped in my room at the inn to collect clean clothes. When I entered my room, Cervantes rubbed his sleek black body against my leg to greet me.

Where have you been? he had asked telepathically, in his soothing Spanish accent. *I've been lonely without you.*

"Sorry," I said aloud. "I've been fighting the Fae and the human militia. I missed you, too."

He rubbed his flanks against my legs while I bent over and scratched behind his ears and beneath his jaw.

Some treats would be a good way to prove you're sincere.

I found a bag on my bedside table and indulged him before stuffing clothes into a tote bag.

Please don't tell me you're leaving again.

"Yeah. I need to hide in motels. Sorry, but they don't allow pets."

Don't you need my help in making magic?

"Not battle magic. I miss working with you, but Cory will still be staying here, and he needs help."

My magic bond is with you.

I crouched and kissed him on the top of his head. "I'll be back, my friend. That's a promise."

Do not put your life at risk.

"You know me all too well."

Here I was, leader of my guild, and all I wanted was to sleep in a familiar bed with my cat lying at my feet. I prayed I would get the chance to do so again.

I finally contacted Joe Romesco. I had been intensely skeptical that informing the public about the governor's perfidy would do any good for our cause. Her supporters wouldn't believe it. People wouldn't truly understand who the Fae were and what they were doing until it was too late and we were already conquered.

However, during my speech, it had dawned on me that the governor's allies in the legislature, the courts, and elsewhere would feel horribly betrayed when they lost their absolute power to the Fae. These were the individuals who needed to learn the truth. A few of them might break with the governor. All we needed were a few brave people to stand up and resist, because eventually, others would follow. That applied not just to the governor's allies, but to us all.

"What do you think?" I asked Joe over the phone, explaining my theory.

"Any chance you can get video of an elf making the accusation?"

"Not much."

"Can you get a signed statement?"

"I'll work on it. What can you do on your end?"

"I know a politics reporter in Orlando who would be interested," Joe replied. "But I'm most excited by your angle of rattling the governor's allies. I'll speak to a few lobbyists in Tallahassee. There's no money to pay them on our behalf, but they love to share juicy gossip with the politicians they schmooze with."

"If they don't believe in faeries, send them the video I gave you of my friend shifting from human to faerie form."

"I will. More people are accepting that faeries exist. Especially after a few indigenous ones have been captured by the militia."

"Does anyone realize that the Fae of the Unseelie Court have actually taken territory?" I asked. "I've seen nothing on the news about the fall of Altman and Luttvale Beach. For all I know, the residents there think their town is now run by an organized-crime gang that demands protection money."

"No one knows yet. You didn't get any video of the battles you've been in?"

"I was too busy trying to stay alive."

"Do me a favor and keep trying."

I laughed. "You bet I will."

It turned out that staying alive would be more difficult than I imagined.

CHAPTER 22

SOPHIE

The Executive Council of the Guilds, of which I was now a member, couldn't agree on a new leader to replace Dr. Noordlun. Fortunately, however, we decided to appoint Rufus military general of the supernaturals. The question now was, could we get enough supernaturals to volunteer to fight?

Diego, Rufus, and I discussed the matter one evening sitting in the pews of the cathedral, a place the militia wouldn't expect us to be. We were evil monsters, after all, right?

With us were Draylee, Baldric's replacement as the Chief of the Guild of Fae and Wee People, and Gaarg, Chief of the Troll, Ogre, and Gnome Alliance. We didn't bother to invite Timothy, President of the Union of Undead Flesh Eaters. Zombies and ghouls were notoriously unreliable and just as likely to eat one of us as any of the enemy. The Psychic Guild and the Memory Guild had few members who would make good fighters, and all would be susceptible to the Fae's phytolucine spell.

"I pledge my own pack and will forcibly persuade the other

packs to join us," said Rufus, who was as alpha as an alpha could be.

"I pledge all the vampires," Diego said, "except those who were too old and feeble when they were turned." Even the preternatural abilities of a vampire weren't sufficient in one who was eighty years old in body age.

I added, "I can promise that all the members of the Magic Guild will support the fight, though some will be noncombatants."

"Same with our guild," said Gaarg, a troll. "Not all the gnomes are willing to fight, though."

"We indigenous faeries are eager to kill the evil members of our species who support the Queene," Draylee said. "The sprites, pixies, and brownies will join us."

"What remains to be seen," said Rufus, "is if we can get hold of enough conventional weapons to arm the species who lack supernatural means of fighting."

"I wish we could find some regular humans to join us," I said.

"Why?" Gaarg looked at me like I was daft. "The Fae's magic would knock them out."

"The spell is difficult to cast and requires preparation. What if humans caught the Fae by surprise?"

Rufus waved his hand. "Let's discuss practical, not fanciful, strategies."

I sensed the dismissive emotions of my peers. Not Diego, though. He smiled at me with encouragement.

"Okay, I'll be practical," I said. "How can we set up defenses for San Marcos before the Fae attack—without the militia stopping us?"

"Good question." Diego smiled at me again. "Your witches are the ones most qualified to set up defenses in advance—with your magic."

"Of course, we'll cast warding spells to alert us when the Fae pass certain locations. And I'll figure out some magical booby traps to inflict damage."

"What about barriers?" Rufus asked. "I mean, barriers that won't block people going about their business before the attack."

"My barrier spell doesn't last long, so I'd need to cast it in specific places and circumstances."

"As for our fighters, my vampires and I can find hiding places near the main roads leading to the city," Diego offered.

"My trolls will be stationed beneath all the bridges on routes to the city," Gaarg said. "Highway overpasses, too. We don't have many ogres, so I'll keep them in reserve. The gnomes. . . I don't know. I'll try to rally them."

"My shifters will patrol the outskirts of the city," said Rufus. "In human or animal form. If we spot opportunities, we'll do hit-and-run attacks on the Fae."

Draylee said that she'd ask the pixies and sprites to make reconnaissance flights. "And we faeries will stay in the city until the attack comes. Not all of us were as loyal as I'd like."

She referred, of course, to Baldric. Those who kept their Fae nature secret wouldn't be in the guild, but even some members probably couldn't be trusted. There were those, like State Senator Poxton, who had always been disloyal to our supernatural community. And I'd heard rumors that emissaries of the Faerie Queene had been trying to recruit indigenous faeries in several towns for years.

"'Tis a pity we don't have a proper army of professional soldiers," Draylee added.

"This is the way it's always been when you're in the resistance," I said. "You're just a bunch of ordinary people who have to rise to the occasion and do extraordinary things."

We sat in silence for a while. I felt a reflective mood among my colleagues. Then the silence was broken by a *click*.

Three uniformed militiamen stood behind us in the cathedral entrance, studying us with weapons at the ready. I guessed that they were assessing if we were here as legitimate worshippers or had nefarious intentions. Draylee was in human, not faerie, form so their eyes quickly alighted on Gaarg. Trolls can't shift. He simply sat there in the pew in all his large, knobby, trollish glory.

The militiamen raised their weapons. My colleagues and I, heads turned toward the threat, tensed.

"Is that some kind of monster y'all are sittin' with?" the man who appeared to be in charge asked.

"We're just members of this diocese," I replied, busily casting a spell.

"The big guy on the left. He looks like a freak."

"Are you insulting me?" Gaarg asked in a hostile tone.

"Easy, don't provoke them," I whispered.

Diego was coiled like a spring, on the verge of leaping from the pew and attacking. Rufus had the glassy-eyed look shifters get before they transform themselves. The others were just as ready to fight.

I cast my immobility spell. The three men were bunched tightly together in an instinctive reaction to the awe of beholding the majestic cathedral and the fear of us. I aimed my spell at all three of them at once.

Diego raced toward them and stopped. The men didn't move. They were frozen in place.

"What did you do?" Diego asked.

"Immobility spell." I left the pew and walked to the men. "It might not last, so be on your guard."

"I'm just going to kill them."

"Jeez Louise, Diego! We're in a church."

"The Church doesn't recognize vampires. And I don't recognize the sanctity of their buildings."

"Knock it off. I want to try talking sense to them."

"You believe your empathy magic will turn them into better men?"

"No. Too late for that." I stood within arm's reach of the men and stared into their eyes. The spell allowed them to blink, but they couldn't rotate their eyeballs toward me. I had to adjust my position to meet them. "Everyone, stay in your seats and don't make any threatening movements toward these guys."

What I hoped to do was to convince the militiamen to focus their ire on other targets. First, I sent them feelings of calm and reassurance. "We will not hurt you. You can trust me."

The feelings radiating from the men included fear and hatred —the usual suspects. I wanted to calm their fear but could do nothing about their hatred. No amount of magic could cure that. But perhaps I could make use of it.

"The leaders of your militia haven't told you the truth," I said, filling my words with a magical power of persuasion. "They think you're stupid and will never learn the reality, which is this: you've been ordered to round up and kill supernaturals simply to make it easier for another supernatural species to conquer humans and make you their slaves."

Holding Orlena's amulet, I pumped feelings of credulity and trust into the men. Their fear and hatred had lessened slightly, replaced by curiosity.

"You've heard of faeries, right?" I asked, though they couldn't answer me. "You might have captured some. They can take on human form when they want to blend in with us. There are many who have lived in Florida longer than humans have. And there's a large population of them that comes from another land.

They call themselves the Fae, and they're ruled by a queen who wants to conquer Florida and the rest of America. That's who you're serving. And that's who's gonna own your butts when she takes over."

They were comprehending me, but with some skepticism. After the Great Unmasking, humans had to accept the existence of creatures they didn't believe in, so they learned to suspend their disbelief. These guys were skeptical simply because they considered me their enemy.

I slathered feelings of trust on them like jam on a scone.

"You think you're working for the governor, but you're working for the Faerie Queene. Because the governor is secretly a faerie and worked out a deal with the Queene. The governor will help the Fae conquer Florida, and in return she gets to continue being in charge as the Queene's puppet. Pretty ironic, right? You're rounding up supernaturals to help a rival species of supernaturals. They're playing you, boys. Treating you like suckers."

Anger and the sense of being wronged poured from them.

"The Faerie Queene is going to enslave you or kill you. No other options. In fact, I've seen faeries kill members of your militia. Outside of Altman, the Fae set up a roadblock and shot to death a bunch of militiamen, just like you, who were only doing their jobs. Shot them down like dogs. Faeries think they're superior to humans. They think nothing of killing you. And I saw it happen again at Luttvale Beach. Four militiamen shot by faeries without hesitation, just for getting in the way. It's prob-ably happened a lot."

I was making progress. These guys were believing me. I increased the magic just to be sure.

"We're going to let you guys go soon," I said, smiling and radiating benevolence. "But if you guys want to continue catching or killing supernaturals, you ought to go after the most dangerous ones—the ones that are going to take over this city and take your homes from you. The Fae. They're coming here really soon. You'll be ordered to leave town right before they get here. If not, you'll be put to sleep by their magic. So, you need to patrol to the south, the west, and the east. You'll find them in Luttvale Beach and Altman. The faeries will probably be driving delivery vehicles to allow them to fit in wherever they go. But they won't be wearing the companies' uniforms."

Finally, I transferred thoughts to each of them telepathically.

I hate the Fae. They are our true enemies. I don't like having monsters live in my neighborhood, but they're my neighbors. They're not foreigners like the Fae. The snotty evil lunatics look down on me and my family and are going to enslave me, humiliating me in front of my family and friends.

I focused on probing their emotions. Sure enough, they hated the Fae now. Oh, they still hated me and the others in the church, but they'd accepted a revised version of their worldview. They believed me that their greatest enemies were the Fae.

I returned to my colleagues in the pews. "Get safely away from here before I release those guys from the spell."

"Did they believe what you said to them?" Diego whispered.

I nodded. "We'll see if it made a difference."

My supernatural friends filed out of the cathedral. I waited in the anteroom where the prayer cards and votive candles were. Standing in the doorway of the nave, I broke my spell, and then ran outside before they saw where I went. Which was a hiding place in a narrow alley nearby.

The three militiamen came out of the cathedral, walking stiffly and looking dazed. After they passed the alley, I emerged and followed them. I magically enhanced my senses to aid my hearing.

"My neighbor, Sam, was taken in yesterday," one of them said. "I didn't know he was a supernatural. He's a great guy, coaches my kid's soccer team. It just doesn't seem right that he's in detention."

They crossed the public plaza and got into a pickup truck parked on the side of the next street. I raced to my rental car, which was parked nearby. I drove across a side street past the plaza and spotted the pickup as it headed toward the Bridge of Memories.

I was behind them at a safe distance when they crossed the bridge and headed east toward the beach. When they reached A1A, they turned south toward Luttvale Beach. I wondered if they were hunting faeries.

Just north of the beach town, a delivery truck approached from the other direction. Delivery vehicles are omnipresent nowadays, but not at 3:00 a.m. The militiamen's pickup swerved sharply left and blocked the other truck, which screeched to a halt before hitting the pickup. I slowed down, holding my breath, hoping a legitimate delivery driver wasn't about to be sent to a prison camp.

To my surprise, the delivery truck driver leaned out of his window and fired a handgun at the pickup. Then, four more faeries in human form exited the truck and sprayed the militiamen with bullets. The men I had enchanted exited their own truck and returned fire as good as they got, taking cover behind the open doors.

Nope, this was not a legitimate delivery truck. It had been carrying a Fae military patrol.

The skirmish was brief and decisive. All five faeries were casualties. Three shrank to their natural forms as they died on the road, bathed by the headlights. The militiamen saw the transformation and must have realized I'd been telling them the truth. One of the trio was seriously wounded, so they placed him in the truck's bed and sped off back toward San Marcos, paying no attention to my car.

The militiamen had learned a valuable lesson that they would share. And I had found a way to fulfill my desire to get regular humans to join our side—though I hadn't imagined it would be militiamen.

Best of all, I had captured everything on video with my phone. I turned around and headed north, pulling over in front of a real estate office as soon as I was far enough away from the scene of the skirmish. I sent the video to Joe Romesco, and as a group text to all the guild leaders.

Fae patrol wiped out by militiamen near Luttvale Beach, I wrote in an accompanying text. *I convinced the militiamen that the Fae were their true enemy, and they acted on it. Let's share this video every-where, so humans learn of the danger they're in and the militia gets second thoughts about their mission.*

Diego was the first to respond. *Brilliant! Are you safe? That video was taken dangerously close to the action.*

Thank you. And yes, I'm safe.

Rufus chimed in next. *Great job! I'm sending someone to the scene to see how law enforcement reacts to it. That will tell us if they're totally in the bag with the Fae.*

Most of the other guild leaders reacted the same way and promised to disseminate the video, as did Joe.

Draylee, I wrote, *how far can your sprites and pixies fly?*

To Palm Beach and back, no problem. And as fast as lightning. Isn't magic wonderful?

Please ask them to look for increased traffic headed north from Palm Beach when the roads would normally be empty, like now. I have a gut feeling that the Fae are going to abandon their strategy of infiltrating with delivery vehicles. They're going to move masses of soldiers our way in any kind of transportation they can.

The Fae were taking too many losses with their original strategy. I was betting they would invade by overwhelming San Marcos with speed and sheer numbers.

The notification of an incoming text woke me in my motel room as the dawn light seeped between the curtains. The text was from Draylee.

Brief surges of heavy traffic seen on I-95 northbound and SR-40 eastbound. The Fae should be ready to attack in a day, two at the most.

CHAPTER 23

DARLA

I screamed when I saw Archibald perched on my bath tile just as I was about to remove my bathrobe and step into the shower. "Do you mind?"

"I have important news," he said, panting with excitement. I'd never seen a gargoyle pant before. "We've located the angel. However, I'm afraid we'll need assistance. He's buried in some human's yard. Can Sophie or Cory use their witchery to keep the humans at bay while we do our work?"

"Sophie has more spells than Cory that suit this situation. If she's not too busy preparing for the invasion, I'll get her to stop by. Now, please disappear so I can take my shower."

It turned out that the yard where the sarcophagus was buried was the same one I'd seen in the video—the home of the nut who'd shot Michael. I recognized it when I showed up at night and parked on the street. There were a couple of lights on in the house, so I parked two houses away to avoid being seen.

Sophie arrived later in a rental car. She got into the passenger seat of my car and kissed me on the cheek. My baby looked like she'd aged years in recent weeks, her eyes and face showing strain and exhaustion.

"Congratulations on becoming the Arch Mage of the Magic Guild," I said, hugging her. "When we hired your first magic tutor, I never imagined you'd make it this far."

"Thanks. It was kind of like a battlefield promotion. I don't have the seniority that some others have, but I guess we need a wartime leader. That describes me, with all my anger issues."

"How are the preparations going for the defense of San Marcos?" I asked.

"About as well as you'd expect, with amateurs facing a professional army." She had no time for my stupid questions.

"Oh. Well, it was lovely weather today, wasn't it?"

"Yes. Lovely. Simply lovely." Her sarcasm was thick. "How are we going to unearth the sarcophagus and crack it open?"

"I assume Archibald has a plan for that. We need you to keep the homeowners from coming outside and shooting us. This is where the woman lives who shot Michael."

Sophie shook her head. "What an idiot."

We're in the backyard now, Archibald said to me telepathically. *If Sophie is here, tell her it's time to work her magic.*

I repeated to his message to Sophie.

"Okay," she said with an enormous sigh as she got out of the car.

I pointed out which home it was and followed her as she crouched and crept up to the house, peering carefully into the window of a lighted room.

She gave me a thumbs up and made strange gestures with her hands. The tingling of supernatural activity ran through my scalp and down my spine.

"The woman and her husband were on the couch watching TV," Sophie whispered. "I cast a sleep spell on them. I'm going to put a locking spell on the home to prevent them from opening doors or windows if the sleeping spell wears off."

After she did that, we went around the house into the back-yard. Archibald and his partner, Jerry, stood on a mound of freshly turned soil. When I say "stood," I mean it looked as if their legs were hidden beneath the soil. I'd never seen their legs before—if they even had any—because they were always attached to a surface of some sort.

The two gargoyles nodded to us. Then the lion and the impish demon dug into the soil and disappeared underground headfirst, just like sand fleas burying themselves in the sand when the surf recedes.

"I didn't know gargoyles could do that," Sophie said.

"They have a kinship with all minerals. Soil contains organic material, too, but it's full of clay and rock particles. That's exactly a gargoyle's cup of tea."

We waited for a while before Archibald's words appeared in my head. *We've reached the sarcophagus.*

How are you going to release the angel?

It's a kind of magic we have. We can undo the bonds that form minerals into stone. See you soon!

A faint rumbling and a cracking sound came from deep below us. I waited, excited.

A whoosh of air rose from the holes the two gargoyles had made. But I realized it wasn't air. It was supernatural energy akin to magic—a wind charged with what I could only describe as the energy of the divine.

Suddenly, Michael, in his full material, physical form, stood facing Sophie and me. His giant white wings unfolded as if stiff from their cramped confinement. I smiled at the angel, but he looked pissed off, like an angel of retribution.

Archibald and Jerry popped up out of their holes.

"Thank you for help—all of you," Michael said. "You are blessed. Now I must perform a bit of divine justice."

"The woman who shot you is inside this house."

"She reacted out of fear and ignorance. The person who trapped me in stone acted out of pure malevolence."

"Ah, that would be Marge Moosebacher. An evil faerie who shifts to human form and goads people into harming all kinds of supernatural creatures."

"I shall pay her a visit," Michael said, glowing with an intense white light before he disappeared. "My biggest pet peeves are hypocrites."

Sophie broke the spells on the couple and their home, and we drove to a coffee shop to have a brief moment alone. That would be such a rare treat. There was a place in Old Town that stayed open late. I ordered a cup of decaf, but not surprisingly, Sophie went for a double espresso. My child never learned how to relax.

I skipped the small talk. "I feel like I'm losing you, dear. You're living like a fugitive."

"I *am* a fugitive, Mom."

"And a war hero. You don't have to take so many risks. Everyone knows you're brave; you don't need to prove it."

"I'm not trying to prove anything."

"We just need to survive the war and all the oppression. Life will return to normal afterward."

"Mom, there won't be an afterward if the Fae and the governor win."

I took a sip of my coffee. "I feel like I'm going to lose you. That you're going to throw away your life in this war."

"Mom, now you know how *I* feel. Like I'm losing you to Danu. She's taking you away from Cory and me."

"I have no choice in that matter. You have a choice, though, in how much you throw yourself into every battle."

She huffed in indignation and took a gulp of espresso. "Must I remind you that there's a warrant for my arrest because the governor wants me dead, and that Marge Moosebacher does, too?"

"The Fae army is not coming just to get you. You keep throwing yourself at them. Cory told me about your bravery at Luttvale Beach."

"Maybe we should avoid war talk. Let's just enjoy each other's company while we still can."

Suddenly, I got choked up. I placed my hand on hers. "Let's do that."

I SAID BEFORE THAT THE INN WAS WHERE YOU NEVER KNEW who—or what—would walk through the door. Or materialize out of nowhere. Brushing my teeth, I was once again interrupted by someone invading my private space. This time, it was the ghost of an ancient druid.

"A long time it's been since I've visited ye," said Bilrog, appearing in my mirror. She wore her usual ghastly face paint and herbs braided into her hair.

"Yes. I went too long without being startled to death in my bathroom. What brings you to the land of the living tonight?"

"I've come to talk about yer daughter. I'm not so certain she understands her destiny."

I had a feeling about where this was going. "What exactly do you mean?"

"When ye become Danu, Sophie will be the daughter of Danu. The last time Danu was on earth, the Tuatha Dé Danann ruled Ireland. They were like demigods—possessing powerful magic and great wisdom. Sophie will be their leader."

"The Tuatha Dé Danann were a mythical race. How can she lead a race that no longer exists? Are they suddenly going to show up in San Marcos?"

"They live here already, they do." Birog wore a big smile, showing off her blackened teeth. "Only they don't use that name. They are the supernaturals—the witches, the faeries, the elves, and the others."

"What about the vampires?"

Birog cackled. "No. Not the undead. Those bloodsuckers have always done their own thing."

"So, why are you telling me all this?"

"You must prepare her for her new responsibilities."

"Sophie has been showing a lot of leadership and initiative lately. I'm actually very proud of it, though she's driving me crazy with fear for her life."

"She doesn't yet realize her destiny and the power she will have. Ye must make her understand."

"Sophie won't listen to me. And she's too busy right now fighting the Fae and the militia that's been attacking supernaturals."

"It is good that she is doing these things," Birog said. "You must prepare her for what will come. When you become Danu, you will anoint her as leader and fulfill her destiny."

"*If* she survives the battles."

"If she is worthy, she will survive."

"That's not very reassuring," I complained. "By the way, exactly when will I become Danu?"

"Only Danu knows."

"And another thing, what happens to my body when I become . . . hello?"

Birog was no longer in my mirror. I turned and surveyed the bathroom to make sure she had truly left. That weird druid was driving me crazy. Was her visit tonight because my transformation was coming soon?

Oh, Danu, please spare me this ordeal, I pleaded. *Please don't make me leave my family.*

CHAPTER 24

SOPHIE

I admit I was curious what sort of revenge the archangel Michael had planned for Marge Moosebacher. It seemed highly unlikely he would kill a faerie, but hopefully he intended to mess her up. If so, it could be my chance to take her down once and for all. Though I didn't know if Michael had struck yet, I drove to her house the next morning to see if I could find out.

The leafy neighborhood was quiet in this early hour, before people left for work and school. The occasional jogger and dog walker were the only people I saw. When I rolled slowly past Marge's home, the sight of Baldric's car still in her driveway made me sick from the memory of what I'd done to him.

This whole empath business truly threw my psyche into chaos. It made me feel guilty for all the brutal things I'd done, but it hadn't erased the old chip-on-my-shoulder Sophie who was prone to strike down enemies ruthlessly. The two sides of me were constantly at war with each other. And while my empathy made me feel bad about killing Baldric, it wasn't preventing me from doing whatever was necessary to stop

Marge. "Whatever was necessary" might prove to be fatal for her.

All faeries are born with some magical abilities, including the ability to shapeshift to match the species they live among. Some faeries, notably Marge, had magical powers of persuasion. That was how she stirred up the public against supernaturals. But Marge was not a powerful sorcerer, like the ones we had encountered in battles. I was a much more powerful magician than she was.

I turned around in a cul-de-sac and passed by the house again, looking for signs of anyone at home. Just as I passed the driveway, I saw the garage door inch upwards. I stopped and cast the spell I use to fry electric motors. The door stopped moving. I jumped from my car and ran up the driveway, dropping to the concrete to slide through the narrow space beneath the door.

A luxury car sat with its driver's door open. Marge, in her natural faerie form, was in the seat, frustrated as she realized her legs were too short to reach the pedals. She was too short to even see over the dashboard.

"Where do you think you're going?" I asked, showing her the naked steel of my sword.

"Get out of my house!" she screeched in her high-pitched faerie voice. Her face was unsettling, a doll-sized version of her human face with her features not of the right proportions.

"You've ruined so many lives. I think it's appropriate to invade your life." I took out my phone with my free hand and snapped a photo of her.

"No pictures!"

"Oh, come on, don't you think it's time for the world to see your true nature? A supernatural creature, who is illegal thanks to jerks like you."

I expected her to cast a Fae version of a protection spell, but she was too rattled. Or maybe she didn't have the powers to do it. She fumbled the glove compartment open and pulled out a pistol. She needed both of her tiny hands to fire it but was struggling. I easily knocked the weapon away and onto the garage floor with my sword.

"If you want to shoot me with a human gun, you should be in human form," I said.

"I can't!" She jumped from the car and skittered away from me, slipping into the house. I ran after her.

Marge ran through the house like a frenzied cat, ducking under furniture, slipping through the stair banister. I couldn't keep up with her as she raced upstairs. Big mistake for her. The only way to escape me now was down the stairs, and I stood at the top of them, blocking her way. I pondered what spell to use to capture her, knowing that much of my repertoire didn't work on faeries.

The sound of a window opening came from a guest bedroom. Yikes! I forgot that faeries could fly. I cast my immobility spell, and thankfully it stopped her before she escaped, her wings having just sprouted.

I approached her, and it finally occurred to me why she was stuck in faerie form. "The angel damaged your ability to shift, right?"

She couldn't answer, but the sudden increase in frustration and anger rising from her told me I was correct. I stared at the creature, who wasn't as tall as my waist, and pondered what I should do with her. A quick, painless execution? A slow, horrible one? How about being empathetic and choosing a more merciful route?

I sensed magic flowing from her. She had placed a protection spell around herself after all. It would block most of my attack spells; however, a crossbow bolt made of ash wood would pierce the bubble and kill her. Not being a Fae sorcerer, she could do little else to stop me. Perhaps my less-aggressive spells would reach her.

"You shouldn't have trapped the angel in concrete," I lectured. "There was no reason to do that other than pure evil."

She whimpered. I couldn't believe Marge Moosebacher had whimpered. I sensed that even she realized she had gone too far, and that I was about to make her regret it even more than Michael had.

No, I would not hurt her. I'd use my empath magic on her and see what happened. That is, if my magic could penetrate her protection spell.

First, I went into a bathroom and found a hand mirror, holding it up in front of her. "Look at you. You're a faerie, a supernatural creature. You're making humans fear and hate people like you. I assume you're doing it to help the Fae conquer us, although you might just be a hateful person who enjoys persecuting others. Maybe that's it.

"If your true motive is to help the Fae," I went on, "you're making a mistake. They are foreign invaders. When they take over, you'll be a second-class citizen because you've been tainted in their eyes by living among humans. The neighbors you've had your entire life and pretend to be one of. Why would you turn against your neighbors and help foreigners who hate you?"

I sensed in her a tiny bit of agreement with me. A minuscule seed of shame. Her protection spell hadn't blocked my empathetic senses, so it was time for a full blast of empath magic. The emotional connection I built served as the conduit for the magically enhanced feelings I sent to her next:

The witch is correct—I'm betraying my species by attacking all supernaturals. I've always known, but didn't want to admit, that the Fae consider indigenous faeries like me to be collaborators with their human enemies. I've always had doubts that the Fae would allow me to share ruling-class status with them. I ignored these doubts.

As I sent these thoughts and feelings, I sensed that the hatred she felt for supernaturals other than faeries was genuine. I riffed on that.

I despise vampires and shifters and witches like this one who is illegally in my home. It's okay that I don't ally myself with the supernaturals I hate, but I should be loyal to my fellow faeries. It's okay if I sit this war out. I'm tired of all the violence and angry mobs. If I can't shift to a human form, it's best to go into hiding and stay safe.

She appeared to accept the thoughts and emotions I had sent, but I couldn't tell if she was fully convinced. Rather than spend hours attempting to brainwash her, I decided to leave. If she remained trapped in her faerie form, she could only continue her Mothers Against Monsters hate mongering behind the scenes. And I had bigger fish to fry.

As soon as I was safely in my car, I released the immobility spell. Then I drove away through the mid-century suburb where I was certain only one resident was a faerie trapped in her diminutive natural form, fuming about all the people she hated, while hopefully recognizing at long last that she was one of them.

I HAD MISSED THE MORNING RUSH HOUR WHILE DEALING WITH Marge. Still, the city was busy as I headed to the official new headquarters of the defenders of San Marcos, a parking garage. Yes, a parking garage in Old Town mainly used by tourists. It was five stories tall, giving us a good view from the top deck of our low-rise city. It was made with reinforced concrete that could withstand bullets and magic fireballs. And it allowed an easy escape should we need it. The only downside was that it cost $20 to park there. I mean, really?

With all the scouts we had on the outskirts of the city, the best use of warding spells would be as an alarm system to protect our headquarters. I parked on the street and walked the perimeter of the parking garage, placing the spells at the vehicle gates as well as pedestrian entrances. Then, I forked over the parking fee and drove into the garage.

I expected to find at least one guild leader on the top deck using binoculars to look for approaching enemies. What I hadn't expected was the crowd of gnomes milling about at the top of the ramp. I parked my car just below the gnomes and walked up to them. I said hello, one of the few words I knew in Gnomish.

They cheered when I passed through them. Were they mistaking me for someone else?

Gaarg was on the top deck, resting his enormous elbows on the concrete wall as he stared through binoculars.

"Where did all the gnomes come from?" I asked.

He turned to face me. "Sophie! Good to see you! I convinced the recalcitrant buggers to join the fight."

"How did you manage that?"

"The gnomes have great respect for you and your mother. Despite all the losses they've suffered, they didn't want to let you down."

"That sounds beautiful," I said. "But tell me what really happened."

"A Fae patrol attacked one of their hamlets, and they want revenge. Their hatred of the Fae is greater than their survival instinct, I guess. I wish all our fighters were like that."

"I'm grateful. We need every soldier we can get."

"Indeed. We need more than we can get. Reports are coming

in of Fae forces on the outskirts of San Marcos. It's about to get real."

My stomach clenched. We were going to engage in a massive battle. But unlike the wars in human history, this one had been fought in secrecy. Humans were going about their business, completely oblivious to what was about to happen. People were working, picking up to-go breakfasts, dropping their kids off at school.

And our everyday world was about to be turned upside down and held by its ankles.

CHAPTER 25

SOPHIE

Gaarg, Draylee, Rufus, and I stood on the upper deck of the parking garage, our makeshift command headquarters complete with a folding table covered with paper maps. We'd found some traffic cones and blocked off the ramp leading to this level. It wouldn't do to have tourists parking their cars up here, wondering why a troll was pacing back and forth, talking on a cellphone.

"It was an honest mistake," Gaarg said into the phone, "but don't attack any other vehicles unless you're certain Fae are inside. Remember, they're not just in delivery trucks anymore." He sighed and turned to the rest of us. "One of my trolls took out a UPP truck with actual packages inside."

"Were there witnesses?" Rufus asked.

"Probably. But remember, it was on I-95 in Florida, where people have seen much stranger things than a troll tossing a truck off a bridge."

"I just heard from my scouts," Draylee said. "They've seen an increase in charter buses and passenger vans heading north to San Marcos."

"My shifters have had no encounters yet. They're looking for Fae traveling overland, like you said they would be," Rufus said to me. "If they're all in vehicles traveling on highways, my shifters can do little."

"All I said was I believed they wouldn't continue hiding in delivery trucks," I replied, annoyed. "The only other thing I know with certainty is that the Fae are more active at night."

"And what are we supposed to do about that?"

"You're our general. It's your decision."

"Yes, it is. I'm ordering my shifters to move closer to the city. The vampires should, too. I'll let Diego know."

A prickling sensation in my brain told me a ward had been triggered by foreign supernatural energy. Had the Fae infiltrated the city already? The energy was coming from behind me, so I walked across the empty parking deck in the direction where it was strongest. I peered over the wall on the other side of the garage from where I'd been standing. Five stories below me, on the other side of the street, was one of San Marcos's many historical museums.

Two white vans were parked by the museum's entrance. The supernatural energy rising from them told me they were being used by faeries. The vans must have been waiting inside the garage and just now exited it, setting off one of the wards. Around ten Fae in human form wearing black stormed inside the museum, too quickly for me to conjure the magic for shooting my lightning. It looked like a robbery in progress. If so, why hadn't they waited until the phytolucine spell knocked out all the humans in the city?

From my high vantage point, I saw a police car a half block away. The police did nothing to stop the robbery. I guess they'd been ordered by someone of high rank to stand down or had been bribed by the Fae.

I was too far away from Rufus to get his attention, so I texted him about what I'd seen.

Gaarg's gnomes are on their way, he replied.

To my surprise, three pickup trucks carrying militiamen arrived and surrounded the vans. I had expected them to have fled San Marcos by now to avoid the inevitable phytolucine spell, but what did I know?

The museum doors burst open, and the Fae soldiers ran out carrying sacks and boxes of whatever relics they had stolen from the museum. And then the unexpected happened: the militiamen blew them away with a withering volley of rifle fire. The militiamen gathered the loot, tossed it inside the museum doors, and drove away.

Wow. This was a remarkably good development. It appeared that more militiamen were realizing the Fae were their enemies and did the right thing by defending the city's historical heritage. I wondered if my changing the minds of the three militiamen had set the ball rolling.

But it left unanswered why the Fae tried to steal items from the museum, and why they did it before their army entered the city. Perhaps they were seeking precious metals or gems they needed for magic they planned to use when they attacked. If so, the militiamen had unwittingly done us a huge favor.

The other guild leaders had joined me after hearing the gunfire from the brief battle on the street below. I explained what had happened.

"Man, that's fantastic about the militiamen. Was this because of you?" Rufus asked me.

I shrugged. "I only convinced them to see the obvious fact that the Fae aren't their friends. The truth is spreading. I want to know what the robbers were seeking. When there's time, I'll ask someone in the museum."

"My guess is gold from the Spanish treasure fleets," Draylee said. "For centuries, humans sought to create gold through alchemy. Faeries use a form of reverse alchemy to turn gold into magic."

My hunch had been correct. They must have been preparing a spell to aid their attack.

"I wonder if we can convince the militia to join us in our defense of the city," Rufus said.

His point was moot. I sensed a powerful spell drifting through the city like a blanket of fog.

"The Fae are sending their phytolucine spell now," I announced. I looked over the wall and saw two pedestrians approaching the museum fall to the sidewalk, unconscious.

We walked the perimeter of the upper deck, looking down at the human civilians lying unconscious in an adjacent park in front of the city's visitor center and in the nearby outdoor cafes. A tour bus sat in front of the visitor center, filled with tourists slumped in their seats.

"It's time for high alert," Rufus said. We got on our phones to spread the word among our forces.

I looked at my watch. The day had flown by and soon darkness would come. And with it would come the attack.

The wizard Maximilian texted me that Fae commandos were breaking into the main water-pumping facility. Draylee passed the word that her faeries saw suspicious activity at an electrical substation.

"They're attempting to destroy the city's infrastructure," Rufus said. "Sophie and Draylee, work together with your fighters to defend it. Gaarg and I will remain at the command center."

Draylee and I rushed downstairs, texting our respective guild members as we went. Draylee agreed to marshal her faeries to attack the Fae at the electrical substation. My witches, firing lightning bolts or fireballs, would not be a good mix with high-tension power lines. Instead, we met at the water plant.

A half-dozen witches and I arrived in time to see heavily armed enemy faeries scaling the chain-link fence that surrounded the main building and the water tanks. Cory's fire-balls, Jocelyn's flame stream, Maximilian's telekinetic powers, and the lightning from my sword knocked the human-sized faeries to the ground. Along with their weapons, the faeries were carrying what appeared to be explosives. The other witches secured them while we four disabled the lock on the main gate and went inside to find the faeries who had already made it over the fence.

We walked through the complex, past workers asleep on the ground. Up ahead, I spotted a group of faeries in their natural forms trying to turn a giant water valve in a pipe that ran from the ground. They must have flown over the fence, while their counterparts were in human form to carry the weapons and explosives.

Before I could even point my sword, Jocelyn had doused the faeries with her fire stream. The one who flew away was knocked from the sky by a fireball from Cory. We searched the facility for more enemies and found them in a control room, tinkering with keyboards beneath a row of large monitors showing bar graphs of water levels, as well as camera footage of pumping substations and reservoirs. Our magic knocked them from their chairs before they even noticed us.

"It looks like they already messed up the controls," Cory said. "How would we know what they did and how to set it right again? Sophie, you're a water witch. Can you protect the city's water supply magically?"

I gestured at the dozens of windows open on the numerous monitors. "Not simultaneously in all these places across the city and county. Better to use a spell to fix the controls. If I can remember how to cast it."

I called it my reset spell. A magic tutor who had taught it to me called it a reversion spell. It returned an object, entity, or system to its previous normal state. In other words, it would undo the changes the faeries had made to the water-system controls.

Searching the hundreds of spells in my mind, I finally recalled the spell's energy structure and its incantation. I cast it standing beside the control board and watched as the keyboard keys clicked on their own and the bars of the graphs moved up and down.

"Okay, back to normal. I believe we should still be able to take showers now," I said. "If we ever have time for one."

A third group of infiltrators has taken over the police station, Rufus texted to the group.

I wasn't surprised. The police couldn't fight back because they were unconscious, but I had doubts they would have resisted even if they weren't.

Just got word that my pack is fighting a convoy of Fae vehicles on Route 1 at the south side of town, Rufus added. *The main battle has begun.*

Night had fallen, and sure enough, the vampires had joined the fight. *We ambushed a large force that came on boats up Mullet Creek and landed near the marina,* Diego wrote. *Still fighting them.*

Mullet Creek flowed from the marshes through the west side of town and emptied into the Sangre River. It frightened me that the Fae were so close to downtown.

Draylee replied, *We're still fighting at the electrical substation, but I can send Gorkee with my remaining faeries to reinforce Diego.*

I'm tired of playing whack-a-mole, Rufus wrote. *Instead of always being on the defensive, we're going to attack the main Fae force.*

We don't know where they are, I responded.

We haven't seen them on the interstate, so I'm guessing they'll come from Luttvale Beach and attack us from the east. I'm sending my remaining shifters there. Gaarg, send your reserve trolls there, too.

We need them to guard Old Town, Gaarg replied.

I'm our general now. That was an order.

The sprites and pixies were off doing reconnaissance, so the only fighters remaining in the center of town were the gnomes and witches. I prayed that would be enough of a force to protect the city if the Fae broke through our forces on the outskirts. Or if they unexpectedly came from the north.

I led my team from the water station back to Old Town to join the rest of the witches. It was eerie walking through a city incapacitated by the Fae's phytolucine spell. The streetlights were on, but nothing moved on the streets. Drivers slept inside cars that had collided with walls or other cars and idled until they ran out of gas. Pedestrians slept on the sidewalk where they had fallen. It was a gloomy, post-apocalyptic scene.

We reached Old Town and climbed the parking garage stairs until we reached the fifth floor, where I had instructed the rest of our witches to wait. It felt safer up here and I preferred the vantage its elevation offered. Gaarg and Rufus ignored us, but I sensed they felt safer with our witches acting as the two leaders' bodyguards.

"Where are the gnomes?" I asked.

"In a nearby park," Gaarg replied. "Just in case the Fae come from the north."

We waited for word about the other battles—engagements

that would make or break our defense of San Marcos. No one texted with news, so we just milled about nervously. My stomach rumbled. It was yet more evidence of how amateurish our army was. We hadn't even thought to bring food.

Faint sounds of gunfire came from the south. I hoped it meant the wind was carrying the sounds and not that the shifters stationed there were being pushed back by the enemy. I was tempted to volunteer some witches to reinforce the shifters.

Until my brain suddenly buzzed from all my warding spells going off at once.

Rufus made a sharp intake of breath. "What the—"

I looked down to the street to find it crawling with Fae in their natural forms. Running to the other sides of the garage, I realized they were everywhere—hundreds of them or more, surrounding our headquarters.

The Fae had not come from the north. No, they had somehow popped up right in the center of town.

CHAPTER 26

SOPHIE

"Jocelyn and Sonya, guard the two stairwells," I commanded. "Juanita, disable the elevator. Maximilian, we need your telekinesis. Come with me. The rest of you, attack the Fae from the upper deck."

"I'll summon the gnomes," Gaarg said.

"No," I said. "These faeries must have come into the city through tunnels. Dang it! My mother told me a tunnel was discovered a while ago. Cory destroyed it, but we should have anticipated that the Fae would dig new ones. Tell the gnomes to search for the tunnel openings and block them. Gnomes have a nose for locating underground passageways."

Rufus stared at me, his bearded mouth open in surprise. I had overstepped my rank, but he knew I was correct.

I had barely finished speaking when Cory unleashed his first fireball downward to the horde below. Others fired with their particular forms of attack magic, various manifestations of energy like Cory's fireballs or my lightning. Some had spells that inflicted pain, while others simply used sleep spells. Juanita had a unique method of sucking energy *away* from her targets, causing the enervated faeries to drop to the ground, unable to move.

More than half of the witches who'd shown up had no spells for fighting. They used more common weapons: guns. Those who didn't want to fight helped by sharing their magical energy with the fighters or by simply waiting to heal the wounded.

Maximilian and I jogged down the ramp to the parking deck below. Fortunately, there was only one two-way ramp per level, because we needed to barricade this one to protect the upper deck.

"Ah, good. Two minivans over there," Maximilian said. "They're tall but also low to the ground."

The wizard was a more powerful magician than I, though not skilled in battle magic. I felt honored that he had voted for me to be the Arch Mage. He walked up to an old brown minivan in a handicapped space beneath flickering fluorescent lights and placed his palms against its side.

A powerful surge of energy radiated from him as he appeared to lift the van with his arms. The truth was, he was using his mind to do so; touching the vehicle enabled a more effective transfer of energy, which was necessary for such a heavy load. He walked with the van up the ramp and placed it sideways in a spot just below the top of the incline. Then, he repeated the proce-dure with a second minivan. This left a small gap between them, which he filled with a Mini Cooper shoved into the space vertically.

The barricade was formidable. It would slow any Fae trying to reach us on the roof but wouldn't stop them completely because they could climb or fly over it. Still, the narrow space remaining below the concrete ceiling would limit the number of faeries squeezing through. They would be easy to pick off.

We headed back to the roof parapet, but only made a few

steps before a faint, high-pitched whine came from the lower decks. It grew louder as it approached us. Soon it was joined by the rumble of hundreds of running feet. The horde was coming.

I made a quick survey of the situation on the roof. The witches were spread across the four sides, shooting downward, but also upward at the flying faeries who attacked with bows and arrows. Rufus fired at them with an assault rifle because shifting to wolf would not be advantageous against flying opponents. Gaarg, whose fingers were too large to fit past a trigger guard, batted faeries away with his giant club. Two witches were on the ground with arrow wounds. Things were looking grim.

I returned to the barricade just in time to shoot lightning from Alfie at the faeries trying to crawl over the vehicles. Maximilian used a percussive form of energy that slammed into his targets, knocking them unconscious and sending them flying backwards.

I looked down through the tiny space between the top of the ramp and the roof and studied the enemy. As was their custom, the Fae fought with traditional weapons when in their true diminutive forms. These included pikes, spears, swords, and arrows. You might think that would put them at a disadvantage, but they were highly skilled fighters. And there were enough of them to keep advancing until we ran out of ammunition and magical energy.

Speaking of which, Maximilian and I were keeping the attackers at bay, but how long could we continue? A faerie appeared with his belly on a minivan roof and threw a spear at me. I dodged it but was left with a graze wound on my neck. Lightning from Alfie made short work of the faerie and each additional one coming after him. I didn't dare cast a protection spell, though. It would use up too much magical energy, limiting my shooting.

Screams came from the roof behind us. The moonlit sky was thick with flying faeries shooting arrows like evil Cupids. Faeries on foot ventured forth from the stairwell that Sonya had been guarding. More witches lay on the parking deck, being tended to by the healers. I began to wish I had allowed the gnomes to come here, but I knew my decision had been correct.

I called to Rufus, "Where are the shifters, vampires, and Gorkee's faeries?"

"The vampires are coming. But the others are stuck in heavy fighting."

We needed reinforcements quickly. As I stared with horror at the swarming faeries in the sky, an idea came to me.

Ronnie, we need your help right away, I called to the dragon telepathically. *We're at the top of the main parking garage in San Marcos and are being overrun by the Fae.*

I waited for a response, but none came.

Ronnie, please save us. We can't let the Fae win.

"We need to retreat," Rufus said.

"We can't retreat," I replied. "The entire garage is teeming with faeries. There's no way out except by jumping."

Rufus shifted to his huge, magnificent white wolf form, loped to the wall, and jumped over.

I left Maximilian to man the barricade and ran to the spot and looked down. Even with his supernatural healing abilities, could a werewolf survive a five-story fall? At first I couldn't see him among the faeries on the street, until the crowed parted and the wolf bounded through them and disappeared into the night.

"Did he just desert his post, or was that a genius tactical move?" Gaarg asked.

"I guess we'll find out."

"My opinion is that he bailed—"

An arrow struck Gaarg in the thigh. He clutched the wound

with both hands and sank to his knees. I was overcome with sympathy, empathy, and the sad realization that I wasn't very good at using magic for healing. For killing, yes, but not for helping the wounded.

I signaled for a healing witch to come help Gaarg. Alma was an herbalist as well as an energy-healer. We helped Gaarg lie on his back, and she got to work.

Ronnie? I called with my mind.

He responded. But not verbally. The moon was briefly obscured by the black silhouettes of dragons flying overhead, dozens of them, more than I could count. My heart soared.

The dragons descended in a V-formation, and then the destruction began. Gliding just above the ground, the dragons disgorged jets of fire upon the masses of faeries surrounding the parking garage and those who had been spreading out through the city. Block after block of San Marcos was illuminated with the yellow blaze of righteous retribution.

The dragons gracefully turned and headed back toward the garage. They circled the structure, ascending from the ground up, shooting their flames into each level at the faeries inside. The sturdy structure shook as cars exploded below us.

"Everyone, get inside the south stairwell!" I shouted.

Maximilian and the surviving witches on the roof dashed to the stairwell we still controlled. Alma and I helped Gaarg limp inside while the other healers dragged in the wounded.

I thought we would roast alive in there from the heat of the flames. The fire door held up against the conflagration, which flickered around the door edges. The jets of fire ceased, and the heat in the stairwell lessened. I opened the door and saw no dragons above us.

Anything else we can do for you? Ronnie asked telepathically.

I checked if Gaarg was conscious. "Gaarg, where else do we need to send the dragons?"

"Luttvale Beach." He grimaced with pain. "Our people are retreating from there yet again. Including all those that Rufus sent."

Luttvale Beach, I told Ronnie. *The Fae are probably in human form. Please try not to damage the town too much. It's so quaint.*

Laughter boomed in my head. *Who thinks about quaintness at times like these?*

Only a few minutes later, a yellow glow appeared on the eastern horizon, a false sunrise that spelled the doom of the Fae forces there.

"Everyone who's in fighting condition, follow me," I ordered. "We have to prevent any more Fae from exiting the tunnels."

"I know where the gnomes found the tunnels, so I'm going with you," Gaarg said. "Alma's magic did wonders for my blasted wound."

The troll headed for the elevator, limping and visibly in pain, but his healing had come a long way. Juanita restored power to the elevator, and I rode it with Gaarg to the ground floor. He was so tall he had to tilt his head to fit inside.

"Until we hear from Rufus," he said, "you're our general now."

"I don't know. . ."

"You've stepped up to every challenge so far. You must do so for this one, too."

The gnomes had located two tunnel openings nearby. One was in a Little League baseball field, and the other was in the backyard of a home in the same neighborhood. The tunnels provided access to San Marcos behind where our forces were, enabling the Fae to attack us from behind. I wondered if they had known they were as near as they were to our command center.

Several gnomes were gathered at the ready around each tunnel exit. I found Skeetch in the baseball field standing beside a three-foot-wide hole behind second base.

"We've stopped the Fae from emerging from the tunnels, but we can't push them out of the other ends," he told me. "It's one-on-one fighting down there."

"Are there any other tunnels besides the two that surfaced in this neighborhood?"

"My gnomes sniffed around quite a bit. They're confident these are the only two tunnels. For now. Because we're guarding the exits, they very well could be digging tunnels branching off from these."

"Should I use my bunker-busting spell?" Cory asked me.

"Not yet. Your spell would collapse the tunnels, and we need the gnomes to explore them. I want to make sure the Fae haven't dug detour tunnels from these."

"It will be a massacre if we go down there now," Skeetch said.

"You're not going now. You're going after my magic takes effect."

"And what magic would that be?" Cory asked.

"There are several layers of porous limestone beneath the soil," I explained. "Much of the drinking water for San Marcos comes from underground water tables sandwiched by the limestone. I'm going to force the water to rise upwards and flood the tunnels. I'm a water witch, after all. But first, did you map out the tunnels?"

"Um, no," Skeetch replied. "Gnomes don't like maps because we use tunnels and burrows to hide our treasure and don't want anyone finding maps of it."

"I see. Is there a gnome who can give me a mental picture of this tunnel?"

"Ginch is who you want." He signaled to a chubby, elderly gnome with a beard that nearly touched the ground. He came over to us, and Skeetch explained what I wanted.

"Picture in your mind, as best you can, the entire length of this tunnel from beginning to end, as if you were looking down at it from the sky," I told him. "I will connect with you telepathically and see what you're picturing."

Skeetch translated what I'd said into Gnomish. Ginch looked at me as if he thought I was crazy, then nodded. I concentrated on him and formed the mental connection, enhanced by empath magic. Soon, a hazy aerial view of San Marcos came into view and became sharper and more focused. It wasn't like a satellite view; buildings and streets were absent. It was more like a detailed topographic map, with a dotted line showing the meandering path of the tunnel, beginning in undeveloped land south of the city and ending up where we stood in the baseball field.

Armed with this information, and keeping the picture in my mind, I cast the water spell. I summoned all the water I could sense beneath the tunnel: rainwater that had descended beneath the soil to the limestone strata along with the natural springs.

Rise! I commanded it, while I simultaneously reduced the air pressure inside the tunnel, drawing the water toward it. I wished I could see the tunnel's interior, but I knew the spell was working when water bubbled up from the hole in the ground.

The bubbling turned into gushing.

Several drenched faeries scrambled out of the tunnel, panting for air, and were immediately captured. I had no doubt others were escaping from the opposite end. I continued the flooding for several minutes until it was likely that no Fae soldiers remained in the tunnel, at least not alive.

I released the spell and could feel in my body the sensation of water receding from the tunnel and sinking back into its home below.

"The tunnel is safe for exploration," I told Skeetch, who ordered a patrol to go underground.

Skeetch and I walked to the nearby home where the other tunnel had its opening. I repeated the same process with the help of a different gnome. We waited for nearly an hour until Skeetch reported that the tunnels were now controlled by the gnome guards, and that there had been no evidence of newly dug tunnels.

Gaarg limped to me as I walked from the home to the street. I was exhausted, but relieved that San Marcos had defeated most, if not all, of the Fae within our borders.

My hopes were dashed when Gaarg reported the news.

"The shifters south of the city have been overrun," he said. "A large force of Fae is headed into the city."

CHAPTER 27

SOPHIE

The original vanguard of the Fae army turned out to be the last of their forces to reach the city, thanks to the shifters in the south who had slowed them. But the shifters were in retreat, and the Fae arrived after we had been battered to pieces. They were in human form, riding in cars and vans. And they were armed to the teeth.

Thankfully, the surviving vampires joined us, along with stragglers from our various retreating fighters. After the dragons wiped out the Fae in Luttvale Beach, the trolls and shifters there returned to the mainland and met up with us as well. Our small numbers of indigenous faeries added to the gnomes, minus those guarding the cleared tunnels. Our surviving witches rounded out our paltry forces. The few pixies and sprites hovered above, ready to attack the Fae like hungry mosquitoes.

We didn't know if the Fae would come via I-95 or U.S. 1, but either route fed into Colonial Street, the main road that ran into the city center. It passed a cemetery, and I placed half of us there to ambush the Fae. The headstones and mausoleums would provide cover when we fired upon the Fae.

I crouched behind a large, overly ornate monument to a Gilded Age family in the front of our forces, close to the street, and immediately sensed a supernatural presence. Several, in fact. At first, I assumed they were ghosts. This was an old cemetery and rumored to be haunted. But no, the energy was more than just spectral. It was corporeal.

Something rustled the grass beside me, making me jump in alarm. The scent of rotting flesh wafted past my nose. Shuffling footsteps approached. Zombies and ghouls were gathering near me.

"Zombies, ghouls, brothers, and sisters," I called out, but not too loudly. "The night of glory has arrived. We are the last of the supernaturals surviving in San Marcos, and we need you to join us. The Fae are marching into our city to conquer us and make us their slaves."

Jawbones clicked in the darkness. I couldn't see the undead creatures yet, but they were very near. Their emotions, however, were unreadable. My empath magic would be of no use. Only my powers of persuasion could affect their rotting brains.

"The Fae are making their final push into the city," I continued. "They'll be coming this way. We need your help to ambush them. We *must* stop them here before they spread out through the streets. I shouldn't have to remind you of this, but the Fae have no use for your kind. If they rule our city, they will wipe out all of you."

Light from a distant streetlamp caught the decaying face of Timothy, President of the Union of Undead Flesh Eaters. Behind him were the dark silhouettes of several shambling figures.

"Timothy! It's good to see you! Can you help us?"

"Unity is the only thing that will save us," he said through a mouth of loose teeth. "As Benjamin Franklin said during the American War of Independence, 'We must all compose ourselves together, or surely we shall all decompose separately.'"

"That's not quite how Franklin put it. But it's the right idea."

"I've eaten Fae brains before," he added. "Quite tasty."

A drone of engines approached on Colonial Street.

"They're coming," I said. "Your guild will have the honor of being the first wave." A wave of mortals would be a suicidal tactic. A wave of zombies and ghouls would suffer many casualties, but they were technically already dead. Right?

Headlights pierced the deserted street. The convoy was an assortment of cars, vans, and trucks—no longer delivery vehicles, but anything with wheels that could transport the Fae. Timothy hid behind the monument with me.

The first vehicle passed us, followed by a second. Finally, I gave the order to attack.

The undead emerged from the cemetery and into the convoy —the stooped figures of animated dead humans and the hideous-looking ghouls: naked humanoids with large, glowing eyes and gaping maws. The creatures swarmed the vehicles, and many were run over. Others clung to the cars and vans, punching through windows and crawling inside.

As soon as the disabled vehicles stopped, the road was blocked, and the undead crowded around each of them, seeking the succulent meat inside as they cracked open the steel and glass like the shells of lobsters.

Meanwhile, the first vehicles that had passed us stopped, and Fae soldiers poured out, firing upon the zombies and ghouls. Purple lightning bolts shot from Alfie, taking them down with the help of Cory's fireballs and Jocelyn's flame stream.

I stepped out into the street, and from this vantage point, I saw how incredibly long the convoy was. After so many Fae casualties, they still had all these soldiers? The vehicles farther back that hadn't been attacked by the undead were emptying their passengers. The Fae soldiers formed into assault teams, one of which went into the cemetery where they battled the witches and indigenous faeries.

Other teams fanned out on both sides of the road into secondary streets and shopping plazas. One team was savagely attacked by vampires, and Fae bodies were tossed into the air. Hundreds of muzzle flashes blinked in the darkness as the enemy fired ineffectively at the vampires.

A large pack of wolves charged from the other side of the road, tearing apart the Fae combat teams. Unfortunately, multiple high-powered rounds from assault rifles can overcome a shifter's preternatural healing abilities. Still, the wolves charged bravely. The pixies and sprites dive-bombed the Fae, but had little effect.

We needed the dragons to rescue us again but calling them in would harm us as much as the Fae. Our forces were mixed with theirs in several melees taking place at the rear of the convoy and on either side of it.

This was the largest battle I had yet seen in the war. Beneath the moonlight, the Fae spread out from the road in terrifying numbers. This part of the city was less urban than Old Town, and there were fewer buildings, allowing the battle to range in parking lots, open spaces, and the wide road itself. It was a strange mixture of modern warfare and medieval hand-to-hand combat. And the outcome was in great doubt.

Diego appeared at my side. "We're falling back into the city," he said. "The vampires are too outnumbered. I'm hoping the shifters will keep up the pressure on the Fae so that we can attack them from a different angle."

Heavy fire came from the opposite side of the cemetery. The

Fae had outflanked us, putting the witches and indigenous faeries in danger of being surrounded.

"We have to fall back too," I said to Diego. He looked into my eyes intensely. For the first time, I sensed his emotions clearly: fear for my life. He truly worried that I would not survive the night. And there was something else.

Love. Yes, it was undeniable.

"Stay close to me," he said. "I want to protect you."

"I'm serving as the leader of our forces. I can't follow you around."

His face and emotions were filled with dismay. "Then I shall follow you." He kissed me, right there in the street, with guns blazing and arrows flying around us.

Generals aren't supposed to kiss in the middle of a battle, but I won't deny that it lit my heart on fire. Until movement approaching Diego caught my eye.

"Behind you!" I shouted, as I blasted my lightning at the group of charging faeries. They were in their natural forms, survivors of those who had come through the tunnels.

Diego turned and eviscerated several faeries before they fled. He wiped blood from his face. "We're surrounded."

A battle horn sang from the south. It sounded like a ram's horn, something you'd hear during a battle in ancient times. Did it signal that even more Fae had arrived on the battlefield? The gunfire increased in that direction. Then, an enemy unit retreated from the cemetery and moved toward the sound. It was followed by another unit.

"What the heck is going on?" I asked, not expecting an answer.

I received a text from Gaarg: *It's the Elves! The Elven army is attacking the Fae from their rear!*

Returning to the cemetery, I climbed up on the highest

monument I could find so I could get a better view. What I saw made me gasp.

The Elves had fielded a gigantic army. They advanced into San Marcos in three columns, the main one following the same road the Fae convoy had traveled. Two smaller columns took secondary streets. As they neared the Fae, each column reformed into a phalanx of sorts, with a center made of dense rows of armored spearmen with weapons twice their height and overlapping shields. On the flanks of the spearmen were rows of archers.

They looked like the soldiers of Alexander the Great. How could they withstand the modern weapons of the Fae in human form?

Quite easily, as it turned out. Bullets bounced off their shields and armor, which I realized were infused with magic. The archers' arrows flew faster and further than seemed possible, thanks to magic, puncturing vehicles and faeries alike. The phalanxes marched forward unceasingly, impaling faeries with their spears and trampling the rest.

Loosely attached to each phalanx were battle mages. When the phalanx came upon a stalled Fae vehicle, the mages would simply blow it to smithereens. I grinned when I recognized Leighnel as one of them. I'd known he was a mage, but I was surprised to see the scientific scholar wielding such powerful attack magic.

Leighnel had studied phytolucine and tried to keep the substance created by trees out of the hands of the Fae. Ironically, the spell the Fae had created with the substance, that had rendered the humans unconscious, was what made it possible for the Elves to appear out in the open with no humans awake to see them. And, I would learn, video security cameras had no ability to capture images of Elves.

The three phalanxes of the Elven forces plowed forward, mopping up scattered Fae units, those in human and faerie forms. Our supernaturals saw this and rallied, coming together in a solid line that marched southward to crush the Fae between us and the Elves.

A red fireball sailed from the disorganized Fae forces and hit the main elf phalanx. The Fae still had a sorcerer among them, despite all the sorcerers we'd dispatched. He sent another fireball at the Elves. I screamed as it went right toward Leighnel.

The elf mage deftly blocked the fireball. A second one hit him in the torso, and Leighnel dropped to the ground, rolling to extinguish the flames. Did he not have the ability to cast a protection spell around himself?

I left Diego's side and sprinted toward the parking lot from where the Fae sorcerer's fireballs had launched. Using magic to enhance my senses, I saw the sorcerer in his natural faerie form, crouched atop a closed dumpster. He looked familiar.

It finally came to me who he was: the bald monster in the red robe was the one who had tortured Mom when she was being held captive by the Faerie Queene. We'd had the opportunity to kill him when the palace was under attack, but we'd been merciful instead.

What a mistake. Even if I used every drop of my empathy, I couldn't bring myself to spare this evil piece of crap who'd shown so much cruelty and may have killed Leighnel. He still hadn't noticed me when I neared the dumpster.

"Remember me?" I asked.

His head darted in my direction, and he opened his mouth with his tongue slightly extended, as if he were a snake searching for my scent.

"You're just a weak human witch," he said, energy radiating from him as he prepared to attack me.

With a satisfying click of my crossbow trigger, the ash-wood bolt slammed into his chest. He fell from his perch and landed on the asphalt of the parking lot, among the empty cans and rotting food strewn beside the dumpster.

I turned and walked away. Two of our ghoul fighters scampered toward the dumpster, excited about the fresh corpse they had just scented. "Get back to the front line," I shouted at them. "Your snack will be waiting for you after the battle."

Surprisingly, they obeyed my order. The fact was, there really wasn't a front line anymore. I led my witches toward the remnants of the Fae army that were trapped between the Elves on one side and our ragtag force of supernaturals on the other. We discovered the only faeries left standing, aside from the indigenous ones on our side, had surrendered to the Elves. The forlorn prisoners stood silently in a group, a few hundred of them, bound by Elven magic.

I found Leighnel alive. His tunic had been scorched, but the elf seemed to be in good health and was beaming at this moment of victory.

"What made the king change his mind and enter the war?" I asked.

"He finally came to terms with the Faerie Queene's treachery after your governor's demand for gold in return for convincing the Queene not to attack us. Our spies confirmed that she was, indeed, planning to attack and break the peace treaty."

"I knew it," I said, though being proved correct gave me no solace. "Anyway, the war is not over until we capture the Faerie Queene and make sure the governor is impeached or forced to resign."

The Florida legislature acted as mere servants to the governor, so impeachment was unlikely. But I was determined to help make life so unpleasant for her she would decide to resign.

I was surprised to see Samson limping toward me. One leg of his trousers was stained with blood.

"Detective, I didn't know you were here tonight. You should be at home recuperating from your imprisonment."

"I couldn't sit at home while the packs were risking their lives for the city I serve." He hesitated and looked at me uncomfortably. "I saw you here just now and came over to . . . well, not to burden you with my paranoia, but I'm worried about your mother."

"Why? What happened?" My stomach clenched.

"Darla and I have always had this connection—kind of telepathic, though I don't have the ability. Anyway, she sent me thoughts about how she was about to enter a great battle. I called and texted her, but she didn't respond."

"She promised me she would stay away from the fighting."

"Not this battle," he said. "Something more cosmic."

I thanked him and searched for Cory among the supernaturals gathered near me. I found him half a block away, staring plaintively at his phone.

"Cory, have you heard from Mom?"

"I talked to her only minutes ago, but how was she even awake? She should have been asleep under the Fae's spell, like every human in town. But she called me and mumbled something cryptic about entering her own battle. Then she abruptly stopped speaking. She didn't end the call but just went silent. I think she's having one of her moments. But I don't understand what she meant about a battle."

I texted Gaarg: *Please take command of our forces. I'm rushing home. There's an emergency with my mother.*

CHAPTER 28

DARLA

When I awoke, everything was clear and obvious to me. I was alone in the cottage and knew that Cory was off somewhere with Sophie, fighting to save the city. I remembered I had been drugged by the Fae's phytolucine spell, but this time I felt none of the cloudy-headedness I'd experienced last time, when I recovered from the spell in Altman.

Most of all, I knew I had a battle of my own to fight. The Elder God was in San Marcos. I understood, at last, what the Tugara had told us: the entity had come to earth because of all the strife and hatred raging around the world, and especially so in my home state. He fed upon the energy given off by all the war, the petty violence, and the destruction. It made him stronger.

He was here tonight, materializing into flesh, because of the Battle of San Marcos.

I called Cory, not sure why I was doing it, but certain that speaking to him was critical.

"Hey, hon! How could you have avoided the Fae spell?" he asked.

"I didn't, but it wore off, and I'm awake. I must enter my own battle now. A fight of cosmic consequences."

The next thing I knew, the phone wasn't in my hand anymore. I dressed quickly and stepped outside. The distant gunfire sounded like firecrackers—wasn't that what witnesses to gun violence always say? But this popping was more insistent and overwhelming, massive like the crashing surf. Occasional louder explosions rang out, but I was relieved to conclude that the Fae were armed as light infantry and not as some modern mechanized army with tanks, drones, rockets, and artillery.

The Elder God was loving the show. I didn't know how I knew that, but I did. I also knew that he was in what we called the bay, where the Sangre River widened and met the ocean inlet on the east side of San Marcos. I was compelled to leave the inn and walk toward the water.

Danu, you are pushing me toward a confrontation with the Elder God, but I don't know what to do. You must help me.

She didn't answer. Still, I continued to walk along the cobblestones of Hidalgo Avenue toward the bay, the sounds of battle not far behind me to the west. There were no humans anywhere, except for those I spotted asleep behind the steering wheels of their stalled cars. I reached the waterfront promenade and surveyed the water. It appeared normal where I was, but when I turned left toward the north, the water was illuminated with a greenish glow. That's where the Elder God was.

Oh, how I wished I could return to my cottage and go back to bed, but my feet propelled me along the promenade. Toward the ultimate conflict.

The entity was just south of the Bridge of Memories, where the green glow was strongest, about a hundred feet out into the bay. Bubbles were rising to the surface and bursting. The smell of rot and sulfur released from the bubbles drifted to me.

Suddenly, all the lights around me and across the water blinked out. The distant gunfire ceased. I wasn't standing on the paved promenade anymore, but on a sandy bank. In fact, the entire city was gone. Behind me was a forest. The sky was filled with an impossible number of stars, so dense it was like a soup of galaxies. Somehow I had gone back in time, possibly to when the Elder God had briefly reigned on this planet.

The nightmarish creature's two eyes popped out of the water and rose above the surface on their stalks. They fixed upon me immediately. The Elder God knew Danu was the only obstacle preventing him from reigning over our planet and solar system. Did he recognize me as Danu? Was I the Goddess at this moment? I didn't feel like my Darla self, but I still retained my fears and frailties.

I blinked, and the lights of the city and the homes across the water returned. The promenade path was beneath my feet again. The battle raged on behind me. This time-shifting was jarring.

The last time the entity and I had met, I had become the Goddess and fought the creature toe to toe, inflicting damage on him. But the fight had ended as a draw. What would make this battle any different? I considered getting into the water and attacking him, but I hesitated at the prospect of climbing over the safety railing and walking on the slippery rocks at the water's edge. Darla's weakness held me back.

A wave appeared in the bay as the Elder God moved his giant underwater bulk toward me. Two of his four crablike claws rose above the surface. He was coming for me, and I had to stop him.

The ancient melody associated with the Goddess played in my head. The familiar burning sensation grew stronger in my gut. Yes, the Goddess was growing stronger in me as I became her and left Darla behind.

The divine power throbbed in my torso and hummed in my head. I pointed my hand at the creature and a beam of pure white energy poured from me, striking the creature's claw and shattering the shell.

The god made a high-pitched screech. And then it charged at me.

On a hundred crablike legs, the bus-sized, blob-like mass of its body clambered over the rocks and broke through the railing. This unnatural creature didn't belong on land. No, it didn't belong on earth at all. But there it was, lumbering across the promenade, waving its three remaining claws at me.

I continually stepped backwards out of its reach. Then, all at once, the weakness of all-too-human Darla took over, pushing the Goddess to the side, and I panicked. I ran away through my city that had become unfamiliar to me, with the human population in comas and the supernaturals waging a desperate battle.

A creature that large, with a body meant to be underwater, shouldn't have moved so quickly. Yet it did. Its shell-encased body on the crab legs scuttled across Bayfront Avenue, its claws knocking cars out of the way, its sensory tentacles flailing. Its feet clicked across the cobblestones accompanied by the squishing sounds of its soft parts, and it carried with it a stench of rotting flesh and seawater. The monstrosity moved toward me faster than I could run.

I had devolved from a goddess to a panicked mouse scampering along the forest floor to escape a predator. All I had were my survival instincts. They told me to flee into the narrow alley I was approaching. I darted inside, and the creature's bulk crashed into the stone walls on either side. There was no way it could fit in here to reach my cowering human body, but the alley ended at a brick wall, and I had no way out.

The creature couldn't enter the alley, but its tentacles easily did. One of them poked inside, touching the walls and ground to feel its way toward me. Somehow, it grew longer as it moved toward me, trapped against the rear wall. My heart was about to explode with fear as the tentacle's slimy tip poked into my stomach.

The proverbial fight-or-flight response had exhausted the flight part, and I turned to the only thing I had left. I slapped the tentacle away, as if that would do any good.

The simple action altered the trajectory of my downfall. Mouse-brained Darla turned into an angry, desperate Darla, and I continued to slap and punch the probing tentacle until it finally reached around my back. I pressed myself against the wall, but the tentacle was stronger than I and slithered past my ribs to emerge on the other side of me, wrapping itself around my torso.

Remember who you are, the Goddess's voice said to me. *You are Danu, a stronger deity than this primitive false god. Use your powers against it.*

"I can't," I said aloud.

You must become me. Fully. Completely. You must shed your old self and fulfill your destiny. You must become Danu without ever going back.

"I'm not sure I'm ready."

Your only choices are to die right now as a human, or live forever as a goddess.

The tentacle squeezed me and pulled me down the alley toward the open jaws of the creature waiting just outside.

My instincts naturally pushed me toward my only chance for survival: abandoning being human. And embracing the divine.

I reached deep inside myself, found the seed Danu had

planted there long ago, and embraced it, germinated it, finally accepted it. My fear faded away as the Goddess's power surged through my veins.

No, it wasn't the Goddess's power. It was mine, Danu's.

I fired a blast of white energy at the tentacle, severing it. The amputated section flopped and twisted on the ground. The wounded tentacle made another grab at me, and my white beam sliced it off closer to its base. But then another tentacle snaked its way toward me. And a second and a third.

I fired at the creature's mouth. It screamed hideously—a sound never before heard on earth. Still, the tentacles reached me and wrapped around me. Strength I'd never had before enabled me to peel them off. I needed to do more, though, to win this battle.

As my consciousness became Danu's, leaving behind the trivial clutter of Darla's mind, the key to defeating this Elder God became clear to me: I knew his name. That made him vulnerable and gave me power over him. Naming our gods was how humans had built stories around them and helped us understand the world. But gods like my foe prefer to go nameless, so that they can defy human understanding.

And as a goddess, I could use his name to control him, if I used my power correctly.

"Yavevi," I shouted. "I know you! Be gone from this world!"

The tentacles were still poised to wrap around me again.

"Yavevi is your name! *Yavevi.* I possess the power of your naming, what defines you. Yes, I know all about you and your secrets. I have seen the emptiness within you. You are a false god. This world is not where you belong. I am the Goddess here, and I will destroy you if you do not leave at once."

He was taken aback, but he did not leave. Sometimes, you have to put an exclamation mark on what you say.

"Hey, Yav baby, here's a little incentive for you to go." I sent a stream of white energy flowing like the cascades of the rivers I commanded, right into his kisser.

His defenses were down because of my naming him, so my attack was devastating. His mandibles and other mouth pieces blew apart and his carapace shattered, fragments of shell flying like shrapnel. The mournful squeal would have been heartbreaking—if you were an Elder God, that is.

Yavevi's physical manifestation was in pretty bad shape, and I continued to dismantle him like I was attending a crab boil. Though I was a mother and nature goddess, I was not above raining death and destruction down upon harmful species, especially ones not native to the earth. Namely, a crab-squid-freak like this one.

Wounding his non-material self—his god entity—was more of a struggle, requiring all my divine powers. I'd never used them together at once like this. After all, I'd never fully been Danu before. The best way to understand what I did is to imagine a bouncer escorting a drunk from a nightclub. I did it quickly and smoothly, while making it clear that any resistance would involve cosmic-level pain on his part. I didn't release my metaphorical grip on the back of his neck until I had tossed him far past the edges of the galaxy.

When I returned to earth, I ended up in my old body again. Talk about an awkward feeling. Mentally and psychologically, I was Danu now; physically, I was still Darla. Her body was exhausted, so I made it walk home and get back into bed. I entered a sleep deeper than I ever had before, with a sensation of sinking into the soft earth without stopping.

"SHE WON'T WAKE UP," CORY'S VOICE SAID. "I THINK SHE'S IN a coma."

"Mom, can you hear me?" Sophie asked. She was crying. "Move a finger or eyelid or anything to show you can hear me."

I could move nothing, so deep in sleep was I.

"It has to be the Fae spell," Cory said. "When she called me earlier, she must have briefly broken through the spell before going back under. There's probably nothing wrong with her. We can't call an ambulance until the humans wake up from the spell, anyway."

"Her mention of a battle worries me," said Sophie. "A while ago she said Danu wanted her to fight an Elder God. I will ask a healing witch to come here, just in case."

Neither healing magic nor medical science could help me, I was certain. All I wanted to do was sleep and wait for what was next.

CHAPTER 29

SOPHIE

Mom was still sleeping when the sun came up on a battle-scarred San Marcos. The Fae's phytolucine spell had worn off, and human residents were waking up to the perplexing scene of streets littered with dead faeries in their natural forms lying among shell casings and spent arrows. The humans had no idea what had happened overnight and demanded answers.

Fortunately, Joe Romesco provided them. He hit social media and the local news with a firestorm of accusations against Governor Witlessin. His previous claims that she was demanding bribes from the Elves and colluding with the Fae, which had fallen on deaf ears, were finally getting the attention they had deserved. After all, the city had obviously been attacked, property had been damaged, and all these scary-looking little folkloric creatures were on the ground dead.

Until this incident most humans hadn't seen faeries, except those hiding in human form. Now that yet another legendary creature had been proven to exist, news spread across the country and the world. More questions were asked about the accusations against the governor. Even if people didn't believe the claims that she was the Faerie Queene's secret agent and a secret faerie herself, they listened to the many other complaints of her soliciting bribes and kickbacks.

However, no one could deny the battle damage to the city and the dead faeries in the streets. Someone had to be blamed, and Joe did his best to point fingers at the governor. Just as much, someone should get credit for saving the city. Joe claimed that the local supernaturals, the very same people the city was oppressing, were the heroes who saved San Marcos. Giving credit was much more difficult that casting blame, because the supernaturals had to remain hidden for their safety and couldn't bask in their deserved glory.

I was grateful for Joe's efforts, but I had other priorities. Capturing the Faerie Queene was one of them, if it wasn't too late. Cory and I commandeered a passenger van abandoned by the Fae army and drove to the Queene's palace in Palm Beach, accompanied by Gaarg, Jocelyn, Gorkee, and a few gnomes. It was a small group, but it was all we could spare. I doubted the Queene's personal guards were at full strength, anyway.

The cities we passed along the way had not been touched by war, and life looked perfectly normal. We listened to news stations on the radio, and their reports of the Battle of San Marcos were somewhat accurate and mentioned Joe's accusations. But as we traveled further south in the state, what had happened in our city was described as "violence involving supernaturals." National reports on public radio and satellite stations called the battle a "riot by supernaturals."

Some people sure couldn't handle the truth, right?

When we drove past the Queene's palace, my heart sank. The place looked deserted, with curtains closed in every window. We parked on a side street and walked to the mansion, leaving the troll Gaarg and the gnomes in the van as backup so they wouldn't draw attention.

A human security guard near the side gate noticed us before dropping to the ground under my sleep spell. I used magic to unlock the gate and the servants' entrance to the building. Our footsteps echoed on the marble floors as we roamed the quiet, empty building. The furniture and artwork were still there, but the palace had clearly been abandoned by the Queene and her retinue.

When we reached the second floor, we were met by faint crying sounds. At first, I thought they came from a kitten. As we got closer to the open door at the end of a long hallway, I realized the cries came from a faerie.

Governor Witlessin, in faerie form, sat on a footstool in front of a human-sized chair that was too large for her. She continued crying, with her face in her little hands, even after we entered the bedroom.

"Governor, what are you doing here?" I asked.

She removed her hands and looked at us as if we were furniture. "The Queene left for the land of Faerie. She offered to take me, but I didn't want to go."

"You should reconsider," Cory said. "You realize that the Fae army was defeated, don't you?"

"Yes. Those total losers. The Queene has abandoned her hopes of conquest."

"Politics might become unpleasant for you right now."

"I don't want to leave my life—the governor's mansion, my private driver, the trips on private jets, the business deals."

"You mean bribes," I snarked. She ignored me.

"Why are you allowing yourself to be seen in faerie form?" Gorkee asked her.

"Because I can't change into my human form!" She sobbed and snorted.

"Why not?"

"Because a demon cursed me," Witlessin replied with anger. "I was sleeping last night and there was this glowing figure above my bed. I thought it was an angel looking after me, but he told me I'd been wicked and must remain in my natural form. Then he disappeared. He must have been a demon, because I tried and tried, but couldn't shapeshift."

"Thank you, Michael," I said. "It wasn't a demon. It was the archangel Michael. If you've been wicked enough to have an angel punish you, you know you've gone too far."

"Don't preach at me, you stupid human."

"Actually, I'm a witch. One of the people you've persecuted. Your hateful campaign to help the Faerie Queene and your career sure backfired."

"Shut up."

"Maybe it's time you asked your legislature to overturn the Supernatural Criminality Act."

"Shut up. Get out of my face."

"Spoken with the diplomacy of a true politician," Cory said. He looked at me. "Should we capture her or something?"

"No. We'll leave her to wallow in her self-pity. Now that she can't fool people by pretending to be human, her career is over. No more private jets for her."

I took a few incriminating photos, and we left the room. Her weeping followed us down the hallway.

WHEN WE RETURNED TO THE INN, MOM WAS STILL IN BED, asleep and unresponsive. Cory wanted to admit her to the hospital, but a gut feeling told me that wouldn't be a wise course of action. First, I wanted a healing witch to check her out because I believed Mom's malady was not medical.

Saul arrived promptly. The white-haired witch was too elderly to participate in the battle last night, but he was the Magic Guild's best healer. After working at home through the night, tending to the wounded supernaturals who'd been brought to him, he came straight here when I called.

Saul used crystals, which I never had the knack for, but also potions, poultices, and spells. He placed the crystals on Mom's pillow and bedside table and held a bouquet of herbs above her head. The witch checked Mom's pulse, then murmured an incantation too quietly for me to hear, his hands on Mom's head.

"I sense no illness in her," Saul said. "Obviously, I'm not a doctor and can't guarantee she doesn't have a physiological disorder, but if she does, I don't believe it's the cause of her not waking up."

"She has a benign cyst in her brain," Cory blurted out.

"I know. I sensed it. She's under the influence of a powerful force of magic that I can't identify. It doesn't resemble any type of witchcraft that I'm familiar with. I believe it's why she won't wake up."

"Is the magic of divine origin?" I asked.

He looked at me strangely. "That's what I was wondering. I've heard gossip that your mother is the human vessel of a goddess. Is that true?"

"Yep. I'm afraid Danu wants to become Mom, or for Mom to become her. I've dreaded it for as long as the Goddess has been in her. Is Mom going to die?"

"She's as healthy as can be. It doesn't seem likely this goddess would want to kill her."

"Well, she would take her away from us," I said. "To me, it's the same thing."

"What a goddess wishes to do is beyond our control. We can only wait and see. I'll give Darla an amulet for luck. Call me if there's any change."

There wasn't. The day went by, then another, and Mom continued to sleep with a half-smile on her face. She wouldn't accept water, and I carried her to the bathroom, but she didn't go. Each night, Cory slept beside her as usual. I stayed upstairs in my room instead of at a motel, unconcerned about anyone coming to kill or arrest me.

I showed up at Cory and Mom's cottage early in the morning and knocked. Cory was probably still asleep. I knocked again, and he opened the door, ashen-faced.

"She's gone," he said, just above a whisper.

"My God!" Tears welled in my eyes. "She passed away overnight?"

"No. She's literally gone. She's not in bed or in the cottage. I never felt her leave the bed. I've been sleeping very lightly lately, and I would have known if she got up."

I followed him into the bedroom. The bed was empty. Mom's nightgown lay on top of the sheets. I checked the closet and found her robe hanging in its usual spot. "Did she wander off naked?"

"I don't think she wandered anywhere," Cory said. "I think she simply disappeared."

"Danu took her."

He nodded. "She took her to wherever goddesses live."

"Why would Danu take Mom's human body?"

"Maybe we're looking at this the wrong way. We speak of Danu like she's a bad actor stealing Darla from us. Maybe Darla simply *became* Danu and ascended to the heavenly realm, or whatever you call it."

"If that's the case, she can descend back to earth whenever she wants to. Right, Mom?" I looked up at the ceiling as if she were above us somewhere. "Mom, we want to see you. Please come back to us."

Behind me, Cory gasped in surprise. "My, oh my. Look at you!"

CHAPTER 30

SOPHIE

T he Goddess Danu was petite and wiry, barely over five feet tall, with the face of a woman in her late fifties. She had a familiar smile and twinkle in her eyes. By all appearances, it was my mother standing there before us. Yet she radiated divine energy and practically glowed with it. Despite being in human form, this woman had transformed to a state beyond human.

Meet my mother, the Goddess.

"Are you just going to gawk at me?" she asked.

Cory reached a tentative hand toward her. "May I?"

My mom, the Goddess, nodded.

He touched her face. "You feel like Darla. A little warm, like you have a fever."

"You know, I've always run a little warm. I figured it would be easier for you guys if I became Darla when I took on a human form. I feel like I've kept my same personality, too."

"It would appear so," I said. "But you definitely have a goddess vibe. How, um, how did you—?"

"How did I become divine? Kind of like a caterpillar becoming a butterfly. It was a bit uncomfortable, to be honest, but Darla literally transformed into Danu. I woke up in the pool beneath the waterfall where I used to visit the Goddess. I went behind the falls, to the cave I'd always feared to enter. Finally, I had the courage to go inside, wading through shallow water through a winding passage. With each step, I felt weaker, until I collapsed into the water, and my heart literally stopped beating."

"You died?" I whispered.

"I appear before you now as Darla, but she doesn't exist anymore."

Danu pointed to the wall beside the bed. Instantly, vine tendrils appeared, snaking in all directions over this wall and the other three, thickening and sprouting leaves.

"Good," Cory said. "Now I don't have to repaint this room."

I became choked up again. "I lost my mother."

"And you gained a goddess. I'm still your mother, but as a new, greater entity. I am the Goddess, and you are the Goddess's daughter. Which means you, too, have some transforming to do."

"Does this have anything to do with the ghost of a druid who showed up in my bathroom?"

Mom—I mean, Danu—laughed. "Ah, Birog. Yes, she had an agenda to see Danu worshiped again and the Tuatha Dé Danann rule the land. The children of Danu. You, as my daughter, will rule them. This is a much different era than when Birog lived. You will not rule the humans, but the supernaturals."

"How could I do that?" I asked. "It was nearly impossible to get the supernaturals to unite to fight the Fae."

"But you accomplished it. And you will continue to keep them united so that they can end the oppression by humans and go on to flourish. First, we have business to take care of." She pointed her hands at me.

I cried out as crippling pain filled my entire body and dropped me to my knees. How could this entity who used to be my mother hurt me like this? My heart raced and my head spun, and I thought I was going to die.

But soon, my heart slowed to a strong, confident rhythm. My head cleared, and the pain evaporated. I felt different somehow. I couldn't figure out what had changed, aside from the optimism and fearlessness that filled me. Remaining on my knees, I struggled to grasp what had happened.

It gradually dawned on me. I no longer feared death. Every human being, no matter how young and cocky, knows that death awaits them. We spend every waking hour with a deadline hanging over us, a clock ticking down our remaining minutes before we perish. To live a full life, we must ignore the deadline, the date of which we don't know. Perhaps we have a guesstimate of the date, if we have a terminal illness; but the clock could strike at any moment, even if we're healthy.

Knowing we will die is an existential dread that is a fundamental aspect of being human. At that moment, I no longer had the dread of death. Not because of some emotional adaptation I had achieved. No, I no longer feared death because I wasn't going to die. Ever. I felt it in every fiber of my being.

I said softly to Danu, "Did you make me immortal?"

"Yes," she said. "As the Goddess's daughter, you shall live forever."

"Ahem." Cory cleared his throat. "I'm not of your blood, but—"

"I shall make an exception for you. Whenever I come to the earth in human form, I want to be with you, and I don't want to see you grow old and die. You shall live forever as the Goddess's husband."

Cory grimaced and sank to his knees as I had done. I watched him with empathy as his body trembled and went through the transformation. A few minutes later, he stood up.

"May I hug you?" he asked Danu.

"Yes. And you, too, Sophie."

I'd always found group hugs to be awkward, but when the three of us embraced, a divine energy swirled in and around us. It was exhilarating. Even Cervantes appeared and rubbed against our calves. The love we had always felt for each other was amplified, and my spirits soared as I reflected that Mom would never be the same, but I still had her in my life. A life that would last forever.

Danu peeled away from us. "We have much work to do. I must begin the long process of healing the earth. You, Sophie, must take up leadership of the supernaturals. And both of you must work to temper the hatred that harms so many humans and supernaturals alike."

"That's a tall order," Cory said.

"You have all the time in the world to do it."

THE EXECUTIVE COUNCIL OF THE SUPERNATURAL GUILDS OF San Marcos was in a giddy mood. With the Fae vanquished and the militia absent from the city, threats against our members had diminished. The police had stopped aggressively hunting us while they appraised which way the political winds were blowing. Our only immediate threats were random vigilante attacks.

The guild leaders were very receptive to my rousing speech

about how we could get the Supernatural Criminality Act over-turned and enter a golden age for us.

"You believe the governor being out of the public eye is enough to make the legislature come around and vote in our favor?" Samson asked. He had become the new Alpha of the shifters after Rufus deserted his post and disappeared from the city.

"Yes, I do," I replied. "Along with threatening to expose the secret faeries in the legislature and all those who colluded with the Fae."

"Even if the act is overturned, we've been unmasked to the public. They know we exist, and there's no going back from that."

"We will behave discreetly like we did before the Great Unmasking, and the public will learn to live with us."

Samson nodded. "Sophie, you know I have a high regard for you. I move we vote on making you the new leader of the Execu-tive Council. I'm not sure if I buy the Celtic mythology stuff, but I'm certain you're the right person for the job."

"I second the motion," Gaarg said. "You were an outstanding leader on the battlefield, and I trust you to lead us through this next phase."

I had thought I would need Danu to show up and convince them, but they voted for me unanimously. I prayed to her to give me the strength to lead the guilds to glory.

A certain vampire pulled me aside. "You have certainly risen to meet the moment time and time again," Diego said. "I have never been so impressed by a human."

"I'm not an ordinary human anymore." I told him about Danu's gift of immortality.

"Good Lord." He leaned toward me and took in my scent. "I'd thought something was different about you. Yes, I can tell—

you truly are immortal now. And you didn't have to return from death's door like I did when I was turned."

"Yes, I think I prefer the divine version of immortality over the undead kind."

Diego smiled wryly. "This changes everything, don't you realize? I was ashamed of my fear of getting hurt by losing you to your mortality. Now I have nothing to fear. At the risk of sounding rash, I ask permission for my attorney to contact yours."

"First, I don't have an attorney. Second, what the heck are you talking about?"

"Betrothal. Marriage. With vampires, we typically begin the process with attorneys because of the complicated financial assets and such."

Talk about being blindsided. "Marriage? Are you serious?"

"*Deadly* serious," he said with a grin.

"Does this mean you're proposing to me?"

"In essence, yes. Once the pre-nuptial agreement is hammered out."

I wanted to marry him, despite the awkwardness of the legalese. Yet, part of me still stung from his having rejected me before because I was a mortal. I decided to amuse myself with him a while before I gave my answer.

"I'll have to think about it before we move forward," I said.

He opened his mouth, but nothing came out. So much for the smooth-talking, worldly vampire.

"There is much work to be done," I continued. "We're still at war, even though we defeated the Fae. We supernaturals are still being persecuted, right?"

"Marriages can thrive even during times of war," he said with sincerity.

"What's the rush? I'm immortal now, like you. Don't vampires have otherworldly patience?"

He took me into his arms. "I also have an otherworldly longing for you that makes my heart ache. I want to be with you for eternity. And I want it to begin now."

"I suppose I will marry you, then. I mean, your attorney can draw up the paperwork. I would hate to see you suffer."

He laughed. "I'm certain our honeymoon period will last for a century, at least."

"It will. And if you marry into *my* family, you'll never become bored. I know how vampires fear boredom."

"I know you well enough to expect to be delighted every day."

"Okay, enough of the sweet talk. What you mean to say is that with me, you expect the unexpected every day. As crazy as it may be."

He smiled and nodded. After all, they say honesty is the key to a great relationship.

PLEASE LEAVE A REVIEW

Dear reader, thank you in advance:
Please give my book a better chance.
Success and sales depend on you,
So kindly post a book review.

AFTERWORD

Alas, this book wraps up the Goddess's Daughter trilogy. However, Sophie, Darla, and the gang just might appear in a future series. In the meantime, I have other irons in the fire, such as my continuing Monsters of Jellyfish Beach paranormal mystery series. Please do check it out.

INTERESTED IN THE BOOKS THAT SPAWNED THE GODDESS'S DAUGHTER?

Check out the Memory Guild Midlife Paranormal Mystery Thrillers

Visit your favorite e-retailer, wardparker.com, or books2read.com/amagictouchmidlifeparanormal

GET A FREE BOOK

GET A FREE E-BOOK

Sign up for my newsletter and get *A Ghostly Touch*, a Memory Guild novella, for free, offered exclusively to my newsletter subscribers. Darla reads the memories of a young woman, murdered in the 1890s, whose ghost begins haunting Darla, looking for justice. As a subscriber, you'll be the first to know about my new releases and lots of free book promotions. The newsletter is delivered only a couple of times a month. No spam at all, and you can unsubscribe at any time.

Visit wardparker.com

ACKNOWLEDGMENTS

I wish to thank my loyal readers, who give me a reason to write more every day. I'm especially grateful to Elizabeth Thurmond for all your editing and proofreading brilliance. To my A Team (you know who you are), thanks for reading and reviewing my ARCs, as well as providing good suggestions. And to my wife, Martha, thank you for your love and moral support.

ABOUT THE AUTHOR

Ward is the author of the Memory Guild midlife paranormal mystery thrillers. The Goddess's Daughter urban fantasy series continues the adventures.

He also writes the Monsters of Jellyfish Beach paranormal mysteries, set in the same world as his Freaky Florida series.

Ward lives in Florida with his wife, several cats, and a demon who wishes to remain anonymous.

Connect with him on Facebook (wardparkerauthor), Book-Bub, Goodreads, Bluesky (wardparker.bsky.social), or Pinterest (WardParkerBooks). Check out his books and sign up for his newsletter at wardparker.com.

PARANORMAL BOOKS BY WARD PARKER

Freaky Florida Humorous Paranormal Novels

Snowbirds of Prey
Invasive Species
Fate Is a Witch
Gnome Coming
Going Batty
Dirty Old Manatee
Gazillions of Reptilians

Hangry as Hell (novella)
Books 1-3 Box Set

The Memory Guild Midlife Paranormal Mystery Thrillers

A Magic Touch (also available in audio)
The Psychic Touch (also available in audio)
A Wicked Touch (also available in audio)
A Haunting Touch
The Wizard's Touch
A Witchy Touch
A Faerie's Touch
The Goddess's Touch
The Vampire's Touch
An Angel's Touch
A Ghostly Touch (novella)
Books 1-3 Box Set (also available in audio)

The Goddess's Daughter

(Continuing the Memory Guild Series.)
Of Envy and Empaths
Of Fear and Fae
Of Valor and Vampires

Monsters of Jellyfish Beach Paranormal Mystery Adventures

The Golden Ghouls
Fiends With Benefits

Get Ogre Yourself
My Funny Frankenstein
Werewolf Art Thou?
In Sprite of Herself
Worms of Endearment